The Olympus Project Leviticus Club

SYDNEY ADDAE

The Olympus Project
Leviticus Club
Sydney Addae
ISBN 978-1-937334-94-9
Copyright 2018 by Sydney Addae
First Edition Electronic July 2018

Thank You So MUCH For Your Support!

Many thanks to my Den-mates for your constant encouragement. To Denise and Vicky, thanks for all of your help. A special thanks to the ladies of NC Cover 2 Cover Interracial Book Club for brainstorming with me and your awesome friendship! Vickie Z, Tristin A. Yolanda, Karen, and Sally! Thanks for all of your help! Love you guys.

THE OLYMPUS PROJECT
The Leviticus Club

Two Groups.
One Serum.
Two Destinies.

With the absence of La Patron's Knights, the Joints Chiefs have enacted a risky plot to create a team of high functioning fighters as replacements. When enlisted soldiers die in the military, they arbitrarily receive a shot of a serum created by the Liege decades ago. If the soldier revives with his mind intact, they are mutated with one or more gifts or power. They are sent to train in the Olympus Project where they receive a new name and destiny.

Before the Joint Chiefs were created, the Liege used humans for their experiments. Hundreds died on the operating table until the Liege changed specimens and began experimenting on full-blood wolves instead. The humans who survived the surgeries mutated with additional gifts and powers, forever changed. Hunted, they eventually escaped the Continent. They arrived in the United States after the Civil War and headed west to hide from the Liege and to survive. Using their unique skillsets, they took on jobs which earned them a stellar reputation. When someone began stoning disabled people to death, they were called to find the killer.

While working on the case, they met Ryan and Ryder, La Patron's grandsons, and learn the Liege Lords are dead and powerless to harm them. They strike a bargain with La Patron and come face to face with Zeus and Hermes, two mutated soldiers in the Olympus Project.

Neither group knew of the other before now. Different origins. Different standards. Different goals. Immediate enemies.

Leviticus Club is the first book in **The Olympus Project**.

·

PROLOGUE

Dressed in white linen tunic, a blue robe and an ephod with 12 stones, the priest spoke in a loud voice, commanding the attention of all in attendance.

"Does not the word of Yahweh in the Holy Book of Leviticus, Chapter 23 say 'For the generations to come none of your descendants who has a defect may come near to offer the food of his God. No man who has any defect may come near: no man who is blind or lame, disfigured or deformed; no man with a crippled foot or hand, or who is a hunchback or a dwarf, or who has any eye defect, or who has festering or running sores or damaged testicles. Because of his defect, he must not go near the curtain or approach the altar, and so desecrate my sanctuary. I am the Lord, who makes them holy."

The people standing around him spoke together. "Yes, that is what Yahweh says."

The priest picked up a brick from the stack in front of him and lifted it above his head toward the others. "What is the penalty for those who disobey the Lord?"

"They are taken outside the camp and stoned to death," the others said as they each picked up bricks, one in each hand.

"Then come, let us leave the altar of Yahweh and go to the outer courts." He led them to a courtyard where a man with shriveled legs lay with outstretched arms tied to stakes in the ground. His eyes were closed as if he were asleep.

"We will cleanse this earth of those who are not worthy to be in Yahweh's presence, for this is our mission. Do we accept it?" he asked.

"Yes, we accept it," they said together.

1

The man's eyes blinked open.

"In the name of Yahweh, we rebuke you, unclean one." The priest threw the first brick, hitting the man in the forehead. The others threw their bricks until the man's body was covered in red.

The priest lifted his eyes upward. "Thank you, Father." He pushed the wheelchair out of his way as he returned to the sanctuary.

CHAPTER 1

Noah Sloan and his cousin Liam sat on the bar stool in a dark, dive of a bar. Liam wanted to get him out of the house, claimed he spent too much time alone. Through daily badgering, he finally convinced Noah to leave the warmth and quiet of his home in the country for lunch, a drink and hopefully more. Noah had no interest in lunch or the more.

Nursing his drink, his mind drifted in and out. He wasn't aware of the menacing, pit-bull vibes he gave off or that everyone except his cousin gave him a wide berth. Thoughts of war, death, and grief clung to him with dogged tenacity no matter how many times he sat in the shrinks' office, he couldn't shake the cloud of despair.

He exhaled and tossed back another shot of tequila out of boredom more than anything else. Alcohol no longer affected him. After his discharge, he'd tried to stop the dreams with drink, didn't work other than to give him more intense headaches.

Liam slapped his back smiling.

Noah glanced at him and read concern despite the smile. They thought he'd snap, completely lose it again. Harm himself or others. Vague memories of debilitating pain, blood, being strapped and confined plagued him. He couldn't remember clearly, and that frustrated him more.

"Stop frowning, we're here to have a good time, breathe fresh air, take in new possibilities," Liam said leaning closer with a grin.

Noah growled and turned away. Liam was the light to Noah's darker personality. Both stood around 6'2", side by side you'd see similar angular shaped faces, sharp cheekbones, blade noses, dark brown hair, although Noah's was long enough for a ponytail and Liam's just brushed his shoulders. Noah's eyes were a mix of blue and brown and lacked the

3

warmth of Liam's lighter blue. Both had muscular builds, but Noah's chest was slightly wider. People often mistook the cousins for brothers, indeed they were best friends and closer than Noah and his much younger brother from his mom's second marriage.

"That chick's been eying you since we stepped inside here. Let's send her and her friend a drink."

Noah didn't respond. There was no let's, Liam was broke. What he meant was for Noah to send them a drink. He pulled out a couple bills, slid them to Liam. "Do whatever you want, but keep me out of it."

Smiling widely, Liam nodded. "Thanks. Pay you back when I get paid next week."

Noah didn't bother acknowledging the statement. Next week would never come. If Liam paid everyone he owed, he wouldn't have a check.

"Another one," Noah told the bartender, sliding the shot glass forward. Since Liam didn't show any signs of leaving soon, he'd keep drinking.

"Thanks for the drink," a husky, female voice said sliding onto the stool next to him.

Noah noticed her long, tanned legs first. His gaze traveled upward, took in the jean shorts, exposed belly button, her barely concealed breasts, reddish-brown hair, interesting light brown eyes and thin lips. She wasn't unattractive but nothing he would stop doing what he was doing to take home either. Which had nothing to do with her and everything to do with the dark images floating through his mind.

He didn't trust himself. Neither should she.

"Liam bought it, thank him," he said tipping his head toward his cousin who sat at the table with the blonde.

"I did. He told me to thank you as well." She placed her hand on his thigh.

He tensed. Since being discharged he disliked being touched by strangers or talking to them. She was losing on both fronts.

"Is there any way I can thank you?" She leaned forward. "I'd love to fuck you."

He read the hunger in her gaze and wondered if her words were supposed to make him horny? Turn him on?

They didn't.

Which meant he was more fucked up upstairs than he realized. There was a time he'd pulled women left and right, would have two in bed, fucking all night long until he passed out. Now the idea of being with her left him cold and limp.

He didn't immediately respond and glanced at Liam and the blond who now sat on Liam's lap, her nipple in his mouth as she bobbed up and down on his dick. No wonder the place had a funky odor.

Dr. Higgins, his therapist, said he needed to rejoin the world, socialize more. Dig deep to find the manners he utilized before the surgery, before becoming a mental patient.

"As charming as that would be, I'm going to pass." He didn't look at her when he spoke, instead, he tossed back his shot and winced at the bite.

"You're turning down free pussy?" she said close to his ear.

"Yeah, I'm on a fast, can't indulge," he lied. The Doctor would be proud of him for not hurting this female's feelings.

"Oh."

Out the corner of his eyes, he saw three large men strode inside. Scruffy looking, lots of tattoos, big round belly's, wore black tees with scarves tied on their heads. Motorcycle jocks, he thought as something crashed behind him.

The sound of a slap and then a low, growl. "Bitch."

Noah looked over his shoulder. Liam stood to the side, eying the three men as he finished repacking and securing his junk. *Priorities*.

"Stop, Big John." The blond was snatched from the floor and all but tossed into the arms of the two other men.

"Shit, told her not to do it," the female sitting next to him murmured. "Big John's crazy. He don't want her but don't want no one else to have her either." She slid off the stool and walked off.

Big John swung, his fist connected with Liam's belly.

Liam grunted.

Must've had the wind knocked out of him. Noah turned around fully to watch. His cousin could handle himself, win or lose, he created the problem. As long as it was just the two of them, Noah wouldn't interfere even though he wanted to.

The idea of beating these three to their bloody knees excited something twisted inside of him. His hand curled into a fist as Big John knocked Liam to the ground.

Liam charged and punched the biker in the gut. Didn't have much impact, not until Liam followed it with several other punches and hit the big guy beneath the chin, snapping his head back.

Big John went down hard.

Glee exploded inside of Noah. He wanted to join in but forced himself to remain still. Shaking it off, he stared at Liam, made sure his cousin was alright to continue. If not, Noah would step in and stop things.

Standing slow, Big John swung and missed. Liam stepped forward and hit him with a series of punches again. People mistook Liam's easy-going ways as a sign of weakness and ended up learning painful lessons. Most people in this area of Texas worked with the land, or some kind of labor with their hands and didn't take shit from anybody.

Big John grabbed Liam in a surprise move, spun him around to his friends who moved forward.

"No." Noah slid off the stool in an easy move as violent anticipation swam through him. His therapist would say he should remain in control, be the peacemaker rather than fight. It was never a good idea for him to lose control. But this was his cousin, brother of his heart, the only person left who mattered. That settled it.

"No." He shook his head. The other two, almost carbon copies of Big John, looked at him, then at Liam. "If this big ass bitch can't win a fight on his own, it's over. You two yahoos aren't helping him." Noah pointed to make sure they understood.

Rather than respond, predictably, they charged him. Noah reached back, grabbed the wood stool he had been sitting on, swung and knocked the closest one upside the head so hard he slammed into the second one. Both hit the ground.

Someone screamed in the background.

Blood ran down the head of the first guy as he lay still. Glaring at Noah with teeth bared, the second guy, cursed as he jumped up and with quick steps swung at Noah.

The fist glanced off Noah's chin, turning him slightly. He ducked the next punch, slammed his fist into the guy's stomach with a hard right, and then hit him with an upper-cut beneath his chin. The guy flew backward and hit an unforgiving hard-wood table.

He didn't get up.

Chest-heaving, Liam stood over Big John, clenching and unclenching his fist. The guy remained moaning on the ground with blood running down his nose and forehead. Several bruises dotted his face and his right eye was swelling shut.

The blond ran to the Biker and placed a kiss on his lips. "Big John, baby talk to me."

Noah looked at the bartender who had watched the entire thing. "I'll pay for the table and chairs."

"Thanks. First time I've seen those three go down. They're a part of a larger group, so watch your back," the bartender said with a slight smile.

The female who offered him a quickie was on the phone while staring at him. It was time to leave if they didn't want to take on a whole gang.

"Liam."

His cousin looked at him and nodded. Noah slapped down three one hundred bills and walked out.

"Don't leave," the female said.

They ignored her and headed to Liam's car.

They didn't say anything for a few moments. "Gotta admit she had a nice rack," Liam said with an unrepentant grin.

"Not worth getting the shit beat out of you, though," Noah said knowing it wouldn't change his cousin's MO.

"Not even. That dude had a serious left." He rolled his bruised cheek a few times.

"Drop me by the house, I've got an appointment with the shrink in a few hours and need to get a bite to eat first." The chicken sandwich the bar served had been inedible. He ate a few of the fries and returned the basket. Now he was starving.

"That's right, forgot about that, what time is it?" Liam asked.

"Appointment's at 4:30."

"Is it helping? Still having nightmares?" Liam asked.

"Part of PTSD." He didn't discuss his problems, not with anybody. They could code him as mentally disabled or anything they wanted but no one knew what was really going on with him. No one knew his brand of crazy.

Noah pulled into the parking lot, looked at the five-story V.A. building and cursed. He would prefer fighting the entire gang of Bikers than dealing with these appointments.

"Fucking hate this shit." He slammed his palm against the steering wheel, closed his eyes and took several deep breaths.

No good. His heart had been racing like a fucking thoroughbred since he rolled over this morning. These dreams or whatever the hell they were would be the death of him. Like bullets or land mines, they exploded in his sleep, taking him places he'd been and others he couldn't imagine. It was like someone was playing a big cosmic joke on him with the things he had seen.

Real or not? He had no way of knowing. Sometimes, he felt intense emotions, colors and smells. Then the mist would roll in, cover everything, sometimes causing pain, other times confusion. God, he wanted his old life back.

He glanced at the dashboard clock and stepped out of his truck. The sooner they started, the sooner he could leave.

"Noah Sloan, 11:00 with Dr. Higgins."

"One moment, I'll call you when she's ready," the receptionist said offering a small smile.

Whenever the receptionist smiled, the doc was having a good day and he might get out early. That would be great, sleep pulled on him. He needed one night without those frigging dreams to catch up on his rest.

"Mr. Sloan, Dr. Higgins will see you now." Again that soft smile.

Moving quickly with a hopeful early departure expectation, he entered her office and sat in the chair in front of her desk.

Young, smart and decent looking with reddish blonde hair, green eyes, and a nice figure, Dr. Higgins inhaled and released her breath slowly. There was no smile, no warm greeting. She looked as if she hadn't slept well last night either. Well, damn. Why was the receptionist smiling?

"Good morning, Master Sargent Sloan."

Noah didn't react. Had she forgotten he no longer responded to his military title? He crossed his legs and looked at her.

An image of a woman in pain flashed across his mind reminding him of something he had seen in his dreams. He closed his eyes for a second and counted to five.

"Bad dream?" she asked when he opened his eyes again.

He didn't respond, never did when she poked into his nightmares.

"It's been a while since we talked, Noah. How've you been?" Her glance flicked from his face to something on her desk and back to him again.

"Been good, Doc. How've you been?"

She smiled but it was off, not quite right. "Headaches? Pain? Still going to physical therapy?"

He hadn't been to PT for two months, she knew that. What was going on with her? "Like I said, I been good. No complaints."

Another flash, he heard a scream, sensed a struggle before it disappeared. This time he counted to ten. When he was tired, exhausted, his dreams tended to follow him.

"What's wrong, Noah?" her voice softened, concerned.

"Nothing, just remnants from a dream. Don't make much sense." He looked at her.

"Tell me about your dream."

She didn't want to hear about the ugly things he saw, the underbelly of society.

"Master —"

"Don't call me that. Not anymore," he snapped.

"Sorry, but I need you to talk to me. The sooner you share something, the sooner I can let you leave."

"You don't understand. They're not real dreams, more like snapshots of action, like a bad movie clip of a jackass slapping a woman around in the back of a white jeep. She hit her head, sees stars, there's blood. Fucking asshole." He rubbed his forehead to ease the pounding in his skull. *When would this stop?* "See? Not a dream, just stupid shit that pisses me off messes with my sleep."

"What did you say?" Her voice wobbled.

He waved his hand, not wanting to see it again. "Nothing. Just rambling. Not even sure anymore."

She stared at him.

"Listen, Doc, are we doing a full session today? I didn't get much sleep last night or the night before and would appreciate it if you could cut it short." When she didn't say anything, he released a long breath and fought down the rising anger of being in this chair.

Her face was white as snow with a few red blotches on her cheeks. She stared at him with lips trembling.

"What's the matter, Doc?" Concerned, he stood and headed toward her.

She held out her hand. "No. Sorry. One moment." She raced out of the room.

Frowning, he looked at the door, returned to his seat and closed his eyes. He must have dozed off for a few minutes because he heard her calling his name.

"Sorry," he said wiping his mouth. "You okay?"

She nodded but didn't say anything for a while. "That was very unprofessional of me, I apologize. Please, I'll let you leave early today but before you go, tell me about your dreams? Are they violent? Places you're familiar with? People, you know?"

He didn't want to discuss the dreams. They were a pain in his ass. Since the surgery the nightmares were bad, but walking through his dreams, seeing the things he saw, was worst.

"Not violent always." *Just most of the time.* "Sometimes I've been to the places I see in the dreams." *Doesn't happen often, though.* "I don't see faces, so it's hard to tell if I know the people in the dreams. I get more of an impression, know what I mean?" *Most times I see faces. But I also know the people even without their faces.*

Just like he now knew, she had been the woman in the back of the Jeep being beaten.

The horrified surprise on Dr. Higgins face made him smile. Maybe she'd back off, stop asking so many questions. The smile faded. There had been so many faces and attacks and crimes in his nightmares. Not being able to help tore him up inside.

CHAPTER 2

Tired and ready to be home, Noah took a short-cut through the town of Littleton. He had just turned onto a side road to cut through a neighborhood before hitting the feeder road out of town.

He slammed on the brakes as a pale, dark-haired woman ran toward the street yelling at the top of her lungs covering her mouth with one hand while waving the other wildly.

"Oh my God, oh my God., no, no, no…help," she screamed with desperation. She heard the screech of his brakes and ran toward his truck, oblivious to the near miss of him hitting her. "Please help," she yelled as tears streamed down her face.

He swerved to the side and parked. "Please help Nate, please God, help him." She bent forward at the waist and cried harder.

Noah looked around, saw nothing out of the ordinary, just a van and a car parked in the driveway nearby. There was no sign of danger that he saw. "What's wrong?" he asked as he stepped out and walked closer.

"Nate." She pointed to the black van parked in the driveway. "Please help him."

He walked over and looked inside. "Shit." He closed his eyes and shook his head, but it was too late. He'd already seen. Pissed and resigned, he pulled out his phone and dialed 9-1-1. "There is a dead man in a van."

<<<<>>>>

Two hours later, exhausted, Noah stood on the sidewalk watching the black coroner's van drive off with the body of Nathaniel Green.

He closed his eyes but still saw the broken body of the older man in the back of the van. Who would kill, not just kill but brutalize an invalid like that? It wasn't right or fair. The old man had no way to run or fight back.

The police had already interviewed him and the woman, Lisa, who worked at the library with the dead guy. When he didn't show up for work, she came to check on him and found him in the driveway. The officers told him to expect the Detective later today or tomorrow.

Noah glanced in Lisa's direction, she was still having a hard time coming to terms with what she'd seen. It had been a horrible sight, but not the worst he had seen. After five tours in the Middle East, and 21 years in the military, he'd seen much worse than this and would probably see worst in his dreams later.

He hated what his life had become. Some days he wished he had died on the battlefield instead of being resuscitated and sent home to live a half-life. Resigned to the idea of difficult days ahead, he turned, headed for his truck and drove out of town to his 15-acre ranch.

In his living room, news blared on the TV as background noise, something he needed these days. His favorite sitcom had come and gone while he was out.

Beer. He needed a beer and remembered there was none in the house, thanks to his cousin, Liam coming over yesterday, cleaning him out.

Unable to sleep, he took several deep breaths, sat in the leather recliner in front of his 60" flat screen TV and half-listened to the news. Instead of the current events, he saw the handicapped van, the way it was left parked in the driveway.

Why hadn't they driven it into the garage? Did they want him to be found sooner, rather than later? Why bash in his head? Where was his wheelchair? Why so violent? The man was a librarian and churchgoer. After the death of his wife from cancer, Nate lived alone and had no kids, at least that's what the woman who found Nate told the police.

His phone rang, he glanced at the caller ID. "Liam?"

"What're you doing?" his cousin asked.

"Just got in." No matter what he was doing, it wouldn't stop Liam from asking for whatever he called for.

"What's wrong?" Liam asked.

Noah had no reason to keep the information to himself. He explained the shortcut through town after his appointment. "Found an old cripple murdered and called the cops." He didn't want to get into how he'd respond later tonight. Liam knew about his nightmares and PTSD but didn't know about walking through his dreams. No one knew about those.

Liam whistled. "You moved to the country to get away from the bloodbath in the city and it happens in your neighborhood? That sucks."

"Wasn't out here, saw it in town," he said wondering how Liam confused the two.

"How much did you see?"

"The body? All of it." The bludgeoned face, crumpled body, bones, dried blood and guts.

Liam cursed. "I'm coming over."

"No, I'll be fine," he lied.

"You won't be fine, and you know it. Damn it. You still have nightmares and don't need to be alone with that shit."

Noah wanted to disagree but wouldn't know until later, much later when his dream woke him.

"You drank the last of my beer," Noah said, giving in.

"I'll pick up a 12 pack on the way."

"Buy two."

Noah disconnected and ordered two extra-large pizzas, it was going to be a long night.

That night, Noah flinched at the sound of gunfire in the distance. Missile strikes exploded nearby blinding him in white-hot bursts. He couldn't see because of the smoke. The mists curled around him, tightening, fouling the air, robbing him of breath. His skin burned. Moans of his men pierced his heart as he dragged himself to the closest sound.

Gotta help 'em.

Just as he reached Johnson, more rounds went off in the distance and some close enough that the ground vibrated.

"Hold on, let me help you," he whispered as he scooted closer and looked into Johnson's vacant eyes. *Too late.* He took in a bit of air, hoisted his rifle and prepared to defend himself. If death came looking for him, so be it but he'd take a few of those bastards with him. Ignoring the pain on his left side and the blood running down his face, Noah searched the area for anyone he could help.

There were a few moving on the ground. He moved toward the closest as the dark mist rolled in blinding him. Remembering the direction of the fallen soldier, he continued as the mist became heavier, deeper with a satiny texture that made breathing hard. Still, he pushed forward, using his outstretched hands to find the fallen.

"You can't help anyone until you help yourself."

Noah whipped around with his weapon ready to fire.

"You can't even control the mist. It stops you from doing what you really want to do. Help others."

Blinded by the mist, Noah refused to give away his position to the enemy even as he continued moving forward, searching for his fallen teammates.

"Will they ever learn?" Followed by a long-suffering sigh. The mist rolled to the side as a man dressed in black with long white hair and gleaming green eyes strode forward. Grass, green as an Irish spring, lay on the ground beneath him instead of the bloodied battlefield from a few moments before.

Shocked, Noah stared at the bare feet of the stranger, unable to reconcile what he was seeing. When the man stopped. Noah slowly looked up and swallowed hard.

"You're on my turf. In my backyard bringing war and death with you. If that's your thing, fine but you need to contain the mist, it's not healthy for the pups." He waved and Noah saw several dark puppies yipping and playing in the distance.

"I'm…" Noah cleared his throat and tried to rise. Surprised by the lack of pain and the absence of bloody injuries, he stood. Clearing his throat again, he wondered why the mist recoiled from the stranger and always wrapped around him. "I'm sorry. I don't know why the mist shows up or why I dream of the war."

The stranger's look called him a liar.

"I'm former military, seen a lot in the war, no doubt that's the cause of the bloody dreams. But this mist." He waved his hand through it, instead of it recoiling it seemed to wrap around his arm. "Don't know what it is or why it's here."

It dawned on Noah that he was dreaming again. "Hey, what are you doing in my dream?" He looked around, saw the puppies. "This is a dream, right?"

"Yes, it is. I have free rein in dreams, I'm called Grandfather and you are?"

"Master…Noah Sloan."

"Well, Noah, you've got quite a problem with that mist, I hope you find a way to fix it, otherwise you'll be miserable while awake and asleep. That's no way to live."

Noah stared at the man standing close but without the annoying mist wrapped around him. "How are you able to be free of the mist in here?"

Grandfather smiled. "I'm a lot older and wiser. Some things must be learned to understand. You'll be waking up soon and forgetting this conversation. I'll be keeping an eye on you, Noah Sloan. You've got heart and good character, the world needs people like you."

"What?" Noah asked, surprised as Grandfather disappeared into the mist. His words rolled over Noah.

"You can't help anyone until you help yourself. You can't even control the mist. It blinds you to what you really want to do. Help others."

CHAPTER 3

General Strait sat in his office at the Pentagon reading a brief regarding several enlisted men in their Olympus Project. He looked at the photos of the men. All good candidates if they could complete their training and control their gifts.

His phone buzzed.

"Yes?"

"You have the files?"

"Looking at it right now. There's only ten, that won't be enough to replace the Knights. We'll need more," the General said.

La Patron, the Alpha of the Wolf Nation had allowed a specially trained group of full-blood wolves to serve in the military for a few years. Those men were unparalleled in their abilities to win against any enemy. Unfortunately, La Patron removed those men from the military and refused to allow them to return after learning that a few of them were being used in the labs for testing. Their departure left a void for high risk, covert jobs. The General believed, hoped, the Olympus Project would fill the void, even if half-way.

"In time the unit will grow."

Considering the serum was injected to enlisted men in the field as a last resort to restart their hearts, the General understood. Those who survived the shot underwent some kind of mutation. Some were stronger than a dozen men, some manipulated the elements, emitted noxious odors or poison, all were faster, with enhanced vision, hearing and smell, just as the Liege research and notes said.

"We could use Zeus and the others now," the General said. All of the soldiers in the project were given names of from Greek mythology and were called Olympians.

"Patience, they're being formed into a solid team learning to use their unique skills. Which brings me to the reason for this call. We need to be moved somewhere private. An island or a facility that cannot be tracked until we can go public."

The General grunted and looked at the pictures again. These men might be their only defense against the Wolf Nation. They were just as fast, with similar vision and strength. At least their skills were similar to some wolves. So far, no one was on the same level as the Knights or KnightForce. According to the Liege files and notes, the mutations evolved over time so it was possible that one day this team would defeat the Knights. The General prayed it happened in his lifetime.

"Understood. I'll have my assistant contact you and secure a location. Don't stop training, bring them up to speed as soon as possible."

"Yes, Sir."

"What about the others? The ones who didn't die from the shot and left the military?"

"We're monitoring them through their doctors to determine if they're developing gifts. So far, most of them are mental and beyond help. We knew that was also a risk with the serum."

The General nodded. "True. I've got some personal family matters to deal with. Death in the family. Might be out of town later this week. Get in touch with my assistant if there's an emergency."

"Will do, Sir. We're on the right track with this team. They'll be able to fight and protect against our enemies."

But will they be able to protect against La Patron? General Strait wondered as he disconnected and looked at five names. Five soldiers who received the shot didn't die but were undergoing treatment for mental instability.

"Such a waste," he murmured as he closed the file and locked it away. He took a deep breath and allowed his thoughts to return to the stoning death of his cousin, Nathaniel. He couldn't believe it, stoned? In the U.S.? In recent years there were reports of stonings in the Middle East, mostly women, but not here. Was this a terrorist group? Homeland Security was looking into it as well. It made no sense.

He flipped through the pages of the investigation report and shook his head. This wasn't the first time either. The FBI investigated five other occurrences across six states. It was a miracle and blessing there were so many other things happening, the press hadn't gotten a whiff of it yet. Still, for this to happen on American soil shook him.

He looked at the photo on his desk with him, his wife and Nathaniel last year at a Florida resort near the theme park. They'd spent five days together and it had been fun. His wife was beside herself with grief.

He wanted justice on behalf of Nate. Anger clenched his chest as he weighed the fallout of getting involved with an active investigation. It wasn't a good idea, he understood that. But neither the FBI nor Homeland Security had made any credible progress since discovering the first stoning.

Determined to get answers, he made several calls pulling in favors until he was granted a small window. Five days and access to classified information. Now to dangle the carrot to get what he needed. He placed the call to a number he wasn't supposed to have. General Jim McNeill accidentally gave him the information when this group got him out the country when he ran from La Patron.

Thomas Mason answered. "Yes?"

"Thomas this is General Strait. I know you asked not to be contacted by the Joint Chiefs, but I need a personal favor. My cousin, Nathaniel Green was murdered. Stoned to death. He's the sixth disabled person, across six states to be killed in that manner. Someone's singling out our disabled for death, I need you and your team to stop them."

"No." His tone was flat, without emotion.

General Strait expected that. The only reason McNeill mentioned this group to him was to help him gain access to highly confidential files the military acquired from their time collaborating with the Liege. It was the only thing this group bartered with back then and hopefully now.

"I would offer you a deal. You've got five days to catch the killer, turn him or them over to the authorities and I'll release copies of the remaining Liege files to you. You've been after those for a while. Of course, we'll pay your normal fee." Strait had no idea why this group was interested in the Liege and at the moment didn't care. They were ghosts and based on Jim's cryptic email letting him know they were safe, these guys delivered.

"What shield would we use?" Thomas asked a few moments later

The General released a pleased, quiet sigh. "Special agents for a special assignment. The agency has given us five days before they step in and take over. If that happens the deal is null."

Thomas grunted. "Send me what you have on this murder and the others, as well as the payment. Send half the Liege files now, the rest when we're done."

"Within the hour," the General said and disconnected. He picked up the photo and stared at Nathaniel. "Whoever did that to you will be found and pay. I promise you that."

<<<>>>

Thomas stared down at the bed where Lizzy, a good friend who had been in the Liege compound with him a century ago, lay immobile, sweating and barely breathing. Unable to move or function she occasionally shuddered as beads of sweat dotted her brow.

He wiped away the blood from her nose and hoped the pain from the killer headache she was experiencing subsided soon. It had been six hours since she fell and seized, two hours longer than before. Like Kenny and Beatrice, she was dying and would join them soon unless he found answers. Damn Liege and their experiments, he wanted those files. Needed them desperately before they all fell to the same end.

"Hang on, Lizzy," he whispered, hoping for a miracle. The message from Strait came through, the fee was in their account and the files, as well as the FBI files, had been sent as well.

Their group was already stretched. If it hadn't been for the chance to get the files, he wouldn't have accepted the job. Now, he needed time to go through the files to search for something to help Lizzy. He had no choice but to send Mia to check out the area until he could join her. Sending her alone didn't sit right with him either but they were running out of options and time.

CHAPTER 4

Special Agent Mia Haddon stepped into the Littleton morgue and showed the attendant her badge. Dressed in black dress pants, button-down white oxford shirt, and a lightweight blazer, she believed she looked the part of a competent government employee.

"I'd like to see the body of —" She looked at her phone to consult her notes. "Nathaniel Green."

"Yes, of course. This way." The short, gray-haired man stared at her, his gaze flicked over her short hair and eyes before glancing at her badge. He walked past two bodies lying on tables into a much cooler room. He pulled out a drawer and stepped back.

Mia's stomach clenched as she looked at the draped body. She hated this part of the assignment. Aware of a mental backlash, she stuffed her emotions into that dark box in the corner of her mind and locked them away for now. She pulled the cover down past his waist. With clinical precision, she stared at his face, took note of the smashed skull, broken neck, arms broken in several places, and ended with his shriveled legs.

Without looking at the examiner, she waved her hand, freezing him in place, disarmed any cameras and locked the door with a thought.

"Let me get a really good look at you, Nathaniel Greene," she murmured pulling up her sleeves. Hands extended, she placed them a few inches above the body. As her palms heated she moved her hands above his smashed skull and then slowly down his body searching for more information of his death. If the victim had been stabbed, shot or poisoned, she would pick up different vibrations. But there was nothing other than the obvious method of death, stoning.

Inhaling deeply, she scanned the body again, searching for the killer's

19

scent or lingering emotions. Considering the death was relatively new, there was a chance she could pick up something to help in the investigation.

Nothing. Another dead end.

She pulled out her phone and videoed the remains to send to the others later. Next, she pulled up all the data in the Medical Examiner's computer regarding the case, downloaded the notes to a flash drive and returned the screen to its previous place.

After gathering all the information, she released the examiner, camera and unlocked the door. "Did you discover any particles in his wounds?" she asked continuing their conversation as if the pause had never been.

"Yes. Red clay. I've got it over here, sent most of it to the lab." He handed her a small vial with small pieces of red clay from the bricks used to kill the victim.

"When are you expecting the test result?" She took pictures of the vial contents before returning it to him.

"Any day now, but it'll go to Detective Gordon, this is his case."

Mia frowned. "Gordon? What's his first name?"

The coroner frowned. "Frank, I think, not sure. An asshole but good at his job."

Mia asked a few more basic questions regarding the time of death, drugs, the amount of blood in the victim's body and stomach contents. Mr. Green hadn't eaten much.

"Thank you very much." She gave him her card. "I'd like to know what that red dust is once you hear from the lab."

"Okay, but you might need to go through Gordon. I'll find out and let him know you were here." He stuffed her card into his lab coat pocket and returned to one of the bodies lying on the table.

The first part of her assignment complete, she left the god-awful smelling place and headed for fresh air. Outside, she slid into the driver's seat of her rental and took several breaths to cleanse the smell of death and blood from her sinuses.

Her stomach growled. She ignored it. There wasn't enough time to go to the police station to speak to the detective but she'd call just in case he could see her today after-hours. She'd been lucky to reach the morgue before the medical examiner left.

While she still had sunlight she needed to record the town to send to the team. She set up her voice-activated recording equipment on the rearview mirror. It was important to have an idea of what appeared to be a sleepy southern town with a stoning victim in the morgue.

Pulling onto Main Street, she drove slowly through the area, noticing a diverse group of people which was always good. There weren't any big-name stores or restaurants which suited her fine. Government offices, library, bank, park and small shops were spread over 10 blocks.

A beep for an incoming text message. She looked at the screen on her phone. "Got it."

Thomas' messages were always succinct, he was miserly with words. After several decades, she was used to it. The hotel where she'd be staying was just outside of town. She pulled into a parking space near one of the small restaurants she'd passed and gone inside.

People at the counter stopped and stared. Rude but not unusual. On the day she chose to celebrate her birthday, she wanted to do something different and cut off her long hair as well as changed its color to a shimmering light brown to match her eyes. She stood to the side and scanned the room.

Mixed bags of emotions buffeted her, it was all she could do not to roll her eyes. This place was a seething hotbed of lusting, hurting, angry, happy, twisted people. She dialed the volume down a notch. All she wanted was food and a hot shower. It had been a long day with Thomas rushing her to get on a flight an hour and a half after taking this job. She hadn't had time to mentally prepare which was why her control was jacked-up right now, the small box in the corner of her mind was overwhelmed.

Eager to get out of here and check in, she pushed the sunglasses up her nose as she moved toward the counter. "May I see a menu please?" she asked the waitress.

"Sure hon," she passed Mia a long, laminated card.

She wasn't picky about food, it had a job to do and she allowed it to do her job. "Two chicken sandwich baskets to go, please."

"Be done in a bit," the over-worked woman said.

Mia stood to the side and listened to the chatter in the room, maybe she would hear something that would help the case. Without looking behind her she cocked her ear to the side to filter through conversations. If they were talking about family or loved ones, she kept moving. She ignored complaints about work or weight or politics or religion. Midway through her search two women were talking in low whispers. Their hearts were heavy, and voices sad.

"Ms. Murphy found him. All day she'd been worried about him at work. He always called if he was going to be late or anything," a soft voice said. "She's really messed up over this."

"Nathaniel was such a nice guy, who would do that to him?"

"I don't know, Twanna. But I'm not walking alone at night anymore. It's not safe."

"Poor Nathaniel, I'm going to miss him."

"Me too," the other voice said.

Mia glanced over her shoulder, noticed two young women, one with long dreads pulled back in a ponytail. The other a slender blond wiping her cheek.

"Here you are, that'll be $9.95." The waitress placed a large bag on the counter and smiled at Mia as she placed $15 in her hand.

"Keep the change," Mia said taking the bag and her drink. She glanced at the two women in the back again and left. On the sidewalk, she looked around. The streetlights were on and few cars traveled the road.

Was this a dangerous town? She didn't get a sense of danger or evil. Not here in town. Maybe nearby, she wasn't sure but planned to check the surrounding area tomorrow. It was time to refuel and bring Thomas current.

CHAPTER 5

Mia checked in and took her things upstairs to her room. If she was staying longer, she would have gotten a suite. But for the few days Thomas planned for her to be in Littleton, this small, basic room with a queen-sized bed, chair, desk with chair, TV, mini-fridge, and microwave, would work.

"Eat first," she murmured as she placed her backpack on the table along with her bag of food. Eager to refuel, she didn't waste time and ate everything quickly. As the food hit her belly, she waited a few moments for it to strengthen her system. It didn't take long, it never did. People often marveled at the amount of food her petite frame required to function at peak performance. It became a joke back at the complex in Wyoming where she lived with the others.

Rejuvenated, she pulled out her laptop, turned it on to upload the video and photos of the remains of Nathaniel Green and sent it to Thomas. He would contact her in a few minutes. Eyes closed, arms above her head she stretched and read the room. Was the last occupant dirty? Clean? Nasty? Her energy spiked as she hoped for a bright-white glow signifying an ultra-clean space. Instead, the room gave off a dim-white glow, not the best or the worst, but typical for this chain of hotels.

"Typical," she said opening her bag to grab the items she needed to prepare for bed. They had all been really lucky. Whatever the Liege injected them with preserved them, she still had the majority of her teeth and wanted to keep them for a long time.

Waiting to hear from Thomas she recalled her earlier feelings when he received the Liege files from Strait. She had refused to leave until he checked for information regarding her or the child taken from her decades

23

ago at the Liege Compound.

There had been nothing.

Disappointed once again, she had prepared to leave for this job in silent agony. Through the years she wondered if the child had survived either childbirth or beneath the heavy-handedness of the Liege. Had it been a boy or girl? Or if the child was happy. The absence of answers ate at her soul like putrid cancer.

Vague memories of her early childhood flitted through her mind from time to time. Her family had been large, lots of adults, smiling faces, good food and fun times. It had been brief, over before she was five summers and woke up in the Liege compound. Boris Lancaster, a skinny, evil bastard and one of the Liege Lords, had teased and told her she came from royal blood. Once he bragged she was related to the Queen of Sheba but later claimed to have lied.

None of that mattered, and even though it would be nice to know her family, she desperately needed to know about her child.

Her phone beeped.

"What did you see?" Thomas' brusque voice demanded.

"Broken bones, definitely a stoning. Wasn't done in anger, definitely deliberate." Mentally, she recalled the vision of him on the steel drawer table.

"No anger? Someone calmly stoned the old man?"

Mia shrugged. "No residual anger, I would've felt it. I didn't. It seems clean, no emotions attached but this is a stoning. They would've stood a distance away which could explain why I'm not picking up anything." That was one of her quirks, Thomas called her oddities gifts.

"Good point," he said. "The Detective any good? Give you any problems?"

"Haven't met him yet." When she reached out to Detective Gordon she'd been told he was unavailable.

"Got the feed you sent of the town, tell me your personal take on Littleton, Texas," he said.

"Not quite farmland rural, a step above maybe. Small town feel. Everybody knows everybody. Low crime rate. Family oriented."

"He should've been safe," Thomas said. "Should've been able to live the rest of his natural life safe. Hmm, what happened?"

"That's what inquiring minds want to find out," she said toeing off her shoes and wiggling her toes.

"Get the feeling this is because of his relationship to the General?"

She thought about it. "No, because it happened five other times with unrelated victims. Whoever's doing this hate disabled people, if not hate, then simply wants to take them out for some reason."

"Yeah, I see that. It fits," he murmured.

Thomas would eventually develop some plan of action and send in whoever he thought would work best to finish the mission. Her abilities to hear the truth, pick up emotions and a few other things made her a good scout for them.

"Lab and toxicology reports?"

"Asked the coroner to inform me when they arrive. Detective Frank Gordon is in charge of this case. Do you know him?"

"No. Should I?"

"It would help if you did. The coroner said he was an asshole." She had no idea if or how Gordon would impact their investigation at all. The team preferred not to use their gifts on law enforcement officials but they only had five days to complete the mission.

"You don't have to work with him, you're authorized to do a separate investigation. If he gives you any problems, call me. I don't want to spend a lot of time on this. We've got other things to do."

"Learn anything interesting from the Liege files?" She hoped he learned something that might help Lizzy. The thought of losing another member of their already shrinking team depressed her.

"Yes, more names, tests, we'll start verifying information soon now that she's stable."

Mia closed her eyes, sent up another prayer that information regarding her child would be in the next installment. "Good. Shouldn't be much longer, right?"

"Hopefully. You know the drill, get more information, send it to the lockbox, I'll review it and decide what to do next. The clock starts ticking tomorrow."

"Day one is tomorrow?" That was a bonus.

"Yeah." He paused. "Take care and don't hurt anyone, keep a low profile, just gather information," he said. Reminding her of the one time she lost it and attacked a crooked cop in Silver Springs. Standing 5'4" and weighing a little under 125 lbs, she shouldn't have been able to lift the 250 plus pound cop over her head and thrown him against the wall. She had blown their cover and it had taken Thomas a couple months to bleach the data that exposed them to the public.

"I'm not going to respond to that. Good night."

"Wait."

"What?"

"You okay?"

She was the youngest by 15 years in their small group and sometimes they treated her like a kid. "Yes dad," she teased. "I'm fine. Got the FBI thing down solid. I've done preliminary before."

"Not alone," he reminded her that this was new territory and that their numbers had shrunk. They didn't have enough people to work the jobs they had.

"I know. I'm just getting information for you and the guys. Don't worry." Some days she felt like a cheerleader for a team who knew it was losing.

"Yeah. See you soon, kid."

She disconnected and headed to the shower. Yawning, she grabbed her supplies, stripped and stepped into the steamy shower.

<<<>>>

The next morning, Mia eyed the darkening sky and bit back a curse. "Not today, please not today," she murmured, quickening her pace wishing she had worn her work boots instead of her comfortable brown loafers. The soft leather wouldn't hold up well in the rain. It was days like today she really missed Kenny. His gift or ability to interrupt the weather for periods of time would have been appreciated right now.

Winters were always great around the complex. Kenny always kept the pool area snow-free while the rest of the vast landscape was blanketed in freezing snow. They would run and jump into the warm pool as if it was a nice summer day or play in the snow making snow angels. Like so many of the others who left the Liege with them, Kenny was dead. She pushed away from the lingering memories and stepped aside to allow an older woman pushing a cart pass.

Hustling down the sidewalk, she reached her destination and slipped inside. Odors of unwashed bodies and urine scented the air of the Littleton Police Station. It was a small compact place with two armless, plastic chairs in the waiting area, and a receptionist seated behind thick Plexiglas as if someone would break into the police station.

"I'd like to speak with Detective Gordon, please." She flashed her Special Agent badge knowing the woman would see what she wanted or needed to see.

"He's not in yet, should be any minute, please take a seat."

Mia scanned the room and was grateful there weren't many people in the building. She settled into the plastic chair and tried to get comfortable, which proved to be an impossible quest. Standing, she read every poster, flipped through the four magazines provided, and walked slowly around the room twice and was beginning a third when the door opened.

Gordon walked through the front door, growled a greeting to the receptionist. The receptionist buzzed him through. He walked without looking around and headed to the back.

Mia glanced at the clock and took a deep breath to calm down over the fact she had waited slightly over 30 minutes. Did things really move that much slower in Texas? She stared at the receptionist for a few seconds and then took a deep breath. The receptionist called her name.

"How can I help you?" the receptionist asked her.

Yes! Moving closer to stand in front of the woman, Mia said. "Let me in to see Detective Gordon," she added a slight bit of compulsion to her voice.

"Of course. Straight back, the last office on the right." She pressed a button; a buzzer went off as the door unlocked.

Pleased, Mia walked in. The back area was smaller than she expected given the size of Littleton and it's growing population. With seven average-length steps, she stood outside the door watching the Detective a few moments before tapping on the door.

Frank Gordon sat stiffly in his chair staring at the monitor as if it was the Holy Grail. The huge, mahogany desk and chair sucked up most of the space in the match-boxed size room. There were no additional chairs, file cabinet or equipment. Too minimized for her tastes.

His gun-metal eyes flicked over her and returned to the screen as if she was a mirage, or invisible. She could've spoken, interrupted him, showed off her badge or slammed his head into the desk, but instead decided to be courteous and wait. Thomas would be proud of her restraint.

When he deigned to speak, she heard the military in his voice and bit back a curse. Those guys were the worst in these positions. They tended to extend their tour of duty to civilian life while nursing a grudge over the way Vets were treated by the government.

"You're with the Feds?" He glanced at her and continued typing.

"Special Agent Mia Haddon. I'm interested in one of your cases and —"

"No."

She blinked and counted to ten. You will not make me angry. You will not make me angry, she repeated mentally over and over.

"No, I'm not going to work with you. I'll share the toxicology report and anything like that, but we won't be working together if that's what you had in mind."

Calming, she spoke. "I appreciate any information you share with me." She did not offer to share her information with him, he was indeed an asshole.

He waved and handed her a sheaf of papers. "Got your message yesterday. Printed them off for you to take with you."

That was no subtle hint. He wanted her gone. It took everything within her to remain polite, civil. She toyed with the idea of delving into his private, personal space and wrecking his day. Or maybe she'd touch the monitor he seemed so fond of and fry it with a nice energy pulse.

Mia handed him her card in silence and debated whether or not to search his computer for additional information. He wouldn't have much more than what was on the pages he gave her.

He stared at it for several moments before looking at her. "The FBI? Here? For what?"

Didn't he ask if she was with the Feds? Who did he think she was with? "We're interested in this case, the murder of Nathaniel Green." Did he know more about this case or was he simply an ass?

His frown deepened. "Really? It's a strange case, but I don't see why it would interest the FBI. Could you explain a little more?"

"No. I'm sorry I cannot." She pointed to another paper on his desk. "Have you heard from the lab?" She planned to examine the van and Mr. Green's home before lunch.

"Yes." He pursed his lips and met her gaze. "What do you want?"

"I need access to the crime scene and the lab report." She tipped her chin toward the paper.

He rubbed his chin and stared at her card. "Let me verify this and then we'll see." He stood, and she was surprised by how tall he was. She looked up at him as he walked to his office door and closed it in her face.

Stepping back, did a quick sweep of the office, searching for hidden cameras or other electronics that would document her time here.

No cameras and little else. She listened to him speak to the person the General set in place to handle this case. When he disconnected she sensed his bafflement. No matter how much he didn't want her there, he wouldn't go against the agency.

The door opened behind her.

Mia took her time turning to face him. "What do you know about Nathaniel Green?" She asked adding compulsion to her voice.

"Nathaniel Green. Cripple. Stoned to death. Before that he worked in the library. Never met him. Never talked to him." The Detective's hollow gaze stared down at her.

She released him. The color returned to his eyes.

"You check out. Here's the address of the victim's house. Crime lab's there don't get in their way," he said grabbing his phone and stuffing it into his pocket. He closed the door behind him as he walked away.

"Thanks." She turned and walked behind him as his long strides reached the door before her.

"Give me your email address, I'll send the notes I have so far."

So, he had been holding out information on her. Good thing she used the compulsion on him, otherwise he would never have admitted that.

He pushed open the outer door and stopped. "Normally I'd tell you to take a fucking leap, don't like you guys coming around. But what happened to that guy, a cripple, is disgusting. That crosses a line and anything you can do to help bring Nathaniel justice I'd appreciate it."

Bring justice? How many times did she hear a detective phrase it like that? Too few. Most were about closing record numbers of cases or seeing their name in the news. Few really cared about justice for the dead. That one comment redeemed him in her eyes.

"Will do. Can you send me the information where the van is? Since he was found dead in the van, I prefer to see it first," she said in a pleasant voice that would make Thomas proud.

"It's around the corner. We use Jake's towing to store cars until someone comes to pick it up. Can't miss it." He pointed as if that meant something to her.

After a quick map search for the towing company, she pulled out of the parking lot and following directions entered through a gate into the compound. She found an attendant who showed her the van.

Pulling on a pair of gloves from her work pouch, she opened the back of the van. Staring at the carpet, she took note and pictures of the blood stains. Lack of blood meant he'd been dead before they tossed him into the back. She ran her hand over the carpet fibers hoping to pick up residual emotions.

Nothing.

Definitely wasn't killed in the van, hadn't been afraid or excited. Next, she pulled out her magnifying glass and looked over every inch of the back. The murderer was meticulous and left no clues that she could find.

Silently she moved to the area behind the driver, searched and found nothing. Nothing in the passenger seat area either. Clean as a whistle. Thomas believed it was more than one person and she had to agree with him. Six stonings, in six states. The only thing the victims had in common was some type of disability.

When she finished, she sent the photos to Thomas and returned to her car. She plugged the victim's address into her phone's GPS and headed out of town. Within 20 minutes she pulled in front of a nice one-story home in an upscale neighborhood with sidewalks and a large nearby park. The yellow police do not enter, tape stretched across the porch.

The sound of a truck engine caught her attention. A heavy-duty silver truck with a 4-door crew cab and short bed stopped a few feet from the curb. The driver wore sunglasses and stared at the house for a few seconds before nodding at her.

"Mornin'," he said in a smoky voice with a bit of southern charm.

"Good morning." Normally Mia ignored nosy neighbors and proceeded to gather information, but something about the way this man looked at the house sent tingles down her spine, she never ignored those. Somehow he was important to the case.

"Did you know Mr. Green?" Curious, she took a few steps toward the truck.

He looked in her direction for several moments. He took so long, she wondered if he would answer. "No. I... I was the one who called 9-1-1.

The lady he worked with was crying and screaming too hard to call it in. She flagged me down." His gaze was drawn back to the house.

"Your name?"

"Noah Sloan."

"Had you seen him before?"

"No. Never saw him before. Didn't deserve what they did to him."

"Why do you think it was more than one person?" She watched him closely. Half of his face was shadowed by the interior of the cab, but she made out the stubble on his square jaw, firm lips and sharp nose. So far he had been truthful even if not forthcoming. She frowned at the null or blank spot she sensed in him. He was hiding something, his emotions for one and possibly something else. Rarely did she meet anyone whose emotions she couldn't read. *Interesting.*

"Could've been one but it's doubtful that one person could've broken all the bones in his body like that. He was a big guy." Noah shrugged. "I could be wrong." The way he said that reminded her of Thomas who would make that statement when he wanted someone to think he was humble, but really believed he was right.

She asked him a few more general questions which he answered in monosyllables. "What made you come through this area instead of going home your normal route?" she asked adding compulsion when he mentioned the detour.

His head turned toward her and she had the feeling of being sized up by a large predator which made no sense. Thomas, Tip, and Max, guys in her family, were all big men who took few prisoners. But for all her gifts and with a powerful group backing her, she felt vulnerable beneath his gaze.

"No real reason, other than wanting to get home," he said after a long period.

Doubtful the compulsion worked, she wanted to end their conversation without coming across as afraid of him or weak. Straightening her back, she nodded, pulled out a card and handed it to him. "If you think of anything else, please contact me."

"Why is the FBI looking into this?" he asked in that slow voice that she would never forget.

"I'm sorry I can't go into that." Turning, she walked at a nice pace toward the porch, flashed her badge to the police officer and entered the victim's home.

Despite telling herself to get a grip, and to focus on the job, she continued thinking of the cowboy in the pickup truck. *Why hadn't she been able to read him?*

CHAPTER 6

Tired, Mia returned to her room around six that evening. She had spent the balance of the day in the library interviewing Nathaniel's co-workers who were heartbroken and moved to the point of tears over his death. Lisa Murphy, the manager, hadn't come into work but talked to Mia at her home. The woman's grief had been difficult to bear.

Mia called Thomas, told him what she discovered so far.

"This isn't good. The killer hasn't broken his pattern and is still operating in an organized manner. How the hell can someone go across the country stoning people to death without leaving clues to his or their identity? There's something we're missing."

Mia agreed. "There's been no demand for recognition or a calling card to rub his success in the police's faces. We're dealing with a different type of criminal. One with controlled anger issues. There are faster easier ways to kill without drawing attention," she said."

"When I researched stonings, I found a few in the middle east, mostly women, adultery that kind of thing. Nothing here in the States. Why start now? What triggered this kind of attack? It comes across personal but none of the Vic's have anything in common other than a type of disability."

"True." She covered her mouth and yawned. Sleep called and she would answer it soon.

"People stoned each other during Biblical days too, several passages in the Book regarding stonings," he said. "We may be dealing with a religious nut."

That pronouncement woke her. She hadn't thought of that and groaned. "No, not again. We said we wouldn't handle those types of cases anymore. Not after the preacher talked those people into killing themselves before we got there. We're not equipped to deal with the emotional fallout. I couldn't sleep through the night for months."

"It's just a guess, should've thought of it when the General mentioned stoning, but —"

"We were too excited to get the Liege files." She sighed. "We would've still taken the job even if we'd known."

"Yes, but I would've added a few conditions for our protection. We'll come up with something to limit your exposure," he said. "What did you think of Noah Sloan?"

It took a second to follow the abrupt change in the conversation. "Rugged. Handsome. Dark."

Thomas snorted. "Is that all?"

"After he explained finding the body and calling the police, he didn't say much. I got the impression the whole thing bothered him, he kept staring at the house without saying anything. Plus I couldn't read him."

"What?"

"I tried and got nothing." Sometimes that happened, so she shouldn't make more out of it than it truly was. But he registered on her radar as a man, a person of personal interest and that was unusual.

"Yeah? Hmm. I'm sending you his bio. Former military, honorable discharge nine months ago, disabled vet, PTSD which could explain the null, excellent record, lots of honors. After what he's seen during 21 years of service including several tours in the Middle East, it's hard to believe seeing a battered body shook him," Thomas said.

"Maybe that's why it did bother him. During the war, you expect to see stuff and aren't surprised. Seeing it when you come home... that's different. Especially in a nice neighborhood and the guy was in a wheelchair." She paused. "The wheelchair was missing."

"What?"

"I checked the van and his house. At the library, they said he used a motorized wheelchair. It wasn't in the van or his home," she said glancing at the notes on her tablet.

"I'll run a check to see if he had a GPS tracking device on the chair. A lot of people use the tracking devices on the more expensive, motorized chairs."

"It would be a huge break if he did," she said afraid to believe the killer would've made that mistake. This was the second wheelchair victim. The first was found in his chair but it wasn't motorized.

"What do you want me to do now? How long should I remain here? I'm out of leads." She stretched and yawned.

"I'm going to check a few things from here. Check with the Detective tomorrow, see if he has any more information and then verify. We may find something. Not returning the wheelchair is a departure, maybe there's more," he said.

"Okay."

"Tip is in Iowa where the last stoning took place. It's a long shot but he may sense something the Feds missed. He'll be to you tomorrow afternoon to go over the house and van, we'll decide the next step after that."

One of Tips abilities included a higher than normal scenting ability similar to a bear. He smelled things other people missed which helped close a lot of their past cases.

"That's good. Hopefully, we'll get a break and finish this one sooner than later."

"Is something going on? Did you learn something from the genealogy companies?" Thomas asked.

Everyone knew she had been searching for clues of her child for decades and tried to help when they could. "Not yet. It's getting harder to stay positive. I wish I could give up the search, but I can't. My heart and mind won't let me."

"Then keep searching, you'll find answers," he encouraged.

She wanted to ask for some sort of guarantee but knew he couldn't, wouldn't do that. "Thanks. I need fuel. Carbs and protein."

"Eat. You know the rules." His voice changed from pity to downright bossy which she preferred.

"As soon as we're done, I've got my food here." She inhaled the takeout of chicken, rice, and sliced chocolate cake.

"Good. Talk to you tomorrow." He disconnected.

Mia sat at the table in the small room and ate. Her mind split between her quest to find the child taken from her on the delivery table and the elusive murderer who stoned the disabled to death.

Evil men did evil deeds for crazy reasons.

When she finished dinner, she set aside thoughts of her lost child. Time to focus on the case. Sitting on the floor in a lotus position, she took several deep calming breaths to center her mind and body.

Snapshots of Nathaniel Green's broken body appeared in her mind, on a slow slider. Inch by inch she reviewed his body. Marks on his arms. They secured him, stretched him out. Standing or on the ground? His smashed face, skull, chest, everything. Guy never had a chance.

Since the day Thomas found and convinced Mia to leave the Liege compound with a small group of people, they took odd jobs to survive. Since arriving in the States they worked as hired mercenaries. Over the years, she saw several chilling murders and foul deeds. It no longer amazed her how cruel people could be to each other, but this was different. Calculated. And made a statement. By stretching him out, one could argue the position was that of the cross. She nibbled on that idea, but didn't like it and continued rolling through ideas.

Arms outstretched and secured to the ground, Green couldn't hide, couldn't cover his face in shame. If he is not blindfolded he saw his attackers or accusers as they… she shook her head to dispel the building vision. That wasn't what she wanted to see before falling asleep.

Mia woke in the middle of a familiar street and looked around. A weird overhead light illuminated the road and Nathaniel Green's house. She inhaled, searching the area. *Nothing.* Just as before when she examined the victim.

"Then why am I here?" she murmured looking around for clues. Obviously, there was something she needed to see. Eager and hoping for a break in the case she moved toward Nathan's home.

The light expanded to include a familiar gray truck in the middle of the road. Just as he had that morning, Noah Sloan stared at the house before looking at her.

Stunned to the point of speechlessness, Mia watched open-mouthed as he removed his sunglasses, stepped out of the truck and looked down at her.

He was pale, big, and tall. The street lights caused a halo effect around his head. But the look he gave her wasn't angelic, not in the least.

"What are you doing here?" he asked frowning, his tone accusing.

No one had ever walked in her dreams before. "What are you doing here?" she countered.

He walked closer. Frosty blue eyes met her gaze with a mixture of curiosity, mistrust, and anger. Shaggy, dark hair curled against his neck as he brushed his fingertips against her cheek.

Her eyes fluttered closed at the intimate touch. Her heartbeat kicked into high gear.

"Are you real or my imagination?" he asked seriously. The low timbre of his voice held a warm, smoky quality, like smooth bourbon.

"I wondered the same thing," she said placing her hand on his chest, feeling his racing heartbeat.

"You walk in dreams?" he stepped back from her touch. Her hand fell to her side.

"Sometimes. You?" She didn't bother explaining it happened when triggered by something else she experienced during her waking hours.

"Yeah, unfortunately." He looked over his shoulder at Nathaniel's house. "Don't see why I'm back here tonight."

"You were here last night?" That surprised her, was he really gifted in walking through dreams? True dream-walkers were rare. She had never met anyone who could walk through dreams. It was a powerful gift that required a strong personality to hold it.

She wielded a fraction of the gift and it drained her whenever it kicked in. She couldn't control when to enter or pick dreams. From what she learned, a dream-walker could go back through time, see events, invade dreams and speak to people through dreams. Noah Sloan deserved another look.

He nodded, stuck his hands in his pocket and looked at the house again.

"How far back are you going?" she asked curiously and a bit excited at the prospect of seeing the full gift in action.

"The day before he was killed, last time his friends saw him."

She and Thomas assumed the victim went somewhere, perhaps met someone who lured him to his death. "How far back can you travel?" She hoped they discovered something that would point them in the direction of the killer.

He eyed her for a few moments as if weighing his decision to tell her anything. She totally understood. People thought the gifted were freaks or crazy and weird, it was one reason she and the others lived together and kept away from non-gifted humans. It could be dangerous.

"Months. Years. Decades." He didn't sound happy about it.

Decades? Hope flared in her chest as she reassessed him. He was the real deal. She had so many questions but settled on one. "Would you mind if I tagged along?"

"Why is the FBI investigating this?" His gaze held hers.

With his skillset, Thomas would want to know everything about him. They didn't meet dream-walkers ever or other gifted people. She answered his question. "There have been several similar murders over the past six months across the country."

He inhaled deeply and released it slowly as a low keening sound swept through the air. A strange gray mist slowly rolled in. He looked at the mist and back down at her. She noticed he hadn't answered her request to tag along.

"You don't think this is weird? Walking and talking to people in dreams?" His voice had a low growling undertone, his eyes were hard as they peered down at her.

Normally, she didn't talk to people in dreams, that wasn't a part of her gift. But kept that to herself. "No, not at all. There's something to see or learn here to help Mr. Green." By reminding him of their purposes she hoped he would take her with him to the day before the murder. She doubted she could do it on her own.

Plus, if Sloan could travel back decades in time, maybe he could help find information about her child. She cautioned herself against being overly optimistic, he hadn't agreed to help with this case yet.

He nodded and looked at the house again. "You're here and I can't get any decent sleep until I complete this search. Let's go, the mist is rising."

Mia had never seen or felt mist with a sinister touch like this. She lifted her hand to touch it and it recoiled.

"Do that again," Noah said, quickly.

She lifted her other hand and the mist flew backward, leaving a clear path for them.

His eyes widened in appreciation. "I've never been able to make it leave, the mist always comes and blocks my vision, making it difficult to see what's in front of me sometimes." He stared at her as if she was an insect to dissect. "How far can you travel?"

"No more than a few days, a week at the absolute most," she admitted moving toward the house. The mist cleared around her with each step.

"Let's take a look at what happened the day before Nate died." He extended his hand.

Raw energy ran up her arm, the moment she touched him. She shuddered. Oh yeah, Thomas would want to know more about him. Noah was strong and not a product of the Liege with a powerful gift.

One moment they stood in front of the house the next it was a new day full of sunshine and possibilities.

Nathaniel pulled out of his garage and drove off to work. Mia and Noah were with him, seeing through the lens of his eyes. He seemed happy, his thoughts were on the job, some new research books had arrived the day before, new computer software.

She looked at Noah who wore a slight frown. "What is it?"

"Nothing."

Nathaniel pulled into the handicapped parking lot at the library, and eventually went inside.

"Stay with him," Noah said before leaving her at the reference desk with Nathaniel.

Mia watched each person who interacted with Nathaniel. Everyone she interviewed at the library had told the truth, he got along well with them all. She could cross them off her very short length. Nathaniel and Lisa were very close friends. She looked out for him and he respected her.

By the time Nathaniel went to lunch, Mia wanted to fast forward the day to see if he interacted with anyone suspicious.

"Noah?" she said his name.

"How'd you do that? I heard you inside my head when you called me."

"I just spoke. Anyway, can we speed this up? I'd like to see the faces of everyone he interacted with that day."

"Yes. Hold on."

The room spun momentarily.

She grabbed the desk and closed her eyes to bring calm and focus. When she re-opened them, everything around her moved quickly as if he pressed a fast-forward button. Nathaniel returned from lunch, people came and went moving fast. Mia stared at every person, gauging their intent. By the time Nathaniel drove home and cooked dinner, she was exhausted and disappointed that she hadn't learned anything to help solve this case.

Noah wrapped his arm around her waist and helped her back to the street. The mist rolled around them, testing her. Aggravated, Mia waved her hands and sat on the sidewalk. "Back off, now."

The mists disappeared as if it'd never been. She stopped and took several deep breaths.

"You expended a lot of energy; did you find anything to help you with your case?" Noah said standing next to her.

"I'm not sure." Later, she would process everything she saw and pick it apart. Right now she needed rest. Dream-walking took too much energy.

"Did you see the books in his bedroom?"

She looked up at him. "Yes." But she hadn't really looked at them. "Why?"

"They dealt with arms, guns, weapons. A pistol was in his glove box and another beneath his seat. Chances are he was proficient with both and would've defended himself. Were they with the car when it was returned with his body?"

She straightened. "No. There were no weapons in the van or proof that a gun had been used. I'll verify the guns and pull that string. Anything else?"

"Just this. What would make a man as careful as Nate stop and get close enough to a stranger to be taken?"

Great question. "You think this was a random killing?"

He thought about it for a second. "No. Too methodical and precise. Were there any traces of drugs in his body? Something that would knock him out?"

"Probably, I'm waiting to see the toxicology report, it hasn't come in yet," she said.

"Have drugs been used in the past?"

"Yes, in every case," she admitted but wouldn't share more without Thomas' permission.

"Someone gets close and shoots them with a fast-acting agent that incapacitates them. After that, it's an easy matter to take the van or walk away as someone else entered the van from the other side. Either way, it would be quick and smooth."

"Did you see that?" She wondered if he saw the murder which would be great.

"No. The day of his murder is blurred, I've never been able to see the actual crime just what happens before it." He looked at her thoughtfully. "You might be able to break through the blur."

She had no idea what he meant and didn't have the energy or inclination to try more right now. Her body screamed for fuel and rest. "Okay, we'll try it after I regroup."

He didn't agree or disagree she noticed. Noah was a very careful, closed off man. She wondered why.

"Tonight's the first time I've ever had this kind of control and it feels great. Feels like it's supposed to happen this way, kind of legitimizes the whole thing, you know?"

Maybe not so closed off. While she was about to fall from exhaustion, he looked as if he could leap tall buildings in a single bound.

"Good, and thanks for your help. Please keep all this confidential. Don't tell anyone we met here or about my abilities." She mustered the energy to meet his gaze.

"Of course. I respect that and will keep it to myself. I ask you to do the same. Do not tell anyone about me either."

She didn't respond.

"You thanked me, now I'll thank you. When I enter this…" he waved. "Normally it's difficult, extremely draining and sometimes leaves me sick for several hours or days depending on the severity of the event. This is the first time I feel great and at peace. Thank you for that."

"You're welcome. I hope we can work together?" she let the question hang.

His face changed, went blank as if the previous joy-lit candle had been abruptly snuffed out. "No. No, we can't."

Disappointed she nodded. He walked off. The next moment she opened her eyes, looked around and took note of the time on the bedside clock. Two hours had passed since she fell asleep.

She rolled over and touched her lips as her eyelids drooped. "Don't be too sure of that, Noah." She knew she'd see him again.

Noah woke and looked at the clock. He hadn't been asleep long, less than two hours and he was wide awake staring up at the ceiling. There were life-changing moments that happened in a person's life that marked them permanently.

The day the Army recruiter talked to him in high school, placed his hand on his shoulder and told him that he would make a great soldier. Told him he would travel the world, see unbelievable things, make lasting friends while defending his country. That five-minute conversation may have been rehearsed and said to hundreds of new recruits, but that fall day, the words hit a chord in Noah. He joined ROTC and never looked back.

Three months after agreeing to be his wife, his fiancee was killed in an automobile accident, she had been two months pregnant. He hadn't seen or touched her in three months. That incident destroyed his faith in women.

One fateful Thursday afternoon, earlier this year, he died. He had no recollection of crossing over or coming back. In fact, if the doctor's hadn't told him he died he wouldn't know anything about it. That day killed his career as a soldier the one thing he loved more than anything.

Looking back, he didn't have much to show for his 39 years of life other than medals, scars, and discomfort. And then the dreams started. Initially, one here and there. As days turned into weeks, to months, the dreams occurred more often. He considered the whole dreaming thing a waste of time because the mist blinded him and drained his energy.

Until tonight.

He ran his hand through his shoulder-length hair and looked at his hands. There were light, occasional tremors, but nothing like his regular shakes. He's spent a couple hours dream-walking and he was awake, alert and not shuddering beneath a blanket. He wanted to pump his fist in the air, scream hallelujah or whatever.

When he met the FBI Agent earlier today, the way she stepped toward him, asking questions, made an indelible impression. Fleeting, of course, but he'd been aware of her in a way he hadn't noticed women in a while. Still, he never expected to see her again.

Seeing her tonight in his dreams, her soft hair appearing golden beneath the light. Long-lashed soft brown eyes filled with confidence instead of fear at being sucked into a dream startled him. Initially, he was certain she was a figment of his overactive imagination until he touched her.

Soft. Her skin had been soft beneath his finger and he wanted to linger just a bit longer until she touched him. Uninvited touches were off limits and he hadn't invited anyone to touch him in a long time.

Fully prepared to reject her request to accompany him, he had no intentions of spending time with someone with the same mental problems as himself. Until she controlled the mist.

Even now he smiled at being free to see without the mist blinding him and draining his energy. Tonight had been nightmare and pain-free. He wanted to laugh from the sheer beauty of it. They'd discovered information that could help find the killer.

The idea of walking through dreams having a beneficial side never occurred to him until he discovered the guns in the van and books in the library. It was possible learning that information could make a difference, assist in bringing in the murderer.

Tonight had been another life-changing moment, one he wouldn't ever forget. Walking through dreams could be positive, could help people. Most importantly, not everyone thought he was crazy.

CHAPTER 7

Yesterday had been a scorcher, hitting the high 90's by mid-afternoon. Today was on track to match or surpass the heat of its predecessor. Steam rose steadily from the streets and sidewalks. Mia wiped the sweat from her forehead as she walked toward the police station to talk to Detective Gordon.

She glanced at her watch and grunted. Thomas had so many questions this morning when she told him about her dream-walking experience last night, she got a late start. If she'd known he would jump on a plane to meet Noah in person, she would've cut the conversation short. As it was, she hoped to catch the Detective to discuss the bit about the guns before Thomas and Tip arrived. She could go around him but didn't want to risk messing up the case with technicalities.

As she reached the corner, a familiar silver truck drove past and parked in a spot not far from where she stood to watch. Curious and pleased to see him, she watched to see if he got out of his truck. He stepped out, locked it and walked toward her with his hands stuffed into his pockets.

Eyes up, don't look down, stay professional. "Good morning," she said when he reached her.

His gaze locked on hers and for a few seconds; she wasn't sure he would respond. "Morning. I have a few questions to ask if you don't mind."

"Questions? I can't discuss the case —"

"No, not about that. About the other... you know. I've never been able to talk to anybody without feeling stupid or weird. You seem comfortable..."

Thomas was on a plane to talk to Noah and could answer his questions

41

much better than she could. Still, she understood the feeling of being the oddball.

"I've got to talk to the Detective about the guns and check on a couple reports. We can talk once I'm done, or I could meet you somewhere later," she offered.

"I'll wait. Not much else to do today." He turned and headed back to his truck.

Aware of the time, she moved toward the station while wondering what he meant. Seems her days were jammed pack with all kinds of things needing to be completed.

"Okay, I'll see you in a bit."

Noah watched Mia walk to the police station and disappear inside. "What are you doing here? Didn't you tell her you wouldn't work with her?" He shook his head in disgust when he had no rational answer other than the truth, he wanted to talk to her about walking in dreams.

Moving to his truck, he leaned against the grill with his arms across his chest and stared at the door of the station. *Mia Haddon.* He recalled the stubborn glint in her eyes while he said he wouldn't work with her. Did she suspect he'd show up today? He wouldn't put it past her.

The petite hurricane stormed into his world shaking it upside down last night. Nothing would ever be the same. *The mist could be controlled.* Walking in dreams had a purpose. Could be beneficial.

He rubbed his jaw as he thought of the sexy, woman with soft, creamy cinnamon skin and short light brown curls all over her head. Her eyes were an interesting shade of brown, shadowed with long dark lashes, high cheekbones, and kissable lips.

Kissable? He snorted not caring for the direction of his thoughts. Even though she looked 10 - 15 years younger than his almost 40, she wasn't a silly girl like the two females in the bar the other day. He sensed Mia was a go-getter. Smart, articulate and someone who most likely had a man waiting at home for her.

Lucky guy.

Noah appreciated the way she looked at him with that direct gaze that said I see you, the real you, and it's okay. By not expending so much energy hiding that part of him, he was free to enjoy a simple thing like hanging out with a beautiful woman.

A sexy, beautiful woman, who mattered. He couldn't explain why it may have been twisted up with her ability to control the mist and freeing him from that prison. Even for one night. Or that her sense of justice, correcting wrongs were similar to his. Or the fact she kept him company in the vast world of dreams. It could be all of those reasons or none of them, he wasn't a shrink. But nothing changed the fact that the short FBI agent mattered.

<<<>>>

Mia saw the Detective in the lobby and caught him before he left. "Morning, Detective."

"Morning." He frowned at her. "I don't have any new information."

"I do," she said. "Have you checked to see if Mr. Green owned a weapon?"

His gaze narrowed. "No. Did he?"

"We should check."

He looked like he would argue but turned and headed to his office. "Have a seat and tell me what new information you have pertaining to my case."

Rather than make a smart comment about his mood or the case, she talked about the books on defense in Green's home and his weapons.

He sat back as he stared at the monitor. "Green had two handguns." He shared the rest of the information regarding the gun registration.

"The guns weren't in the house or the van," she said.

He shook his head and glanced up at her. "How'd they get the drop on an armed man? That's the whole purpose of carrying a weapon, to protect yourself."

"Drugs? If they someone got close enough, they could've shot drugs in his system before he could reach his gun."

"Soon as I get that report, I'll let you know. But I'm thinking you're onto something. Hard to understand why they took his guns after shooting him up with drugs. He was a cripple, couldn't run."

"He was driving his van and could escape that way," she reminded him, not appreciating his cutting remarks about the victim.

"That's possible." He released a sigh.

"About Green's guns?" What did he plan to do about the missing weapons?

"I'll send a couple guys over to look through the house again. Maybe we overlooked something."

"Is there a pawn shop in town or a nearby town that buys guns?" *Seriously? Why isn't he doing the basics?*

"Yes, there is, I'll let him know to look out for it."

"Detective, if someone stole those guns and sells them anywhere in this country, we need to know about it. It is important to this case." Their gazes clashed.

"I'll make sure the word gets out." He glanced at his watch, stood, stepped around her and walked out. "I've got another appointment and will talk with him later today."

<<<>>>

Mia appreciated Noah offering to tag along with her to the pawn shops in the three adjoining counties. His large frame seemed cramped in her small rental but she didn't want to ride in his truck, besides, he had questions.

"How long have you been able to… you know," he started once they hit the highway out of town. His voice had a gravelly quality to it as if he didn't use it much.

"Most of my life, what about you?" she asked.

True, she lived an abnormally long time. At the age of four or five, she'd been taken to the Liege compound. The operations started early and stopped when she when she started her menstrual cycle. The repeated rapes happened shortly after. Then the pregnancy and delivery. She remained a few more years before escaping with Thomas and a few others.

"Just started for me this year. Metal from an explosive lodged in my brain, induced coma. After the surgery everything was different. Always had dreams but they were stronger, more vibrant, and then I was pulled into them." He paused as if he said too much. When she didn't say anything, he continued. "Saw people I knew, friends who had died. Spent time watching them, learning stuff, went to places I've never been, saw things I wished I hadn't. Then the mist started, changed things again. It's harder to go places, hurts now, and drains me. That ever happen to you?"

The drive to the first pawn shop was an hour and a half out of town, more than enough time for Noah to ask questions and her to answer.

"No. When I dream walk, it's usually based on something I've seen during the day that triggers it. Even then, it's limited to the immediate area that I've already seen. Nowhere near what you can do. You said you could go back decades, that's awesome. How did you develop it?" *And if you could access the days after they took my child, I'd be overjoyed.*

He snorted but seemed to relax a bit, wasn't as stiff as when they started. "Develop it? It just happens, does its own thing. Wrecks my sleep. Can't get out of bed some days, steals my strength. I wouldn't say I developed anything, more like sitting in the passenger seat along for the ride, taking in the sights." He huffed. "Fucked up, really fucked up."

She hadn't experienced any of that but then again she wasn't as strong as him either.

"Any ideas how to stop it?" he asked. She felt the heat of his gaze on the side of her face.

"If I did we'd all have done it by now." She bit her lip and hoped he didn't ask about her friends.

"We? There's more of you? In the FBI?" He turned in the seat to face her. "There's a group of people with shit like me working in the FBI?"

Shocked surprised laced his voice.

She cleared her throat. "A special group for special assignments from time to time."

"Really?" He looked at his hands for a few seconds. "How does that work? Did they come looking for you? Ran tests? Did you sign up? I mean, this dream thing is so out of the box, it's hard to believe you go through regular channels."

"Not that I'm aware of. Thomas gets the jobs, handles the assignments. He brought me in. He's flying in and will be here later today."

"How many?"

She thought of Lizzy and sent a prayer for her full recovery. "Six."

He whistled. "Thought there'd be more."

"No question there is. Making commitments to use your gifts for the greater good is the real challenge. Not everyone wants to be identified as gifted or an oddball." She smiled.

"Yeah. Yeah, you're right."

When he didn't say anything for a few seconds she glanced at him. "Come from a big family?"

"Not really. My mom died when I was in basic. Have no idea who my old man is. Half-brother lives in Alaska with his wife, no kids. He's 12 years younger, we were never really close. My cousin is like a brother and the only family I have. You?"

She swallowed hard and gave her standard answer. "The team's my family."

He asked no more questions and she was grateful when they pulled into the parking lot of the first pawn shop. The Detective hadn't reached out to the owner yet, fortunately, there had been no guns purchased, or sold in over a month. After giving the owner her card to contact her in case someone came in with the revolver, they headed to the next pawn shop in the next county.

"Why didn't you call and ask if the gun had been turned in?" Noah asked as they pulled onto the highway.

"I can pick up more in person." She had to be careful not to over-share anything that would put the team at risk. Although he seemed okay, Thomas had to check him out to ensure he wasn't a threat.

"Like what?"

"Scents, residual energy, deceit, some I can get over the phone, but not most. Plus I wouldn't have been able to do anything about it." She shrugged. "Just more efficient to deal face to face."

"Wait, you can tell if someone's lying?"

"Deceit has a certain smell and ting in the voice so it's fairly easy to detect," she said.

"Bet that comes in handy in your line of work… must be hell in your social life."

She glanced at him as she stopped at the light. "Why?"

"Means people need to always be on the up and up, honest around you," he said watching her closely.

"Why wouldn't they?"

He shrugged.

"Lies are a waste of time and energy, we don't bother. Do you?" she asked.

"What?" He looked at her.

"Lie?"

"Sometimes. Working on it though. Gotta find a way, to be honest, and not hurt someone's feelings. That sucks," he said with feeling.

She wondered what put that frown on his face. "Painful truth is better than a lie, always," she said.

"Makes sense if you can detect a lie," he said looking out the window.

"Also when you're certain a person never lies, you don't question what they say. Makes for a smoother life in the end, don't you think?" she asked.

Noah scratched his head and looked out the window. "Sure does." He thought of the female in the bar the other day. Why hadn't he told her he wasn't interested? It was the truth. Why hadn't he told Dr. Higgins he recognized people in his dreams? He didn't want to deal with the fallout of their feelings being hurt.

In the good doctor's case, she'd been so upset she left the room for over 10 minutes because he told half the truth. Would it have been better to have told her the full truth? Somehow he didn't think so. Most people really couldn't handle the truth.

"Is everyone on your team, like me... like us? With some kind of gift?" Last night had been phenomenal. He woke energized with total recall.

This morning he sensed a call of purpose similar to when he enlisted. For the first time ever, he didn't feel weird or like he was losing his mind.

She nodded and chuckled. "Yeah, a bunch of mutts, mutated mutts, get it?"

Hearing the word "mutated" stunned him.

"Hey, it's a joke," she said softly.

He nodded. "Good name, appropriate I suppose. Mostly women or men on the team?"

"Even, three and three."

"Are they all coming here?" She was easy to talk to and really pretty. Driving around with her wasn't a bad way to spend a few hours, not at all.

"Doubt it. They're finishing up a job out of the country," she said.

"Yeah?" He paused. "What kind of gifts do they have."

"That I can't say. Wait, and see."

Noah glanced at her, saw her smile and relaxed further. He wanted to walk through more dreams with her, ask her to teach him to control the mist. He wanted to see how far he could go and perhaps do more than observe. Her being in his dream last night opened a whole new vista he wanted to explore.

CHAPTER 8

Thomas and Tip met her in the hotel restaurant after she and Noah returned from the pawn shops. Their plates had just arrived when she sensed Thomas' presence. Mia breathed a sigh of relief. He could answer Noah's questions and provide direction for the job. Maybe now she could finish her steak, potato, and cheesecake.

"Hello," Thomas said as he reached their table. Both men were almost a foot taller than her 5'4". Thomas could've been a successful linebacker in the NFL with his wide barrel chest, tree trunk sized thighs and wide neck. His no-fucks-to-give aura typically caused men to scurry out of his way without him speaking.

Noah stilled, looked up into Thomas' face and then at Tip. He didn't respond to the greeting, not yet anyway.

"Hey Princess," Tip said teasing her as he always did since she told him she was a descendant of the Queen of Sheba several decades ago. He was almost as pale as Thomas with a smaller muscular build, dreamy green eyes, and dimpled chin. His easy-going personality made him her favorite.

"Hi, guys." She smiled up at them. "This is Noah. Noah, my team-mates, Thomas and Tip." She frowned. "Do you have a last name, Tip?"

He grinned as he glanced at her. "Not that I know of. Been Tip all my life."

"Can we join you?" Thomas asked, watching Noah.

Noah looked at Mia.

Men. "Sure. You just got in?" She asked as they took the empty seats between her and Noah.

"Yeah. What did you learn?" Thomas looked at her, capturing her gaze with his penetrating silver-blue eyes.

49

She told him about her discussion with the Detective.

Thomas nodded. "Tip will go look at the van, and then the house again. Anything else?"

"Not yet," she said.

He looked at Noah. "Former military?"

Noah nodded.

"PTSD?"

Noah frowned and didn't answer. He looked at Mia and her heart plummeted. She hoped he would be different, strong enough to deal with Thomas and the others. If he became offended with these two... whoa.

What are you thinking? It had been nice working with him, no one else on the team had ever dream walked. Whenever the gift kicked in, it could be a lonely experience.

"Why?" Noah asked, reverting to the man she met the first day, giving monosyllabic answers.

Thomas shrugged. "Just curious, you have that look of a man wrongly diagnosed. Been there myself, know what it's like." He turned to Mia. "Address for the van and house?"

She sent it to him and Tip via text.

Thomas' phone beeped. He read his text and cursed. "Another body dropped. Found in Tennessee 48-hours ago. Another cripple," he growled and looked at Tip. "Hit the van and the house and prepare to fly to Tennessee."

Surprised that Tip would act as a scout, Mia stared at Thomas while Tip stood.

"Got it. Nice meeting you," Tip told Noah and grinned down at her. "See you around, Princess. Duty calls."

She smiled but glanced at Noah's blank face. It was as if the entire morning they spent together never happened. Damn it. She would have to wait to discuss going back in time to the Liege Compound to get answers about her son or daughter. "Later, Tip," she said.

Thomas stared at the wall for several moments. "What're we missing?"

Mia and Noah had been discussing that in the car.

"We briefly touched on the Middle East stonings the other night. Is it possible they have a sect here?" she asked.

To his credit, Thomas thought about it a minute or two longer than when she realized it was a bad idea.

"I don't see it," he said, looked at Noah. "What do you think?"

"I don't see it either," Noah said and then clenched his jaws. "Did you tell him?" he asked her. "Did you tell him about... you know?"

Mia's eyes widened. "What?"

Noah stood and walked out without a backward glance.

Another one bites the dust. She glared at Thomas. "You had to go there, didn't you?"

He met her unflinching gaze. "Five days, four-and-a-half to go. If he has information, we need it. He's the real deal, Mia and we need him. Don't think he realizes his gift —"

"I know he's the real deal, Thomas. But this is new for him. He thought he was going crazy and is just beginning to believe that's not the case. He may work with us if he trusts what and who we are," she said. Sometimes Thomas acted like a bull in a china-shop. There was no reason to ask Noah's opinion if it wasn't freely given.

Thomas stroked his clean-shaven, square chin and stared at the table. The waiter placed a glass of water beside him. "Can I get you anything?"

"No," Thomas snapped without looking up.

Mia offered the waiter a brief smile when he looked surprised at Thomas' rudeness. The man often forgot the basics they had been forced to learn to fit in with the changing world.

"I'm done, thank you," she said, earning a small smile from the waiter. She'd be sure to leave him a large tip.

As soon as the waiter cleared the table and left, Thomas looked at her, his gaze an eery gray. "Hate groups."

"Hate groups?" She tried to catch up. "What about them?"

He stood. "I need to check a few things out. Have Noah walk through the scene again, try to look into the van on the day of the murder. Help him to see more." He strode out.

Mia had no idea how to reach Noah and hated Thomas pushed him away before she could learn more about him personally. She pulled out her phone to contact Thomas.

"I don't know how to reach him," she said when he answered.

"I'll send his address." He hung up before she could say anything else.

She headed toward her car as her phone beeped with Noah's address. Following the GPS instructions, she drove out of town where the landscape changed. She saw cows, horses, ranches, and farms. It was quiet, peaceful. Eventually, she turned down a dirt road which stopped in front of a large ranch style home with a wide porch. Seeing Noah's truck, she stepped out and headed toward the porch.

He opened it before she knocked.

"What?"

Mia blinked at his growly tone. "What do you mean, what?"

"Why are you here? I don't want anything to do with you, didn't you get that?"

She hadn't, not really. The people in her life blew up at each other often but it didn't mean stay away, more like go away for now.

"Um, I... we need your help." This was unusual turf for her. He didn't share her goals, wasn't on the team, had no real reason to cooperate.

"Tough." He closed the door in her face.

She stared at the door for a few moments and then turned the knob. The door opened and she walked in.

"What the hell?" he said from his chair in front of the television. "You're trespassing. I should call the cops."

Mia frowned. Granted, she had been born in a different century but common courtesy was still common. "Why are you so angry? I don't understand." Baffled, she watched the red spots enlarge on his face as his jaw clenched. Her gaze zeroed in on the fast pulse in his neck before searching his gaze. "You're troubled."

"I don't want you here," he growled.

Heat raced to her cheeks as she understood she was the source of his anger. Since she'd never caused that reaction in anyone that she could recall, she took a deep breath and released it slowly. Uncertain of how to proceed, she decided it best to retreat.

"I see. Well, I will leave you for now and see you later. Tonight." She backed toward the door.

"No." It came out like a low rumbling sound.

She stopped and looked at him. "No?"

"No, I won't see you tonight or tomorrow night or any night. I just want to be left alone."

Frowning she faced him. "You have control over your dreams?" When he didn't answer she continued. "If so I'd love to learn that skill. It would make life so much better." She tilted her head, took in his mulish glare and sighed.

"Doesn't matter. I won't work with anyone who breaks their word. I refuse to help you. Now go away, and don't come back."

"You're rude," she said to hide her hurt feelings.

"You're a liar," he growled his blue eyes like polished marbles.

"Am not. I never agreed to keep what happened to myself. For goodness sake, I'm here on an assignment, of course, I have to report what I find out. You were in the military and should know that."

His mouth opened and closed. "Get out."

She turned on a huff and stomped down the porch. *Ungrateful...*the next time she saw him wallowing in the mist, she wouldn't help.

CHAPTER 9

Unaccustomed to such treatment, anger ripped through Mia. She whipped the rental car around and sped down the dirt road until she hit the street. Her car bounced and swerved to the side as she heard the horn of an oncoming vehicle.

She pulled the wheel hard and hit the embankment on the other side of the road. It took a few moments to catch her breath before she looked over her shoulder at the truck she almost hit.

Two gorgeous, dark-haired hunks were running to her car.

"Are you alright?"

"Where did you come from?"

Mia blinked as her vision sharpened. "Twins?"

The first one grinned, the other stared at her. "Are you alright?" he asked again.

She pushed open the door and stood beside it. "Yes, thanks." She looked at the car. "It's a rental."

One of them walked around and looked it over. "Seems okay, you might want to start it to be sure."

"I'm Mia." Her gaze darted from one to the other.

"Ryder." He pointed to the other one. "Ryan."

She nodded and inhaled. Her smile dropped. "You're..."

Ryder's eyes chilled as he inhaled.

Ryan stood next to him. "I'm what?"

"Different." She inhaled again. "Can't place my finger on it, though."

"So are you," Ryder said watching her closely and then looking over her shoulder. "You flew out into the road, somebody chasing you?"

She had forgotten about Noah and waved it off. "No. Just pissed."

Head tilted, she stared at the two. "Are you gifted?"

"Gifted?" Ryder asked before looking at his brother. "What do you mean?"

"Never mind." She stretched, looked toward Noah's house and hoped she hadn't ruined their mission by angering him.

"Come on, share. What did you mean by gifted?" Ryder asked, with a wide grin.

"Extra-sensory gifts." Certain he was more than human, but unsure what, she met his stare.

Ryder ran his hand through his hair as she stared into dark eyes that held multiple secrets. "Naw, don't have anything like that. You?" he asked in a teasing tone. He suspected she was more than human but wasn't sure what or how she suspected he or his brother were more. They were human-deep, with their beasts locked down.

She smiled and opened the car door. "Let me see if it cranks."

Ryder suspected it would and wasn't surprised when it did. The hair stood up on his arms and neck. *"What do you think? Should we call this into Alpha Theron?"*

"She's human, not wolf," Ryan said watching her.

"More than human," Ryder corrected. *"He may want to know there are strange breeds in the state."*

"Dad would want to know," Ryan said. *"La Patron too."*

"Yeah. We need to let them in, but let's try to learn more," Ryder said as he leaned forward, his face near the window. "Everything alright?"

She looked at him and nodded. "Yeah, seems fine. Thanks."

"Can I buy you a drink? Dinner?" he asked still smiling. "We're not far from a restaurant that serves the best seafood and steaks in Texas."

Her brow arched. "In Texas?" she said in a dry tone.

He liked her spunk. "Yeah, pinky swear." He held out his little finger to her. She laughed, it was a tinkling sound that ran through him as she caught his pinky with her own.

"I've got a little downtime, lead on," she said.

Still smiling Ryder returned to the passenger side of the truck, turned and led the way to the Lucky G restaurant. During the drive, he contacted Tyrone, his dad, and Alpha Theron. Both told him to be careful and to let them know what he learned after their meal.

As soon as Mia pulled out to follow the truck, she contacted Thomas, gave him a brief update of what happened at Noah's, the near miss accident, and her current destination.

"Didn't you just eat?" Thomas asked.

She rolled her eyes. Food was fuel she constantly burned. "Yes, is there a point to that question?"

He laughed. They all ate a lot but for some reason, he and Tip enjoyed teasing her about her capacity to eat large quantities.

"No. As far as Noah, the two of you will meet up again whether he wants it or not. The two men could be… well, I'll wait to hear what you discover."

"Could be what?" she asked refusing to allow him to withhold information. It was a rule. They shared all information.

"Were you at the Liege compound when they brought in wolf pups?" he asked.

She frowned and tried to remember. After giving birth she worked as a housekeeper and remained in the dorms. "Could've been there, but I wouldn't have known. Wait, wolf pups? Those bastards experimented on animals too?"

"More than animals. If I'm correct, they experimented on dual-natured humans. Part wolf, part human could be other breeds out there too, don't know. I heard some humans who worked on that side of the building where they housed the wolf pups talk about it once we escaped. What they did to us was nothing compared to how the dual-natureds were treated. From what I remember, they're the reason the Liege stopped running tests on us and focused on them. They're stronger and handled the technology better."

Mia whistled. "Holy shit. I didn't know." Her entire focus had been on surviving and then searching for her child. Seems she missed huge gaps in learning what was happening in the world.

"What can you tell me about them? Are they dangerous? Will they attack me?" Her throat tightened as she followed the truck.

"They have an Alpha in charge of the whole country, La Patron, he's serious and no one to play with. The Joint Chiefs tried to mess him over and got their asses kicked. Every state has another Alpha beneath him. If they realize you're not 100% human —"

"I am 100% human."

"Yeah, right. They'll report it in, the Alphas make the decisions on what to do. For the most part, they don't or won't get involved in human affairs, so I doubt they'll attack. They do speak mind to mind, have keen vision and eyesight, but so do you."

"I don't speak mind to mind," she said.

"No, but we all have similar skills, speed, vision, hearing, ability to hear deceit, courtesy of the Liege. Some can enter your thoughts, so lock down your mind."

"Locking it," she said.

"As far as dangerous? That depends. If you're a threat to them or their way of life, they'll kill you without blinking. Don't tell them you know what they are and it should be alright."

"Sounds like this might be a bad idea all around," she muttered.

"Yeah, but you're on their radar now. They wouldn't have bothered with you unless they sensed you weren't 100% human either."

She scowled at the phone and didn't correct him since he had a point. "How much can I say?"

"About yourself? Be honest, won't hurt. Maybe it'll help, we could use some right about now. If we're lucky, one of their Alphas will contact us and we may learn more about these killings. Or they may have files on the Liege and be willing to share."

Her heart leaped with hope. "Maybe we can come to some sort of arrangement with them. Help each other out."

Thomas snorted. "We don't have anything to offer them. There's millions of them in the States alone, and just a few of us."

She thought about it. "We really don't know how many of us there are. Could be more. They could help us find others."

"Why would they do that? Why would they get involved with humans?"

"I don't know yet when I have an answer I'll let you know. Nothing happens by coincidence. Not meeting Noah or these twins. Something's brewing and we need to be prepared for anything."

Silence filled the car for several moments. "You're right." He sighed. "With Lizzy fading, and the team shrinking, I'm about ready to fade into the sunset myself. Haven't given much thought to a future, hell after 163 years I'm tired. But you're right, there is a hint of expectancy in the air. I didn't want to acknowledge it but that doesn't change anything. Thanks, and be careful."

"Will do. Talk to you later." She disconnected and pulled into the parking lot behind them.

There was nothing lucky looking about the Lucky G restaurant. It was an old wood building with a wrap-around porch filled with rocking chairs, in the middle of a large field. Several cars parked haphazardly around the front and sides.

Mia wasn't impressed with the building but she *was* curious about the twins. *Wolf Shifters.* She stared at them as they left the cab of their truck. Tall, wide shoulders, lean waist, dark shaggy hair, Ryder wore a close-shaven beard, while Ryan's face was clean. She could see them as wolves now and blanked her expression as they approached and opened her door.

"May not look like much, but the food's best in these parts," Ryder said as Ryan stood a few feet behind her watching.

Smiling, she slid out the front seat with her purse strap on her shoulder and inhaled the air. "Smells good." And it did. Her mouth watered and stomach growled in appreciation as she followed Ryan, while Ryder followed her.

Inside, she sensed more people like the twins. Several eyes followed them as they sat at a large table that would easily accommodate her entire team. Once Ryder and Ryan sat she understood the reason for oversized seating, those two ate up most of the room.

An older woman walked over to them, smiling. "Guys, I've got your beers coming up, what would you like to drink, Ma'am."

"Water for now, but I'll want something to go with dessert, maybe a beer then."

"Gotcha, Honey." The woman turned and left them. Ryan handed her a menu.

Mia was impressed by the selections. Tired of chicken, she decided on the pulled-pork barbecue and all the fixings. "Thanks, this is nice." She looked around in appreciation of the laid-back place and atmosphere.

"What's a fine, looking chocolate drop like you doing in Littleton, Texas?" Ryder asked with a devilish grin. These guys were sexy, handsome and young.

Mindful that everyone in the building would probably hear her, she smiled. "Work, what else."

Ryder's brow cocked. "What kind of work?"

She stared at him for a few seconds, glanced at Ryan and then spoke. "A murder investigation."

The sudden stillness in the restaurant proved everyone heard her even though she had lowered her voice.

Ryan frowned.

She pulled out her badge, placed it on the table and leaned forward. "Please keep this quiet."

Ryder lifted her badge, showed it to Ryan and returned it to her. Neither spoke for several moments.

Were they mind-speaking to each other or someone else? She had no way of telling and picked up a soft roll from the basket the waitress had placed on the table when she took their order.

"Ohmigod, this is so good. I need to take a few of these back with me." She took a sip of water and continued eating. When the brush against her forehead happened, she ignored it. No one could access her mind without her permission, once again, thanks to brain tampering from the Liege.

"Glad you like 'em," Ryder said. "I'll have Rita bag a dozen for you to take with you. Food should be out soon."

She licked the butter from her fingers, did a quick sweep around the room. There were fewer people but still a sizable amount.

"Thanks. If the barbecue is as good as the rolls, I owe you."

"There's' been a murder in the area? One that the Feds are interested in?" Ryan asked.

Mia wondered if this was their version of good cop, bad cop. "There's been a murder in the area and I'm here to investigate." Her voice changed, became more serious.

Ryan nodded.

A few minutes later, the waitress returned with two platters. She placed one in front of Mia, the other Ryan. Smiling, she inhaled the sweet aroma and picked up a fry, eyeballed the corn on the cob, beans, and barbecue. Perfect.

Eager for a taste, she scooped a fork-full of barbecue into her mouth and moaned in appreciation as the perfectly blended seasonings hit her tongue. Eyes closed, she smacked her lips and took another bite.

"This is too good to be true." She looked at her hosts who wore slight smiles, watching her.

"You enjoy your food," Ryan said giving her his first genuine smile since they met.

"Correction, good food. I love good food," she said taking another bite as Ryder's platter was set in front of him.

Rita smiled brightly at her. "Glad you like it, if you need anything else, holler."

"Thanks, Rita. I want to take some rolls with me," she said.

"The twins already ordered it," Rita said then winced.

Mia ignored Rita's mistake of mentioning their mind to mind communicating and continued eating. The meal was completed in silence with an occasional moan from her.

When she finished the platter, she reached for the menu to look at desserts. The last time she dream-walked with Noah she was so drained she could barely stand. Tonight, she needed extra fuel to try and push through the mists that prevented him from seeing Nathaniel on the day of his death.

Ryan chuckled.

She looked at him briefly and then decided on a slice of coconut cake. "Are you guys having dessert?" She held up her menu.

"I might," Ryder said.

Ryan shook his head. "I'm good."

"You guys live around here? Near Noah?"

Ryder frowned. "Noah? Don't know him."

She waved it off. "You live near here?"

"Got a place about 10 miles from where you almost ran into us," Ryder said with a slight smile.

"I apologize for that. Normally, I'm a great driver, and don't make those kinds of mistakes," she said with feeling.

"What happened to make you react like that?" Ryder asked.

"Misunderstanding." She clamped her lips tight and watched Rita walk toward them. "I'd like a slice of cake please."

Rita removed her platter with a smile. "Bring that right out to you."

With thoughts of cake and murder on her mind, Mia didn't say anything for a few moments.

"Nathaniel Green," Ryan said. "The librarian was found dead in his driveway a couple days ago. Hasn't been buried and you're here investigating his death. Was there a problem?"

She sensed a subtle push and bit back a smile. Instead, she frowned, debated whether to share as if pushed or ignore it, which would prove she was gifted. In the end, she did neither.

"Problem?"

Ryan nodded. "Feds don't get involved —"

"Why do you care? I'm not questioning your whereabouts at the time the crime was committed. Do you know anything about it?"

His eyes widened and turned cold. Like chips of frosty onyx, he stared at her. "No, unfortunately, I don't otherwise I'd try to help you. I live in this area and when someone, anyone is snuffed like that, as a citizen I'm concerned."

They locked gazes for a few seconds. It seemed the entire building held its breath.

She nodded. "Thanks. I needed this break, a moment of downtime to enjoy a meal without complications. I can't discuss an open, ongoing investigation." Her gaze sharpened as it flicked over both of them.

The restaurant had all but emptied. Mia sensed something was happening and forced herself to relax. Whatever happened, happened.

"I understand," Ryan said. "Just threw me for a loop when you went all cop and accused me—"

"Didn't accuse you of anything, just told you to back off in a way you related to. Most people stop with questions when they're pulled into them." She shrugged and finished the water in her glass.

Rita placed the cake in front of her and a bag. "Your rolls."

"Thank you, my compliments to the chef, everything was delicious," Mia said.

Rita smiled at her as she left with the remaining dishes.

"Did I cause any damage to your truck?" she asked and then took a bite of cake. Moaning, she inhaled. "So damn good."

"No, you didn't hit us," Ryder said. "You're so sexy when you eat. Never seen anything like it."

Mia's eyes flew open. Slack-jawed, she met Ryder's hot gaze. "What?"

"You didn't hit our truck," Ryan said, drawing her attention.

Perhaps she misheard, although she knew she hadn't. She would go along for now. "Good." She patted her lips and glanced up as what she considered to be a giant strode inside, looked around and headed toward them.

Definitely, dual-natured, she thought wide-eyed. He had to be at least

6'5" or more with a barrel chest, thick muscular arms and legs, and long dark hair. But it was his metallic gray eyes that pinned her to the seat like a bug beneath a microscope. For the life of her, she couldn't move or look away. He tried to pry into her mind. She slapped at him.

His eyes went remarkably darker as he stood at the table, staring down at her. "Who are you?" his deep voice filled the space.

"Mia Haddon."

He tilted his head and tried to enter her mind again, harder this time and he wasn't alone. She slapped them both and continued to meet his gaze.

"That's rude," she said when he frowned at her.

"What?" Ryder said.

She finished her cake and hoped she'd get another glass of water when she noticed her empty glass.

"You can have mine." Ryder slid his untouched glass of water to her.

"Thanks. That was delicious." She drank half the glass and looked toward the front where Rita and a man wearing a chef hat stood watching them. "Can I have a slice of that cake to go as well?"

Rita glanced at the tall man standing at their table and then nodded. "Sure."

Mia noticed everyone had left and they were the only patrons inside. "Thanks." She patted her mouth and looked at the twins who stared at her as if she were some unknown species. "What? Something on my face? Teeth?"

Ryan laughed. "No. Not at all." He looked up. "Pull up a chair, Theron. She's going to be leaving soon if you have questions go ahead and ask."

Mia frowned. "I told you I can't discuss the investigation." She looked at Theron. "Do you have information regarding the death of Nathaniel Green?"

"No. I've nothing to do with that, can't be involved." He inhaled and released it slowly. "What are you?"

Mia's brow rose. "Beg your pardon?"

He scowled. "Don't play games with me or mine. You're more than human and I need to know what and how much more?"

She opened her mouth and closed it tight.

Theron leaned forward, with his clasped hands on the table. "See, I'm thinking you know what I am, what we all are, and it doesn't bother you. You've been honest with everything you've said and done. No deceit. But there's more to you, can't deny that."

"Is that a problem?" she asked meeting his gaze. There was something, no someone else just behind his eyes watching her.

"Could be, but not necessarily," he said.

She shook her head. "I cannot say, as I'm sure you cannot or you would have already. But I will say this. I am here to investigate the death of

Nathaniel Green and that is all."

A few moments later he nodded. "Okay, Mia Haddon. I have no other questions for you, but that does not mean there will be no further questions. It's important to me and others to know of any and all kinds of people in the States. We don't know you or yours."

Understanding, she nodded, pulled out her wallet and tossed several $20's on the table. "No problem. We're hoping to get a break in this case before —"

"Before the next one," Ryan said watching her.

She didn't respond. Standing she grabbed her to-go bags, inhaled again and released it slowly. "Thanks, guys, I needed this break of normalcy and good food. Now, I've got to get back to work." She pushed back her chair.

"What if we helped?" Ryan offered.

Frowning, she stopped and looked down at him. "Helped? You don't have information."

"We could help you find information," Ryan said. "We know this area."

She searched his gaze. They wanted someone to tag along with her team to find out more information about them, not the investigation. Maybe this would work.

"I can't authorize that. Thomas is team leader. When I inform him of our lunch, I'll tell him about your offer."

"He's here? In Littleton?" Theron asked.

"Yes. I'm going to meet with him in a bit."

"You have to meet them to communicate?" Theron pressed.

We don't mind-speak, she thought and wondered if it was a skill they could acquire. It would certainly be helpful. Frowning, she nodded. "Of course."

Ryder pushed the bills back to her. "We invited you, we pay."

She smiled without picking them up. "I ate, and I pay my own way. Company policy." She strode out of the restaurant with a quick wave to Rita and the chef.

Inside the car, she did a quick energy scan of the vehicle, stepped out, removed the tracker from behind her license plate and another from the wheel well of the left tire. She walked around it again for good measure and slid behind the driver's side. When she drove a few miles, she turned into a shopping center, removed the last tracker and placed it on a parked tow-truck before heading back into town.

CHAPTER 10

Silas Knight, La Patron and Alpha of the Wolf Nation sat at his desk staring at the pretty, young, curly-haired woman eating cake as if it was the most important thing in her world.

A hint of a smile crept on his face. Maybe it was. Theron, Alpha of Texas had reached out to him slightly before his son Tyrone had, with the same question. *"What is Mia Haddon?"*

Ryan believed she knew what they were, but never let on. Her energy levels were off the charts, it was no wonder she ate huge quantities of food. She registered human when she had to be more. For one thing, he and his Alphas could access most human minds with no trouble.

Neither he nor Theron had been able to read her thoughts and had received an energy slap for their trouble. She knew they'd tried, probably knew what they were but never let down her guard. The petite woman sat in a room full of wolves eating as though totally oblivious to the danger. At his or Theron's order, Ryan, Ryder or Rita would've snapped her neck, tossed her in the back of the truck and sent her body where it would never be discovered.

The fact she didn't fear that scenario caused them all to pause. He would ask the Goddess but needed more information. Was she a new, different breed? Of course, she was, but of what? Her human form held and molded energy, but for what purpose? He sensed no malice from her, neither did Theron but there was more going on.

"Tell her you'll assist in the investigation, that seems to be what's driving her now. Once you meet the rest of her team, ask direct questions," Silas told his grandson, Ryan.

"Thomas is the person we should talk to," said Tyrone, his son and Ryan and

Ryder's father. The twins had reached out to Tyrone while on the side of the road when they noticed her energy and unique scent.

Silas didn't feel this woman was an enemy which was the only reason he agreed for Tyrone to go to Littleton, Texas to meet with Thomas. Once they had answers, knew and understood what breed of humans they were, Silas would catalog the information for future use if necessary and leave them alone. But there was no way a new breed of human could appear in this country and he not investigate.

"Fly down and meet with Thomas. Find out what they are, how they came to be, what else they do besides masquerade as law officials and how long they'll be in Texas."

"Will do. I'll take Rose and the girls. We'll stay with the boys at their ranch for a nice visit. Haven't seen them since the wedding. We'll leave in a couple hours," Tyrone said.

"Make sure you see your mom before you leave," Silas said thinking of his mate, Jasmine. *"She may want to send something to the boys, they'll expect it."*

Tyrone laughed. *"Amazing how spoiled they are when it comes to mom."*

"She loves spoiling them," Silas said as he watched Mia leave the restaurant, wave to the staff and leave the building.

"What does she do outside?" Silas asked Theron as the Alpha and the others moved to watch.

He was disappointed when she slid into the front seat without checking the vehicle. When she stepped out, removed two of the three he smiled. *"She's got skills similar to Asia,"* he said thinking of his wife's best friend and his lead defender.

"She missed one," Theron said.

Silas frowned for a few seconds. *"If she did, it was deliberate. Be prepared for the last tracker to go off in wild directions. She's smart, held her cool in the midst of the pack, ate without fear. Refueling would be my guess, and not once did I sense anxiety or guile."*

"I agree, Alpha," Theron said. *"Different but not a threat is my take."*

Silas thought about it a few moments longer. *"Agreed but I'm sending Tyrone to get more information. I need to know what they are."*

"Yes, Sir. It'll be good to see him again."

Silas sat back in his chair and allowed his thoughts to wander. Her thoughts had been locked down tighter than a vault, it was different, he'd never come across anything like it before. Her confidence and good-natured personality reminded him of his mate. She liked the twins but wasn't interested in them other than cordial friends, so mating wasn't an issue. Thank the Goddess for that. Working for the government she would know how to draw those lines.

She hadn't pumped them for information, hadn't mentioned any of the specifics. Tyrone had given Ryan the information that he spouted regarding the dead librarian. She hadn't seemed surprised, not even when Rita mentioned the twins ordering the rolls, she didn't blink.

The more he thought about what he saw and heard, his certainty grew. She knew about wolf-shifters. Knew about the pack, Alphas and minimally how they operated. He contacted Tyrone.

"When you meet with Thomas, tell him enough about us for him to feel comfortable sharing their information."

"You think they already know?"

"Positive they do," Silas said. *"Open up, lay it on the table, explain why you're meeting with him. We can't make them talk, can't do anything to them without violating the rules set in place by the Goddess, but we can befriend them. Share information to prime the pump, let's see what happens. If that doesn't work I'll reach out to my contacts in the Pentagon."*

"Yes, Sir."

CHAPTER 11

That evening Mia sat at the small round table in Thomas' room watching him pace. It had been a long day. They hadn't come up with any hate groups in the area. Tip hadn't picked up anything new at the house or inside the van.

There was no sign of any guns, bullets, altercations, nothing that would imply the victim fought for his life or was in the van when he died. In short, they had nothing. Meeting the twin wolf-shifters was the highlight of her day, she refused to think about Noah.

The clock was ticking.

"Good job, Mia. The way you played it at the restaurant was perfect. I'll be meeting with Tyrone Bennett, La Patron's son, no less, first thing in the morning. He pushed to meet tonight but I need to know what you and Noah discover later tonight." He glanced at her.

"She's going to be okay," Mia said in a soft voice, thinking of Lizzy.

Thomas stopped pacing and stared at her. "You don't know that," he snapped. "We don't know when we'll burn out, and die. None of us do." He waved at her.

"No, we don't. So we live each day as if it could be our last. Do things we won't be ashamed of and be the best we can be," she said, leaning forward. "We've lived longer than most, seen the world change, experienced the unexplainable. Life's been a gift, to me anyway. When my time comes don't grieve or try to keep me beyond my expiration date."

"I'm not..." Thomas inhaled and exhaled slowly before sitting. "We're dying. I don't know what to do. How to help. It's killing me to watch." He didn't meet her gaze. The words hung in the air for several moments.

"Or we're changing," Mia said softly. "Lately my appetite has been off the charts. I see and hear keener than ever before. I pick up, and manipulate energy faster with better accuracy, than ever before." She looked at Thomas. "I smell it. Things are changing and that scares me more than dying. Death is a given, a time of rest before meeting my maker." She nodded. "That I understand. But change. Noticing different things inside of me? That's seriously scary stuff."

"When did you notice this?" Thomas asked a few seconds later.

She thought back. "Since I've been here, dream-walking especially."

"I haven't noticed any changes, but you've picked up things I missed. You caught them before they hit my radar."

"Are you off because you're worried about Lizzy?" she asked.

"I'm concerned about our future," Thomas said. "If we lose team members, how do we protect the complex? Granted we work to stay on top of our game, money… finances aren't an issue because of our investments but we've got to stay on top of things.…" He shook his head. "People cannot learn how long we live, or about our gifts. Not even the military can know everything. Especially if they think we gained anything from the Liege experiments. They'll start them up again under some fake banner of helping mankind. I worry about all of that, in addition to Lizzy. She's like my sister and she's suffering. I hate it and want to help ease that for her."

Mia nodded. "Understood." She did understand and totally agreed with him. They were family as well as team-mates who lived and worked together.

They owned 153 acres in Wyoming with a large home complex, in the middle. The basement was twice the size of the above grade 3,100 sf house. Fortunately, the house was built before records were kept and there was no data of the original owners or floor plan. Every 50 years they changed the names of the heirs for the land and home, rotating within the group. It helped give the illusion that they died out.

When they escaped to America a century ago there had been 23 of them, Mia had barely seen 13 summers when they arrived and headed west. Now they were down to 6 and one of them was dying.

Thomas ran his hand through his hair. "Get some sleep, Mia. Dream and push to see the day Nathaniel Green died. Anything the two of you learn will help."

She pushed up from her chair and nodded. "I'm sleepy anyway. See you in the morning." She looked at Thomas. Since wolf-shifters could hear through walls they employed the use of sealed rooms to converse.

"Release the seal so I can leave."

"Yeah, right. Sorry."

She left his room, took a right and headed to hers. Inside, she dropped her bag, sealed her room and took a shower. Bone-tired, she pulled on an over-sized tee and fell into bed.

It seemed she had just fallen asleep when she woke. That same weird light illuminated the road and Nathaniel Green's house. She did a quick scan. No one was around. Her hopes of a productive night dropped.

She rubbed her arms and realized she wore the same tee-shirt she'd worn to bed instead of her work clothes that showed up in the last dream. Intent on finding more clothes, she headed to the house.

"What are you doing here?"

Mia stopped but didn't turn at the hostility in Noah's voice. Boy, could he hold a grudge. A chill swept across her arms and legs. Sensing the mist that followed him, she headed inside to find a sweater, or jacket or long pants.

"Go home, I don't want you here." He hadn't yelled or raised his voice, but the words stabbed her just the same.

Rather than respond to his petty remarks, she entered the house. It was warm, inviting, filled with love and joy. She frowned. Those were new emotions, she hadn't sensed them the first time she searched the house. In the front coat closet, she pulled out a long, navy, raincoat and put it on. She headed to the kitchen for a drink of water, the sink didn't work and the refrigerator was empty.

"Better get this over with," she murmured and headed outside. The mist was thick around the house. She waved her hand. It recoiled and cleared a path for her.

Noah stood in the middle of the road surrounded by the mist, shaking, punching and trying to rid himself of the cloying fog without success. It coiled around him tighter until she barely saw his face.

Mia ran forward. "Get out of here," she snapped and waved her arms. The mist rolled backward several feet but remained on the sides of the road as if Noah was roadkill it expected to finish off.

She placed her hand on his shoulder. His eyelids fluttered, teeth chattered and his body shook. Surprised, she stared at him for a few seconds before removing her coat and wrapping it around him. She took his hands in hers and rubbed them.

"Be warm." She thought of heat, a warm cozy fire in a small room. Moments later he stopped shaking. His teeth stopped making that noise and finally, his eyes opened, blinked a few times before he snatched his hands from hers. He stepped backward, looked at the mist and then at her again.

"How do you control it?" he gasped staring down at her. Red-cheeked he remained in the area surrounding her rather than stepping back into the waiting mist.

She grabbed the coat he discarded when he moved and put it back on before looking up at him with a narrowed gaze. Hand on one hip and finger pointed she spoke. "I need answers regarding the death of Nathaniel

Green. I want to see the day he died."

He stared at her for a few moments. "I can't see the day of his death," he said frowning.

"Let's try. The other night you said I might be able to help you push past the blurred lines. Let's do that tonight," she said, still miffed over his rejection. she stuffed her hands in the pockets of the coat to keep from punching him. How could he be so mean? Hateful? Especially after she helped him.

"And then you'll tell me how you control the mist?" he asked, his gaze flicked to the side and back at her.

"Yes, that's the deal," she said pulling the ends of the belt tight around her waist, rather than around his throat.

"I'm not working with you," he snapped as if just remembering their earlier argument.

Anger spiked and raced through her. She itched to let the mist get his ass. Remembering the case, she took a deep breath and spoke calmly to prove he had no impact on her at all. "That's fine. I'm not working with you either. Just let me see that day, I'll do my own investigation and control the mist." Amped by her anger, energy thrummed through her. She glared at the annoying thick mist, wondering why it followed and attacked him. She'd discuss it with Thomas and Tip, maybe one of the others heard of something reacting that way.

It seemed as if he debated a long time when it was just a few moments before he extended his hand. She placed her hand in his and flew backward to stop in front of what could have been wide bands of police tape without words and in orange rather than yellow colors.

She touched the orange band and jerked back from the burn. "Ouch." Leaning forward, she could see a street with traffic but not clearly. "Give me your hand." Without looking at him she extended hers.

He took it. Warmth curled in her belly. She ignored it and pressed forward. This time her hand went through, she followed and pulled him alongside. They were in the van. The fog was thick. She couldn't make out much.

"Do you see anything?" she asked remaining in the same spot.

"Some," he said moving about. "Sounds like a lot of people are around."

She listened hard.

"I'm thinking of dropping that class, Professor Mark's a moron," someone said.

Another voice. "Sorority party tomorrow, come please."

"It's a college campus. Green was at a college campus." She tried to open the door and couldn't. Right now, this was as far as they could go.

"He's not here. Does that mean he was taken on a college campus?"

Noah asked as he dropped to the floor. "His gun is under the seat. So they took it after they killed him."

Mia couldn't see Noah on the floor.

"There's a pamphlet in the seat, I can't make it out. See if you can." His hands touched her feet and made their way up her body.

She tried not to respond to the rough texture of his fingers but it was impossible. By the time he grabbed her hand and thrust the brochure into it, her mind envisioned turned-down sheets and hot nights riding this cowboy.

"Do you see anything?" he asked.

Jerked from her fantasy make-out session, she put the brochure next to her face and couldn't read it. It was blank with stripes of gold and black. "Nothing," she said to conserve her energy. "Don't have much more time, here," she said weakening.

"Okay. I've never gotten this far before." He took her hand and they returned to the street in front of Nathaniel Green's house.

Mia took several deep breaths as she sat in the middle of the road with her forehead on her knees. Good thing she ate two rolls and a piece of cake an hour ago, she thought. Otherwise, they wouldn't have gotten the information they had.

He placed his hand on her shoulder, sending delicious warm tingles through her body. "You okay?"

She nodded hoping for a truce and afraid if she spoke it would spook him into moving his hand.

"Good. His van was at a college campus. Someone had to have seen it, right?" he said speaking too fast for her to keep up.

She nodded again.

"He had taken a brochure, colors gold and black," he murmured and started to pace. "Wonder if the colors mean anything? Could be the college or specific school colors, or if he was there for an organization or group, might be their colors. Or they might not mean anything at all."

Little by little, she regained her strength but wouldn't discuss the case with him, he wasn't on the team. Thomas and Tip would tear everything apart once she told them about it.

"What's up with the mist?" She looked at the rolling gray cloud surrounding them.

"Don't know. It shows up whenever I enter here. Most time I can't do much and just wait to wake-up."

Did he realize the mist tortured him? Added depth to nightmares and robbed him of his rest. She didn't think he realized it and probably wouldn't appreciate her mentioning it either.

She glanced up at him. He wasn't pretty, his face had too much character for that. The light hit his hair and kept his face shadowed so that his cheekbones stood out and his lips appeared fuller. His hair brushed against his shoulders giving him a roguish appearance that displayed more of his personality than he realized. With the mist in the background, he looked primal, a throwback to an uncivilized time.

"What?" he said. "Why're you looking at me?" He brushed his face with the back of his hand.

"Just wondering if you planned to offer me a hand up like any gentleman would." Her face warmed that he caught her staring at him. When he extended his hand, she appreciated his strength as he pulled her up and close with ease.

She stepped back and looked at the road, the mist and the house beyond.

"Now will you tell me how you control the mist?" he asked, stuffing his hands in his pockets while watching her.

"My energy moves it." She shrugged. "I guess it's stronger than the mist and it obeys me."

"Energy?"

She nodded. "We all have it, some more than others."

Neither spoke for several seconds. "Are there a lot of others? People, who use energy?"

"Or people like you who walk through dreams?" she snapped. She wasn't a weirdo like his voice implied.

He met her gaze and nodded. "Yeah, or people like me?"

Stop being so sensitive, she thought and released another breath. "Yes, there are." She raised her hand to stop his next question. "I can't discuss it with you, Thomas can and will. He knows a lot more about it than I do."

"The guy at lunch?"

"Yes, he knows a lot and would like to talk to you."

"He told you to tell me that?"

She thought about it. "No, he didn't actually. But he'd talk to you."

He rubbed the back of his neck. "I thought about it, and you were right, you never agreed to keep our discussion a secret," he said.

"Sorry, for the misunderstanding." She accepted his olive branch. "Sure would be nice to dream-walk to the beach or watch a sunrise or sunset, something fun or pleasurable." She paused. "I'd never really thought about that before, kinda sucks that I've never been able to do that."

He chuckled. "Never heard of anybody wanting to go to the beach in their dreams. You're definitely one of a kind Mia."

She liked the way her name sounded on his tongue and smiled. "Thanks, I think. Sleeps pulling me under. Come to the hotel in the morning for debriefing, we'll put our heads together see what we come up with." And talk to Thomas she thought.

Her eyes grew heavy as she left the dream and fell into a deep sleep.

CHAPTER 12

Mia rolled over ignoring the ringing of the phone. With one eye open, she glanced at the clock and groaned "Go away, Thomas." It stopped ringing and started again.

She released a breath, grabbed her phone. "Too early."

"Not really. I'm meeting with Tyrone Bennett in an hour. What did you learn?"

She pulled the covers over her head and huffed. "The van was at some college, don't know which, but I'm thinking one in the area. There was a pamphlet, with gold and black colors. Not sure what that means." She paused. "Oh yeah, the pistol was under the driver's seat."

"Really?"

She nodded. "Yeah. Noah showed it to me."

"Why college campus and not high school?"

She repeated the students' conversations she overheard.

"Sounds like a college. Thanks. I want you and Noah on that, take a picture of the van, see if you can find out something. Soon as I finish this meeting I'll join you. Tip hasn't reported in but I expect to hear from him soon. He'll find something that'll connect the dots and we can move forward."

"We'll go together, Noah's not on the team. He made that clear."

"Did he?"

"Crystal," she groused.

"Hmm, okay, get some rest. I'll contact you once the meeting's done."

Mia punched her fist into the pillow and tried to get back to sleep. Instead of returning to her peaceful rest, the gray mist rolled toward her as if blown by a strong, turbulent wind. It twisted and danced around her in graceful swirls. If it hadn't been cold as a late winter morning she would've thought it beautiful. The cold chill seeped through the covers, through her skin and rubbed against her bones.

"Cold," she whispered into her pillow, shivering.

The mist moved closer, darkening to the point she couldn't see her hand in front of her. The pain of thousands of needles ran up, down and across her skin. Her back arched as she opened her mouth in a silent scream. Sucked away as through a tunnel she heard gunfire, explosions, yells, screams, and finally moans. The acrid smell of death and weapons stung her nostrils. Body parts lay across the unforgiving ground soaked in blood.

Her heart hitched as she recoiled from the gruesome sight. Uniformed soldiers crawled, scooted and moved slowly on the ground as more rounds exploded in the distance. Haunted eyes filled with fear and desperation stared upward as they prayed to different gods for help.

Tears filled her eyes at the devastation, pain, and loss. She screamed in pain as she was sucked away and dropped in a hospital. The smell of blood and death co-mingled in the air creating a sinister blend. She tightened her eyelids shut unwilling to see more.

The voices, the sobs of human suffering pulled at her until she had to see. She opened one eye and then the other. In the midst of pain and despair, the sweet smell of compassion rose and breathed relief into her senses.

Doctors, nurses and medical personnel moved with a sense of purpose and one singular goal, to help those in need. To bring a bit of humanity back to those who had been in the war.

Just as her heartbeat slowed, she was sucked back to her bed, surrounded by that damnable mist. "Stop," she whispered

The mist rolled back but didn't leave.

She rolled over, lifted her hand and spoke with more authority. "Stop, go away and don't come back."

The mist twisted and turned and dissipated as if touched by the heat of the morning sun. Her heart raced as if she had run a mile. She lay limp with her arm slung over her eyes.

"What the hell?" she whispered, wondering why the mist kidnapped her. What was the purpose of all that? Did it have something to do with the case? Nathaniel Green hadn't been in the military.

Remembering Noah's bio she froze. *The mist.* Did it torture him with those memories? Still, why pull her into it? She shivered as the war scene rolled across her vision again. Her stomach rolled as she curled into a ball taking several small sips of air to calm down.

One question stood out in her mind. "Why had the mist come to her?"

CHAPTER 13

Thomas wasn't sure what he expected, but a calm, well-mannered and easy-going smile wasn't his idea of a wolf-shifter. In the past, the shifters he'd met had been rogues and quite feral. None were well-dress or polished like the man greeting him with a warm smile.

"Thomas, I'm Tyrone. Pleasure to meet you."

Thomas accepted the handshake and waved to the small table in his room.

"Same here, please come, have a seat. I'll seal the room so we can talk."

Tyrone nodded and took a seat.

Thomas sealed the room and offered coffee or pastries, sausage or bacon from the tray he'd ordered in advance.

"No, I had breakfast with my mate, I'm good. Don't let me stop you."

Thomas fixed a plate and a cup of coffee. When he sat he met Tyrone's curious gaze.

"Human for sure," Tyrone said with a slight smile.

Thomas nodded and swallowed his coffee. "For sure."

"But more," Tyrone said, leaning forward, interested.

"What can I do for you, Tyrone? You wanted to meet with me," Thomas reminded him.

"Yes. Of course." He pursed his lips. "Here's the thing. My father is La Patron, Alpha of the Wolf Nation. We don't get involved with human activities, we have more than enough on our plates. However, we do need to know when a different species or group hits the radar. Especially when they're throwing off high levels of energy."

Thomas nodded. "I see. Thank you for your honesty, and candor. I can see why you'd be concerned and have questions. What do you want to know?"

"What are you?" Tyrone waved his hand. "Human and what?"

"The Liege experimented on hundreds of humans first, are you aware of that?"

Tyrone stilled. His gaze narrowed. "No. But others I know may know about that. Are you saying you were tampered with by the Liege?"

Thomas released a long sigh. "Tampered with?" he snorted. "Such a tame word that can't scratch the surface for what they did. Most of the humans died on the operating tables. Those who survived underwent multiple surgeries until they died or went crazy. By the time I came along, they were bringing in pups so I, we, didn't get the full impact of their experiments. But we're fucked up just the same." He read the horrified sympathy on Tyrone's gaze.

"Imagine living with a fucked up mind and no idea how to control your energy. After escaping the compound, humans hunted us like common criminals for being different. No place was safe." He crossed his leg and took another long sip from his cup. "It's been tough hiding the past century and a half.

"You've lived over 150 years?" Tyrone asked in awe.

Thomas nodded. "Don't get too excited, we're not immortal. We're dying. Whatever they did extend our lives, there are some other benefits as well. I've been trying to get hold of the Liege's files to help my friends who're suffering." He shook his head and looked at Tyrone. "So, that's it. A small group of people unlucky enough to fall on the Liege's operating table and live through several operations which changed us permanently."

"You work for the Federal—"

"No. Just this job. Don't trust those assholes further than I can see them. General Strait promised to give us files from the Liege. I'm hoping to find information to save one of our team members." He paused and leaned forward, staring out the window. "This is an ugly case, never seen anything like it. Just had another death in Tennessee, could be a serial killer. We've got five days, three now to solve it before the FBI steps in."

Tyrone frowned but didn't say anything for a few seconds. "What is it you do? Why haven't we detected you before? Where's your base? In the States?"

"When we work together, combine our skills, we're uniquely qualified mercenaries and work mostly international jobs. Rarely do we work in the states. Like I said, the General had the right bait and we took it." He shrugged.

"Before you answer the other questions, let me put your mind at ease, my father's raid of the Liege's compounds and satellite venues have produced tons of files and data which he's informed me you're free to have copies of. I promise it'll be more complete than whatever the General cherry-picks for you."

Excitement and gratitude raced through Thomas as he met Tyrone's sincere gaze. "Thank you. Thank you very much, I appreciate your kind offer."

"Even working out of the country, we never picked up your energy," Tyrone said.

Thomas gave it some thought. "Most of our complex is below ground, and in the States. We've held it for decades. I don't know the answer to that question."

Tyrone sat still for a few moments. "What's going on with this case that makes it so strange?"

Thomas realized he was, in fact, being interviewed by La Patron, a part of him was honored. The other, uncertain. "Someone is stoning disabled men to death. Seven so far, the last one in Tennessee, 48-hours ago. Tip's there now, searching for clues. We got a lead here and will be checking it out."

Tyrone frowned. "Did you say stoning? They threw rocks —"

"Bricks, red clay bricks. The most common building component in the states of the reported deaths. Never seen anything like it. They stake them to the ground, arms wide and…"

"Goddess, no," Tyrone whispered as his face paled.

"They're neat, tidy, organized. But we'll get them. Maybe not within the five days, but we'll get them." Thomas sense of outrage and justice wouldn't allow this crime to go unpunished. They didn't normally handle these cases but it was theirs now.

"The Nation is forbidden to become involved in human affairs, which certain people in Washington choose to forget when it's convenient," Tyrone muttered. "However, we can help you and your team."

Thomas hadn't expected that. "Can you help Lizzy? She's dying," he asked without thinking.

Tyrone frowned. "Lizzy?"

"She's like a sister to me. We were at the Liege during the same time, and she's fading. I don't know how to help her." He fought to keep the pleading from his voice but would beg if it would save the life of one of his team. They were family, the only family he had.

Tyrone nodded slowly. "Is she here?"

"No, she's at the complex. I can have her sent wherever you want," Thomas said eager.

Hawke can take a look —"

Thomas stood fast. "Hawke? The Liege's Hawke? You know him?"

Tyrone nodded. "Yes. Do you?"

Thomas shook his head, thoughts tumbling one after the other. "No, just by reputation. Word has it that he's brilliant and may be the one person in the world who can tell us what the hell the Liege did to us. We searched everywhere for him but he disappeared like a vapor." He stared at Tyrone. "And you actually know him? Seriously? Are we talking about the same person?"

Tyrone grinned. "Probably. Hawke's smart, that's for sure."

"No. The Hawke who ran the labs at the compound was a fucking genius, computerized brain, everyone knew he was the real brains at the compound."

Tyrone rubbed his neck while smiling. "I think it's the same guy, only we don't quite praise him the way you're doing. Gotta keep the big guy humble."

Thomas met Tyrone's amused gaze and smiled. "I see. Thank you. It's just... we've searched for him, for answers for so long, it's... it's hard to believe you have access to him. For the information, we've needed for decades. The lives that could've..." He inhaled and released a breath. Thinking of those already transitioned wasn't productive. "Thank you for your help. We need answers, badly."

"I'll be honest with you, Thomas. We want answers to, it's the reason we're going to help. Because for humans to handle energy the way your team does, without being consumed, the longevity of your life and additional skills, we want to know how it's done."

Thomas stiffened as flashes of being caged or on metal tables flashed across his mind. "We won't be experimented on again."

Tyrone frowned as if offended. "Of course not. We're talking examinations and blood work, questions, answers that kind of thing."

Thomas thought it over. "Where would this take place?" He hadn't mentioned the location of their complex but with Pack in every state, if La Patron really wanted to find them he could.

"Hawke and his team will go to Lizzy. They could also do preliminary work on the others at that same location." Tyrone held up his hand to stop Thomas' objections. "You're asking for more than what a quick evaluation can provide. For Hawke to identify what the Liege did to each of you, he'll need to examine you where he has sophisticated equipment which is in La Patron's compound. Before that happens, a thorough background check will be completed on each of you. It sounds as if Lizzy does not have that kind of time, so Hawke is willing to travel to whatever state she's in and make use of the Alpha's health centers there."

Thomas heard the take it or leave it in Tyrone's voice. He hadn't been kidding when he told Mia they had nothing to offer the Pack and he was grateful for their assistance.

He bowed his head in gratitude. "Thank you. Lizzy is in Wyoming. Where do you want her sent?"

Tyrone held up his finger. Moments later he spoke. "Alpha Crimson is setting things up. Take her to this address within two hours. Hawke will be there with his team." He wrote the address on a piece of paper and handed it to Thomas. "You have to take her. Alpha Crimson has your description and will not allow any other humans into the facility."

Grateful and filled with hope Thomas accepted the slip of paper. "Thank you. We'll be there." Tip was in Tennessee, Mia around the corner asleep and the other two team members were in Italy and returning soon. There was no one else to take Lizzy anyway. Mia never worked an op alone and there could be some fall out there when he canceled with the General. But the opportunity to discover more about them and possibly save Lizzy was too great to pass up.

When Tyrone stood, Thomas stood as well working through scenarios to get everything done. He would leave within the hour to ensure Lizzy was at the clinic on time. As soon as this meeting was done he'd have Mia start packing and tell Tip to return to base for his exam with Hawke's team. Finally, they could get answers. Mia nailed it. Things were changing.

Tyrone extended his hand.

Thomas shook it and unsecured the room. "Thanks for everything." What else was there to say when someone offered to save the lives of him and his friends.

"On behalf of La Patron, you're welcome." He walked to the door and left.

Thomas called Tip and then Mia. He would cancel the op, let the time run out, return a part of the money to General Strait and they'd leave. Mia had never worked an op alone and he refused to leave her behind. As the youngest in their group, they'd all protected and sheltered her through the years, allowing her to search for a child possibly long dead. It made her happy and they were okay with it.

Maybe there would be something in La Patron's files about Mia's child. He hoped he could find answers for most of their problems and prepared to check out.

CHAPTER 14

Noah rolled over, opened one eye and looked out the window. Another blazing hot day in Texas, no big surprise there. What did surprise him was the sound of a rabbit or small creature nibbling on something, in the field beyond his home, over a 100 yards away. Other sounds, the hum of the AC, his refrigerator, even the back porch ceiling fan that he never turned off, all buzzed in his ears.

With his hand on his chest, he continued staring outside, listening in wonder to everything around him. Swallowing hard, he slid out of bed, walked to the window and stared at his detached garage where he stored his tools for his workshop in the back. His gaze slid over the grassy field that separated his land from his neighbors and zeroed in on a rabbit, in the middle of the field surrounded by grass and debris, eating.

"Whoa." He blinked, uncertain he was seeing correctly and looked for the rabbit again. It moved a few feet, stopped and continued eating. Noah didn't know what to think. "What the hell?"

He grabbed his jeans from the floor and headed to the back porch. Pants unsnapped, he stood outside, inhaled and sneezed. Strong scents assailed him. Wiping his nose, he tried to rid his nostrils of the odors he'd picked up and failed. Eyes watering, he returned to the house, sat in one of the kitchen chairs and took shallow sips of air, refusing to breathe through his nose. When the sensations eased, he inhaled lightly, the scents were strong but not debilitating.

Something happened to him.

Thirsty, he grabbed a glass from the cabinet, filled it with water from the sink, and drank it down fast. Heart racing, he closed his eyes to think.

Last night he dreamed.

His eyes flew opened and he looked at his hands. No shakes. No pain. No nausea. He was clear-headed, alert and remembered everything like the last time she walked with him in dreams but turned up several notches. Stunned, he returned to the chair staring at his steady hand.

Shocked and elated, he smiled and then not trusting the reprieve, he frowned. They broke through some kind of barrier last night. For the first time, he saw the day of the crime and found relevant clues.

First time.

Those two words ran through his mind on a loop. Was that it? Mia had pushed into an area he hadn't been able to see before. Is that the reason for feeling fucking awesome?

He'd given her a hard time even though he knew she was right. Thoughts of how she boldly walked into his house yesterday with attitude floated through his mind. Cute too. He kept coming back to her body, it was a work of art.

He'd noticed. She mattered.

The fella Tip seemed to like her and she had given him a big smile too when he left. They weren't a couple, but maybe they had a history. He stopped smiling, ran his hand through his thick hair and stared at his fist.

"You're trying to rob the cradle these days?" He'd be 40 in a couple months, she had to be in her early 20's, still, he couldn't help the attraction, especially when they walked in dreams together. There was something magical, intimate about that which transcended anything he'd ever experienced.

Last night, the mist had come at him with a vengeance, the sights, and sounds of war-battered his mind. He was back on the battlefield fighting for his life. She saw him at his absolute worst when she pulled him out wearing that ridiculously oversized, long coat. She looked like a teen playing grown-up and utterly adorable.

He had wanted to kiss her so bad he shook with it. Embarrassed by his wild need, he rebuked her. Strong and feisty, she turned the tables and probably saved him, again by pushing through that barrier. He moved his hardening cock to the side, knowing there would be no relief from what he wanted most, to plunge into the silky smooth depths of Special Agent Mia Haddon.

Hunger pangs hit his belly. In the kitchen, he pulled out bacon, eggs, potatoes and started breakfast. Unable to get Mia and the things he wanted to do to her out of his mind, he placed a call to the number on the back of the card she gave him.

"Hello?" she sounded cautious.

"Morning, just thought I'd invite you over for breakfast and before we go over what we learned last night." He turned over the bacon and pulled out a can of biscuits, he was hungry.

She sighed. "That's a good idea. I just… never mind. I'll be there in a few minutes."

He frowned. "Are you already out?" It wasn't nine o'clock yet. The offices in town didn't open until nine.

"Yes and no. I'll explain when I get there. It's going to be a long day." She disconnected.

Noah stared at the phone, shrugged and stuffed it back into his pocket. Listening to various sounds of nature and light jazz that played in his bedroom he continued cooking. By the time he heard Mia's car, he had prepared a feast of bacon, sausage, biscuits, eggs with cheese, spinach and mushrooms sauteed in butter, tea, and orange juice.

"Come on in, I'm in the kitchen," he yelled.

Her scent speared through the aroma of everything in the kitchen and teased his nostrils. Strange how he sensed her before she spoke. Smiling, he looked over his shoulder. She stood at the entrance staring at the food and then looked at him. Today she wore a pair of navy trousers with a navy and white pinstriped dress shirt. Classy but still touchable. He liked it.

"Smells good." She took the plate he offered and filled her plate. Pleased he provided this service for her, he filled his plate and followed her to the table.

They ate in silence.

Spirits high, he had so many questions, wanted to share what happened to him, and get her take on this change in his life. When he looked at her, she didn't return his smile. Didn't look at him. She seemed dim. Preoccupied but not quite the bright bulb of confidence he was accustomed to seeing.

"What's wrong?" He missed her smile and the light in her large doe shaped eyes.

She looked at him and shrugged. "Thomas left. He had to go back to handle something important."

Okay, that wasn't what he expected to hear. But it must be a big deal for her to look so glum. "When's he coming back?" Not that it mattered to him, especially if it meant they'd be able to spend more time together exploring dreams without Thomas' interference. That was a bonus.

She shrugged again and continued eating.

Unsure if now was a good time to discuss his good news or ask questions about last night, he remained silent wishing he could ease her discomfort.

"I'm going to continue working on the case, solve it if possible," she said as if trying to convince herself.

Surprised, not by what she said, but by the doubt in her voice. "You wanna do that?"

She rolled her eyes before glaring at him. "Of course I do, that's why

I'm here. It's just…" she exhaled and looked away. "I've never run an op by myself. Everybody else is busy or out of the country. Thomas isn't sure how much support he'll be able to give me. He wanted me to leave with him, cancel the op, didn't think I could handle it." The last few words were said with a bite of anger.

She took a sip of juice and cleared her throat. "I looked up the closest colleges and was researching them when you called. I plan to go check them out, see if anyone remembers seeing his van. We've only got a few more days to locate the killer."

Noah had a couple ideas on how to play her announcement. For one, he was happy as hell Mia was alone. He would definitely encroach on her time. Age be damned. Another, she was unsure how to run an op, something he had a lot of experience with, but he wasn't a member of her team. She seemed reluctant to allow him to get close because of that pesky detail.

Since becoming a civilian and moving here, Noah hadn't dated or been with a woman. He hadn't wanted to expose anyone to his new brand of crazy. But Mia was like him, with her own kind of crazy. Normal rules didn't necessarily apply. He wasn't alone anymore. Plus, his dick was rock hard from watching her eat scrambled eggs. He'd cancel his next therapist appointment, hell, he was cured.

"Yeah, what colleges are on your list?" If she shared, let him in, he'd walk through that door and stay for a while. They'd start their own team. He liked that idea.

She named three. The junior college was five miles from the victim's house and the place she would hit first.

"Good call." He finished his food. "Want some company? I can ride with you, another pair of eyes."

She looked at him surprised. "Oh, Ryan and Ryder will be there." She frowned. "Or maybe just Ryder or Ryan." She waved the hand holding her fork. "One of them, they offered to help. I split the list with them this morning, we're going to meet at the Lucky G for lunch, go over what we find."

Disbelief raced through him, chased by anger. Noah stared at her. "What? Who?"

"Ryder and Ryan, the twins I met yesterday when I left here. We went to lunch."

He shook his head and pushed down the anger bubbling beneath the surface.

"Dream-walkers?"

"No. They aren't gifted," she said.

That made him feel somewhat better. "You told them about the investigation?" She hadn't told him a damned thing until he met her in their dream.

"No. They were aware the victim died. They offered to help and since I'm short on assistance I agreed." She shrugged, finished her juice and pushed back from the table. "That was delicious, you're a good cook. Do you need help with the dishes?"

He looked up at her wary eyes and counted to ten. His jaw clenched and unclenched. Why the hell was he so pissed? He just met her a couple of days ago. Basically, he told her to get lost and stay away from him.

They walked through dreams together to solve a case. That wasn't a big deal. Then why did he want to break something or someone? Unreasonable anger festered beneath his skin. She should've come to him for help.

She did, you told her to get out, and go away, he argued. *That was before last night. Last night changed everything*, he defended.

For you, maybe. But not her. It was the truth and he didn't like it.

"Yes, please. If you'll rinse the dishes and place them in the dishwasher I'll go get dressed." He stood and walked out, leaving her staring at his back.

Mia stared at Noah's broad back and wondered how had she missed the fact he hadn't worn a shirt during breakfast. The sight of his pale skin stretched across a muscular back snapped her out of her morose thoughts.

She picked up their plates, carried them to the sink to rinse and placed them in the dishwasher. Moments passed. Her thoughts returned to the confrontation she had with Thomas this morning.

Shame coated her throat.

She'd been angry, more than angry but she shouldn't have said the things she had. Fear had taken over her mind and fed her tongue when he explained he wasn't abandoning her as she claimed, but accepting help from a possible ally. In the back of her mind, she agreed they needed La Patron's assistance to attempt to save Lizzy and learn more about the Liege's experiments. The fact he found Hawke when they had been searching for the reclusive scientist for decades was unbelievably awesome.

Her rational side knew Thomas had to take the opportunity. However, fear was irrational and it locked onto her the moment he told her to pack up and prepare to leave for home. She wasn't a child, and challenged him, something she rarely did.

"Would you tell any of the others to leave the job like this?"

Her question caught him by surprise. Hell, it surprised her that she actually wanted to stay and work the job. That hadn't been in her mind until he ordered her to drop everything to go home.

"No. But they have experience."

"This will give me experience," she argued.

"I know. But I might not be able to assist you. Tip won't either, not directly. I don't feel comfortable leaving you here working on this. Plus we haven't made enough progress on the case."

She reminded him what they discovered in the dream. "I'm not leaving until there's nothing left to investigate. That's not how we operate and you know it. Ryan and Ryder offered to help, we'll hit the colleges, show the victim's picture and van, see if we learn anything."

They stared at each other for several uncomfortable moments before he sighed. "Mia please."

She'd never seen him so conflicted before and knew if the deal with La Patron hadn't been on the table he wouldn't have left.

"I'll be fine, Thomas. I'm a part of this team and it's past time I do more than scout or administrative work. Go, find out what you can to save the rest of us. I'll be fine." At the time, she meant it. Once he agreed and left, fear rose and choked her.

Up until an hour ago, she'd been coasting, reporting what she saw with the expectations of Thomas figuring everything out. Now, all of that changed. Nathaniel Green and several other victims fell into her lap. Their silent voices cried for justice, how could she give them answers? Peace? Truly, she didn't know.

Thomas agreed with her plan of action, which made her feel somewhat better. When he mentioned Noah, she shut him down with an evil eye that clearly said "no." Noah wanted nothing to do with her or their team. Last night… well, last night was about the mission and saving him from the mist. They both got what they wanted.

"Good, you're almost done." He strode into the kitchen taking up most of the space and stepped close.

He smelled damn good standing next to her finishing the dishes. Realizing she stood there like a paralyzed fool, gazing at his square jaw and long lashes, she took a step back, grabbed her purse from the seat and walked into the living room.

Yesterday it seemed smaller, but it was actually a nice size with solid furniture that looked both comfortable and stylish. There were photos of him and others in uniforms. She looked at each picture, several of the same men were in each photo. The last photo was him and an older woman and a guy with a wide grin who could've been his brother except they looked similar in age.

"My aunt and cousin," Noah said standing near the door.

"Oh." She spun around as he picked up his sunglasses and slid them on.

"She died a couple years back. He's all the family I have left, I don't really count my younger brother," he added as he held the door open for her.

Heat raced to her cheeks as she strode toward him and outside.

"I'll drive," he said.

"No, I'll—"

"My legs are too long for that compact car. Please, let me drive this time," he asked with a slight grin.

It was the naughty boy grin that did it for her, well and the fact he smelled yummy, like wood, oranges, and vanilla.

"Let me get my bag." She grabbed her work case that held her laptop and information she had printed this morning. He stood next to the passenger seat and assisted her up. It was either that or a step-ladder she thought after fastening her seatbelt.

He pulled out and onto the road. "These guys you're meeting later, they live around here?"

Thoughts on Thomas' suggestions for the case, Mia nodded. Once they reached the college, she would head to the security office, show the photos of the victim's van. It was possible someone saw the van on campus or they might have security cams. Thomas had looked as if he felt bad dumping all of this on her, which made her feel like a big crybaby for crying when he left her room.

"What are their names? I might know them," he asked.

"Ryan and Ryder," she murmured while scrolling through data to get the phone number and address of the security department on campus.

"Don't know them, are you sure they're locals and not someone from out of town?"

"I'm sure."

"How can you be sure? Does your gift...oh, that's right, can't lie to you."

She nodded without looking at him. They continued the drive in relative silence as she keyed the address for their destination into her GPS.

"You interested in them?"

"Huh?" Frowning, she glanced at him.

He shrugged. "Asked if you were interested in them, you know."

"Interested how? I don't understand what you mean." She returned to search for the next college and the security address just in case the twins didn't come through. Ultimately it was her responsibility to handle the search.

"Guy likes girl, dates, that kind of interest," he said a few moments later.

"No." Seriously? Ryder and Ryan were babies in her mind even though they were grown, human men. They were fun and cute, but nothing more than that. When was the last time someone interested her? She looked out the passenger window, watched the trees and grass fly by as disappointment settled in her gut.

She couldn't remember.

All of her spare time and energy had been utilized for the search of the child that disappeared minutes after she pushed him or her into the world. It totally drained her resources and she had nothing to show for it. No lover. No fond memories. Nothing. Worst, she didn't see that changing anytime soon.

Noah didn't speak again until the GPS led him in front of a small building in the back of the campus. He pulled out a disabled placard and hung it on his rear view mirror.

Mia looked at it but didn't question him as he walked around to help her down. Folder and ID in hand, they entered the building.

A motherly looking woman with round spectacles perched on her nose smiled at them. "Hello, how can I help you?"

Mia showed her badge and asked to speak to whoever was in charge of the department while second-guessing herself the entire time. Should she have started at the top, spoken to the President? Or someone in charge of student affairs? Heart racing, she remained cool, steady while answering a few of the woman's questions while she spoke to someone on the phone.

"Mr. Grain will be here in a few moments, please be seated. Can I get you something to drink? Coffee? Tea? Water?"

"No, thank you," Mia said, taking a seat.

Noah walked around the small waiting area looking at everything. Five minutes later the door opened and a tall, lanky male with sandy red hair and freckles entered. He took several deep breaths as he pulled on his waistband.

"Hello, Kevin Grain. I'm in charge of campus security, how can I help you?" he asked Noah.

Aggravated, Mia stood and looked at him. "Special Agent Haddon." She extended her hand to him.

His gaze flew to her hand to her face to Noah who met his gaze. "Um, sorry. How can I help you?" He shook her hand and stepped in her direction.

"Is there someplace we can talk?" she asked politely.

"Oh yes, this way please." He strode down the hall, opened a door and waited until she and Noah entered. He closed the door behind them.

"Mr. Grain, during the process of an ongoing investigation, we've discovered the victim in that investigation was seen on a college campus. This campus is within five miles of the victim's residence." She pulled out a photo of the van. "As you can see it's handicapped equipped and unique. We need to speak to your staff and if you have surveillance cameras we'd like to see them as well."

Gran rubbed his jaw while staring at the photo. "How far back you need to go?"

She told him the date of the murder.

He nodded. "Not too long ago, we can do that. Come with me." Down the hall, to the right, he entered another door. Two women sat in front of monitors watching screens and speaking on headsets.

"Our emergency operators," he said as he opened another door. Inside this room were monitors and computer equipment. He sat in front of a monitor, pulled up a keyboard and started typing. "I'll have that day up for you in a few seconds. There are cameras all over campus, you can load four at a time."

Inwardly, Mia groaned. This would take some time.

"Good news is it covers all entrances and exits, so if you don't see the van enter, you can scratch us off the list," Grain said. "Was he a student here?"

"No," she said, certain for some reason. Nothing in his home suggested it. Besides, Lisa, his boss would've mentioned it. "But please verify to be sure." Second guessing again as she gave him the name.

"No, not a student," Grain said. "It's all set up." He moved from the chair.

Mia hesitated a second and then sat. This was one thing she would've been grateful to have Noah handle.

CHAPTER 15

By noon, Mia's stomach rumbled. No way she'd make it to the Lucky G for lunch.

"That was the last one," Noah said from the seat beside her. He'd been a champ, assisting her as she looked through the all the tapes. Even though Lisa and the others said he'd been at work the day before and she had seen it when they dream walked, she insisted on reviewing everything on that day. It had taken over three hours.

Standing, she stretched before pulling out her phone to contact the twins. They hadn't reached out to her since this morning. If they hadn't been able to hit the University she would head there now.

"Hey, I was going to call you in a few. We showed the van and the victim's photo to the security team looked at the footage from that day and asked around campus. He's not a student and there's no proof the van was here," Ryder said.

Mia heard female voices in the background and hoped the twins took the search seriously. She couldn't afford to mess up.

"How did it go there?" Ryder asked.

"Nothing, we looked through the security feed as well. Headed to the last college within 30 miles of Littleton, now. Hard to believe he traveled that far."

"Who knows, people do strange things. Want us to meet you there?" Ryder asked.

She thought about it. "No, that's okay. Noah's driving, won't take long. I've already called campus security, they're getting things ready. Thanks so much for your help today, I really appreciate it."

"Any time. Call if you need anything. Maybe we'll hit the Lucky G again.

I love watching you eat."

She smiled. "And I'm outta rolls. I need my fix. We'll do it again soon." She disconnected and looked at Noah who stared at her.

"Ready? One more campus and that's a wrap," she said.

"Can we grab something to eat first? I'm hungry." He stood and opened the door.

"Me too. Maybe that buffet across the street, what do you think?" She pointed to a building in a shopping center that advertised all you can eat southern cooking.

Shrugging, he followed her out. Mr. Grain said goodbye before leaving for an earlier meeting. They waved at the receptionist and headed to the truck.

Once in her seat, she glanced at the disabled placard. When he slid into the driver's side she pointed at it. "What's up with that?"

"Mental disability. When they took the metal out of my skull, I was messed up. Just started driving four months ago, my doctor insisted I get one of these. I only use it when parking is tight."

Why allow someone with a mental disability to drive? she wondered before realizing there must be degrees to these disabilities. "Green had one."

Noah nodded. "Yeah, he did." They drove across the street from campus to the Golden Buffet. It was crowded. Noah pulled into a handicapped parking space.

Before he opened his door a really pretty blonde with bright green eyes approached him with a wide smile.

Mia disliked her staring up at him on the spot.

"Hello and blessings from Yahweh. I'm Tiffany and would like to share a positive word with you today. She held a brochure in her extended hand.

"Take it," Mia whispered her gaze latching onto the gold bars at the top of the paper.

"Thanks," Noah accepted the brochure.

"Many blessings from Yahweh," Tiffany said and quoted two scriptures as she stared at Noah. When she finished, she asked. "Do you need any help?"

"No. No thank you," he said, sounding surprised or embarrassed.

Mia looked in the side and rear view mirror to see if Tiffany was alone. There were college students everywhere in the parking lot because of other stores and a large supercenter on the other end.

Was it possible the victim came here? Or to one of the stores in the shopping center? It was definitely a thought. She searched for a gas station. There was one near another entrance to the shopping center. What if Mr. Green bought gas? That would be more likely since there hadn't been a large amount of food in his system. Thomas had pulled the victim's credit card info, there had been no purchases on the day of his death or the day before. Cash was still king, so that didn't mean he hadn't purchased gas.

When Tiffany walked off to bless someone else, Mia watched for a few moments and looked at the brochure. "The Leviticus Club?"

"Never heard of it," Noah said. "Probably some local college organization. We eating here or what?"

"Go to the gas station over there." She pointed while reading the group information.

"For gas? Tank's almost full."

"No, I want to see if you're approached again." The brochure was filled with religious information about the goodness of God. Nothing wrong with that. But it felt wrong.

He started the truck, pulled out and headed to the gas station on the other side of the center. As soon as he pulled in, another person, brunette female this time, approached with a smile, another blessing, and a brochure.

"Don't get out," she hissed when his hand went to the door.

Mia all but dropped to the ground, thinking he needed a step stool. She watched the young woman who was as bright and pretty as Tiffany talking to people about her faith. After putting five bucks in the tank, Mia climbed back in and fastened her seatbelt.

Noah started the truck. "Where to?"

"Someplace nearby to eat and do a computer search," she said.

"Not the buffet?"

"No, not there. Any restaurant will do. With a booth or large table," she said using her phone to start researching the Leviticus Club.

When they pulled into the parking lot of a Chinese buffet, she looked at him and shook her head. "Chinese food has no staying power, you know that, right?"

"True, but I can eat as much as I want within a minute of taking a seat." He stepped out and opened her door to assist her. They took a booth at the back. He headed to the buffet while she ordered their drinks. Once he returned with two loaded plates, she went to the buffet and did the same.

They didn't talk until they were done eating.

She turned on the laptop and searched for everything she could find on the club.

Her phone rang.

"Ryder?"

"Yeah, how's it going?"

She told him what about Tiffany and the other female at the gas station.

"So… they were nice, religious groupies. Is that a problem?"

"Not really but I noticed they didn't approach other cars the same way. It was as if they targeted the disabled vehicles. There were cars in disabled spots with these brochures beneath the windshield wipers while other cars had none. I watched one of them work while we were at the gas station. They picked and chose who got the information."

"That's not very Christian-like is it?"

"No. It's a long shot. Another thread to pull. I'm looking into the organization now."

"Yeah. Give me the name, I'll have my dad do a deep search and send it to your email tonight," Ryder said.

Grateful, she smiled. "Thanks a bunch. I appreciate it." After giving him the name of the group and her email address, she disconnected. Things were looking up. Once she returned to the hotel, she would send Thomas an update, see if he had any suggestions.

"You didn't mention that."

She looked across the table at Noah. "What?"

"You didn't tell me all of that was going on and I was sitting next to you."

Was he angry? She couldn't tell. Couldn't read his face. "I'm sorry." She sighed and ran her fingers through her short curls. "I don't know how to do this. You say you won't work with me, tell me to get away, then you ask to come along. I don't know if I should share information or what's going on. So tell me, what's this all about? Why are you helping when you said you wouldn't?"

Noah met her serious gaze, read the frustration and recognized the signs. Mia was close to the edge. He needed to handle this correctly or everything would blow up in his face. She had a valid point. He hadn't told her about last night or this morning when everything changed for him.

"No. I apologize. You're right. I've been all over the place with you. First, I want to help, to work with you to solve this, as a team if possible."

Her gaze widened as she leaned forward. "You want to join our team?"

No. He didn't know them or about them. He wanted to work with her. "Maybe. Right now, I want to be on your team."

She frowned. "My team? I don't have a team."

"Yes, you do. You're in charge of this op, calling the shots and we're helping you," he said gently reading the fear and doubt in her gaze. "You've got great instincts, Mia. I didn't notice what you did and it's important. At the very least it starts the conversation, why are they targeting people with disabled tags?"

Her gaze narrowed for a few seconds and then she nodded. "Yeah, good question. We need answers. Eat up and then we'll head back to their campus, talk to a few people."

"As the FBI?" That wasn't the best move but he didn't want it to appear he was taking over.

She met his gaze and bit down on her lower lip for a few seconds. "Ryder." She placed the call and shared what she wanted to be done.

"There are a few people in the area who would be perfect and can get the information you need in less than 30 minutes," Ryder said. "Stay there, eat, breathe and eat some more."

"Okay. Thirty minutes?" she asked.

"Or less," Ryder assured her.

Mia returned her phone to the table and looked at him. "Ryder's going over, he's young and will bring the information soon. I'm getting another plate." She went to refill her plate.

Noah remained seated, all of his senses were jacked. He heard both sides of her conversation, had heard it the entire day and had been struggling to deal with the new changes. They drove with the window down to dilute her scent. He heard every sigh and small noise she made which made his dick harder than steel. Thank God she was preoccupied and hadn't caught on.

She returned and sat down. "You okay?"

He nodded. *No lies.* "No. Not really." He met her surprised gaze and told her what happened this morning, his senses being off the chart, feeling great, better than he had in years.

"Feels like I can see clearly again, no pain, nothing." He waited for her prognosis.

"That's great, you deserve it," she said seriously without explaining what happened to him as he thought she would.

His smile dropped a bit. "Why do you say that?"

She tilted her head and stared into his eyes. "You served in the military, put your life on the line for everybody, it's not right that your life is messed up because of that. You've given enough."

He thought of the men who died on the battlefield. "Some gave more. Gave their all."

She nodded. "And God will bless them for their sacrifice, just as He's given you this opportunity. Don't waste it."

He met her gaze and nodded slowly. "No, I won't. Just... how can I tone it down? Some of the things I smell, I'd rather not."

She smiled and it was as if the sun peaked from behind a cloud warming him from the inside. "Think about what you want, tell your body what to do."

Sounded simple. He tried over and over again until he felt normal again. By that time Ryder and Ryan entered the restaurant.

The twins could've been college students, they looked young, masculine, vibrant and drew the attention of several men and women as they strode through the restaurant.

"Over here," Mia said waving her hand.

They reached the table and she introduced them to Noah. Ryan stared at Noah a few seconds longer while Ryder slid in next to her.

"Strange group. Not sure what they really believe. The woman in the student union who approached us couldn't really tell us much about the group, instead, she wanted us to go to some meeting they're having."

Mia arched her brow. "What kind of meeting?"

Ryder shrugged. "I got the feeling that's all they do, invite you to these groups and once you're there try to sell you something. Maybe they're selling religion. Who knows?"

"Hmm. When is the meeting?" she asked watching Ryder.

"Don't know." He looked at Ryan. "Did she say?"

"Maybe, I wasn't listening, she was weird. Kept saying the same scriptures over and over, about the third time I tuned her out. But she wanted us to come to the meeting, that I remember," Ryan said.

Mia read the brochure again. Other than the normal God loves you stuff and how great He is, there was little about the purpose of the group. What made it different than going to chapel on campus?

Noah whistled.

She hadn't realized he pulled her laptop across the table. "This is a large organization. They're located in almost every state with over a hundred chapters, mostly on college campuses but not all. There's nothing about the corporate office, not on this page. I'll keep looking, see who started it and who runs it now," Noah said.

Mia pulled out her phone and looked at the information for the other murders. "Check to see if there are any organizations near these locations." She gave him the names of the towns where the bodies were found.

"Every one of them is within five to ten miles of a Leviticus Club campus," Noah said before looking at her.

Even though she knew there was a connection, it made no sense. "Why?" she looked at Noah, then Ryder and last Ryan. "I don't see why."

"You don't see a motive?" Noah clarified.

She shook her head.

"Could be because you don't know what these folks believe yet. By tomorrow, you'll know and have a better idea. My guts' telling me they're involved somehow," Ryder said.

"Yeah, we watched them from a distance before coming inside, you're right. They're definitely more interested in helping those with disabilities than without," Ryan said.

"Almost asked one straight out but didn't want to do anything to jeopardize your op," Ryder said and shook his head. "Times have changed when we suspect people for doing evil for what could be a simple kindness."

That was true. What was wrong with asking the handicapped if they needed help or spiritual guidance? Nothing. Perhaps that group of people was more inclined to shy from faith.

Still… she sensed they were on the right track even if she had no idea where the track would lead. "Guys, we need to go to a meeting." She looked at Noah. He wanted to be on her team, well, they'd spend an evening investigating this group.

He didn't turn from her gaze and nodded.

"Can you get us in?" she asked the twins.

Ryder stood. "Yeah. We'll go back, see if she's still there." They turned and left.

"What are they?" Noah asked when they were alone.

Mia shook her head and mouthed. "Not here."

Surprise flashed across his face as his gaze flicked around the restaurant. He sat back and stared at her. "You light up my life."

She frowned. "Huh?"

"It's an old song but totally appropriate for how alive and excited I'm feeling right now. Today's a great day." He nodded and winked at her.

"You're in a strange mood. Hang onto it because I think we'll be in a meeting of some sort tonight." She called to cancel the meeting at the last college, it really was too far to be practical.

He frowned, disconcerted that she dismissed his romantic gesture. "You do?"

"I bet they have some sort of orientation every day. You don't grow that large, that quick, without constantly recruiting. Bet they have quotas to move up in the organization or something like that." She looked at her empty plate, wondered when she had eaten it and stood. "I need something sweet to hold me until later."

Noah watched her hips for a few moments before noticing a few other men watched as well. He didn't like it but couldn't do much about it. Things were tenuous with them and he didn't like it. He needed to make his thoughts about her plain.

When she returned, she ate while reading the monitor. The moment she finished she started typing. "Updating Tip and Thomas about everything. Tip can check out the campus in his area as well."

"They'll be impressed," Noah said.

Her gaze flicked from the screen to him as she smiled. "Surprised for sure. Hell, I'm surprised. Never thought we'd find anything." She looked around and leaned forward. "This group is relatively new, five years old. How'd they grow so fast? Plus, it's a religious group, typically those are avoided like the plague."

"Which is why college students are recruiting in shopping centers," he said. "Makes you wonder if their numbers are inflated."

She nodded and continued typing. "Probably."

"Are you dating anyone?"

Mia's gaze widened as she looked at him. "What?"

Energized, feeling more like himself than he had in decades, he repeated the question without hesitation.

"No. I don't date." She sounded embarrassed by the question.

"Why not?"

"Because I'm... different, you know that." She huffed and continued typing.

Noah understood. She was in the same head space he had been until this morning. "I'm different."

When she stared at him this time, her eyes widened slightly as his gaze lingered over her lips. "That's true. You want to date me?"

He nodded. Although he wanted a lot more, he'd start with dating. "Yes, I do."

She frowned. "Is this normal? I mean is this how people go about dating?"

Since it was how he did it, he nodded.

"We'll talk about it later." She looked up. "Ryder, what did you find out?"

"There's a meeting tonight. Here's the location. They must get points or something because she told me to make sure I use these tickets to get in. Starts in an hour and a half on the other side of town in a hotel."

"Have you guys eaten?" she asked.

"Yeah, but we'll grab a few burgers on the way." He gave her two tickets. "Meet you there. Should be interesting."

Mia agreed.

CHAPTER 16

The drive to the meeting was done in silent contemplation. Noah had removed the handicapped placard and stored it in his glove compartment.

Earlier, Mia did a good job hiding her shock and elation. *"Dating?"* What did she know about any of that? Sure she had sex with other members of the group from time to time, it was more like scratching an itch, or meeting a basic need, but that stopped over 10 years ago, and all of those guys were dead.

She peeked at Noah's strong hands on the steering wheel and imagined them on her body. Warmth coursed through her. "Stop," she silently demanded before the scent of her arousal seeped across the seat to him.

"Nervous?" he asked.

"Not really." She forced her thoughts away from his long, thick fingers to the case. Her case. "It'll be interesting to hear what they're selling."

"You think it's a sham?" He sounded surprised.

"Yes. The women in the shopping centers are serious believers, that came through. They were probably told to focus on the handicapped. Helping the disadvantaged is an easy sell. But I don't think we'll find the same level of devotion at the top."

"Is that one of your …um, gifts?"

"Empath. Reading the brochure, the club comes across as fake. Plus, there's no mention of Christ anywhere, just Yahweh."

"So?"

"Christ is all about love, peace, and joy, at least that's my take from the books I've read. Old Testament Yahweh dealt with a lot of land taking, wars, killing, laws, and punishment. Which personality would appeal to murderers?"

He whistled. "Don't know much about the Old Testament. Grew up Baptist dealing mostly with the New. But the Middle East is a hotbed of a mess because of land disputes in the Bible. So this group focuses on a particular book of the Bible which is about —"

"Laws. Leviticus means the law of the priests. Deals a lot with procedures."

Noah frowned. "Laws of priests? They made a club about that?"

"Strange, right?" They turned into the parking lot of the hotel on the outskirts of town and pulled next to Ryder's truck.

"Hey," she said after Noah helped her from the cab.

"Hey. Not that many takers from what we noticed when we peeked inside," Ryder said as they headed to the entrance.

Inside the meeting room, they were greeted by several smiling faces of men and women who welcomed them enthusiastically.

Taking seats on the third row, Mia counted 12 other guests seated nearby. Some looked bored. Others talked amongst themselves. One fella was asleep.

The meeting started on time. A young, blond, handsome guy greeted them and gave a spiel about the love of God. How God loves everyone and we owe it to Him to offer our service with our whole being. It wasn't a long speech, didn't put her to sleep or anything but it came across... practiced. Like a recital and she wondered how many times had he said the exact same words? Her gut said every night.

Next, he opened a large book that had been on a stand slightly behind him and started reading. "Leviticus 19."

As he read, the members of the group stood with their hands on their chests as if they were making a pledge of some kind. When he read verse 14, "Do not curse the deaf or put a stumbling block in front of the blind, but fear your God. I am the Lord," Mia's eyebrow rose and she glanced at Noah. A blind man had been stoned.

When the meeting ended, Mia still wasn't sure she understood what they believed or what the group was about.

"Thank you for coming, I'm Saul, we hope you'll consider joining Leviticus Club," the man who had read the scripture said, shaking Noah's hand, then Ryder and Ryan's. He didn't even glance at her.

"Sounds good, but I'm not sure what the group stands for," Ryan said moving between her and the rude man.

Mia bit back her frustration and allowed *the men* to gain answers.

"We believe the entire Bible but take our marching orders from the instructions given to the Priests. Each of us sees ourselves as Priests of God and strive to live in a way that meets His requirements."

She listened a few more minutes and watched the others. Most were tall, thin, could be models on a runway. Frowning she looked at the men, noticed a similar quality. Whether blond or brunette, they were all the same type of pretty. Listening to the females, she wasn't surprised by their discussions centered on fashion and beauty.

She walked to the women, noticed their surprise and forced smiles as they stared down at her. What? Don't they like short people?

"Hi, can I say you are so pretty, both of you. Your skin…it's glowing." Feed their vanity first she thought. "All of you are, that's a powerful recommendation to join your group."

"Yes, that and a serious health-care regimen," one of the females twittered, covering her mouth with her hand as she grinned. "Some of the most beautiful people in the world are members of the Leviticus Club because of Biblical requirements to remain clean. Honestly, if more people would just obey the Bible, we wouldn't have so many ugly—" She stopped. "Ugly wars and problems in the world."

"You're so right. How long have you been a member?"

"Two years," she lied and Mia wondered why.

"You'll meet a lot of great people at the conferences, become friends for life," the other female said. *Deceit.*

"Is he in charge of the conferences?" she tipped her head to Saul.

One of the females smiled. The other shook her head. "No. Regional leaders are in charge of the events, sometimes our Priest comes. He's our leader and trains the Holy Priests. You're really pretty, you should come, you'll love it."

Smiling brightly, while cringing inside, Mia said. "Thanks for explaining things, you've convinced me this club is what I've been looking for. You two are the greatest in addition to being beautiful."

Both ladies blushed as they smiled. "Yahweh is all," one of them said as they walked out. Rather than return to Saul and the guys, Mia headed to the lobby to see if she could pick up anything from the attendees.

A few members were talking one on one with their guests but most had left. Taking a seat in the lobby, Mia listened in on their conversations. No one stressed the religious aspects of the group. One talked about a sponsor, Purity Products and how they gave away skin and hair care products, gym memberships, things that fed the body as well as the soul.

The other member kept telling the two women how beautiful they were and that the club was always looking for more beautiful people. Fortunately, the women didn't seem impressed and declined the membership. When they left he stared hungrily at them in a way that had nothing to do with the 10 Commandments.

Turning, he headed to the bar and ordered a drink. Mia closed her eyes and focused to hear his conversation in the other room.

"Any luck?" the bartender asked.

"Naw. Thought I had them, but they bolted. Damn, I need three more to make my quota for this month. You know anyone?"

"Gave you everybody I know already."

"I know, appreciate it. I might have to get another job, this one's not panning out. Head guy's on my ass for not hitting the numbers. Can't help it if the recruiters aren't sending in the right people."

"Every time Saul reads those scriptures, gives me hives, man. That's the killer right there. Makes people nervous, if you ask me," the bartender said.

"It's the one thing that can't be changed. Gotta read it." He sighed. "Let me know if you meet anyone who needs free spiritual guidance and direction."

"Lots of people need that, man. Problem is, you don't really want just anyone," the bartender said.

Mia leaned forward, listening hard.

"Unfortunately not, gotta be without a spot or blemish."

"Heard that," the bartender said.

Moments later the guy walked out of the bar and out of the building. Noah, Ryder, and Ryan strode out a few moments later.

"Why'd you leave?" Ryder asked.

As they walked to their vehicles, she shared her conversation with the females and then what she overheard.

"I hadn't noticed that about the people," Ryder murmured. "Now that you mention it, they all had a similar look. You think that's what this is all about. Pretty people?" he made it sound like a joke but she wasn't sure he hadn't hit the nail on the head. Emotions were all over the place, greed, fear, envy. Love, peace, and joy were conspicuously absent.

She shrugged. "I'll listen to the book of Leviticus so I have a better understanding of what they're supposed to be about. Honestly, I don't see a parallel between the scriptures he read and what they were saying. Seems the more I learn, the more confusing it becomes. Maybe Thomas will have some insight."

"There's the main guy, a Priest, did they say where he was located? Does he travel? What about that group of priests?" Noah asked.

"They mentioned them but didn't give details," she said wishing she had pushed Saul a bit. He was the only one who might've known about the top tiers in the organization. "Today was a good day, thanks so much guys, really appreciate your help."

Ryan looked at Noah and then her. "You need to help him control his voice. When he asked Saul a question, the man almost passed out from the compulsion. It doesn't work if they can't hear you."

"What?" Her gaze flew to Noah's.

"I didn't realize I could do that until they helped Saul sit. Ryder explained it to me after I told him what happened this morning." Noah looked sheepish. "It's still new."

"And unexpected," she said wondering what was going on. This was not the time to fly off the handle with the unexpected.

"Because of Noah, Saul gave us two names," Ryan said. "Aaron Mosely and Peter Drum. One is the Priest, one is the regional director. We can look them up too."

Mia nodded slowly, watching Noah. "The Priest? That's good information. You didn't kill him did you?"

Noah scowled at her. "No. I don't think he realized he said anything, just claimed a headache and walked off." He extended his hand to Ryan. "Thanks for working with me on that, I don't smell everything anymore and my hearing levels are good. It's been a crazy day with all of that out of whack."

Ryan shook his hand. "No worries. Just remember, you can't ever betray what we told you. It's a death sentence, seriously."

Noah nodded and clapped him on the shoulder. "No worries there. After walking in my dreams, and the day I've had, nothing much would surprise me."

"Good." Ryan looked at Mia. "My father sent that information regarding the club to your email. We'll talk with you tomorrow." He and Ryder headed to their vehicle.

"Ready?" Noah asked.

"Yeah." She waved at the twins and slid into the passenger seat. "You okay?" she asked when he started the car. "I didn't fully process what today was like for you until just now."

With a ridiculous boyish grin, he nodded. "I've got super-fucking powers."

She stared at him and then laughed. "Goof-ball."

By the time they reached the hotel, Mia was a quivering mass of contradictions. Noah had lost his mind. The man smiled continually, held her hand and sang, yes, sang along with the radio. She didn't know how to deal with him. What happened to the surly, closed off, refused to smile Noah she met? Him she could handle.

The new Noah scared and excited her.

He opened the door for her and his hand lingered on her back as they walked toward the entrance. Since he carried her bag with her computer, she couldn't send him away and he refused to give it to her.

The elevator ride to the third floor was silent. Nervous, she fidgeted until she realized her actions and forced her body to remain still.

"If I had my computer, I could help with the research," he offered as they turned the corner to her room. "Do you have a flash drive?"

"Yes. I have a few, why?"

"We can use the business center downstairs and I can help you." They entered her room.

"That's a good idea, give me a minute." Mind back in the game, she pushed aside the hum in her body, the tingles spiking her core and searched through her supplies. Finding the drives she nodded. "Let's go." He walked behind her. She felt his hot gaze on her ass.

Her skin sizzled, something she'd never felt before with the few men she had sex with. Throat tight, she remained silent during the short ride down and as they walked to the business center. Inside he grabbed the lone computer and waited for her to do the same with her laptop.

Over the next hour, they read the information sent by Tyrone and researched Aaron Mosely, Peter Drum, Purity Products and Saul. By the time they finished, she was exhausted and hoped they didn't dream that night. She printed specific pages from the email and sent everything to Thomas.

So far, he hadn't responded to anything she sent, neither had Tip. Since she all but demanded to remain behind to finish the op, she tried not to be angry. He told her he would be out of touch for a few days when he asked her to go with him. Still, there was a part of her that wanted his approval, just a nod saying she was heading in the right direction.

For now, she believed Leviticus Club was definitely involved with the murders but had no definitive proof.

"Let's take this upstairs," she said packing up her laptop and receiving the flash drive from him with his research. She yawned, it was well after midnight.

Upstairs, she placed her bag on the table and moved quickly to the bathroom. She'd been holding it in for the past 30 minutes and breathed a sigh of relief.

Noah sat at the small table watching her when she re-entered the bedroom. "Too tired to talk?" he asked.

She was tired but they needed to talk. "No, what's on your mind." She sat on the edge of the bed and looked at him.

Leaning forward, with his elbows on his knees and hands dangling between them he snared her gaze. "I'm damaged. My last tour I was hit by something that lodged in my head. Took a while to pull it back together. Had to relearn basics, walking, my speech was off, processing information was a bitch. Spent months in physical therapy. They say I'm a walking miracle." He snorted. "I talk to a therapist. From time to time I'm right back there, right in the fight, seeing my buddies on the ground. Guys I'd just eaten a meal with, gone in an instant. Fucks with me, so I obey my doctor and talk to a shrink." He paused. "Never thought I'd smile again or want to. The dreams are a nuisance. The mist chokes and paralyzes me. At least it did until you entered my dreams."

The intensity of his gaze stopped her from swallowing or responding. She forced herself to breathe.

"Whatever you did last night when you broke through that barrier, freed something in me. I don't think I'll ever be able to fully explain to you how I felt today. It's like I've got my life back, and anything's possible. Didn't expect the extras but they're worth it to be whole or as whole as I'm going to be."

Unable to speak through her tight throat, she nodded.

"Like I said, I'm damaged and yet as whole as I'm going to be. I like you, Mia. I want to get to know you better, spend my days and nights with you. Earlier, I said I wanted to be on your team, I meant that. Maybe when Thomas and the others get it together we'll talk but right now, this isn't about them. It's about me and you. I want all of you or as much as you can give me."

"You want me?" Her eyes widened slightly.

"Yes, you." He pointed at her with a soft smile.

How pathetic was it that no one had ever uttered those words to her before? The ring of truth, intertwined with a ping of certainty delivered his response with clarity. Her heart expanded as she continued staring at him.

"I know there's an age difference between us, but it's just a number," he said. "We can make it work if you give me a shot."

"Age difference?" She cocked her brow at him.

"Figure I got, what 10 - 15 years on you?"

She laughed, more like she had 95 or more years on him. She'd have to calculate it. She stood and entered his embrace. Now wasn't the time to share her past with him, she needed Thomas' okay for that. It was a part of their pact. But for now, she would relish the sweet words he spoke and hold them close to her heart.

"It's time to rest, we'll talk in the morning." She turned off the light and undressed with the assurance he watched her every move.

"The twins are coming to my place in the morning to work with me," he said shoving his jeans and boxers down his long legs.

She faced him and allowed her gaze to drop. His cock rose as she stared at it. "In the morning?" she asked meeting his gaze.

"Yeah, don't want to talk about them now." He kicked off his pants and pulled his shirt over his head, revealing a scarred, wide muscular chest.

She traced one long wicked scar that trailed from his nipple to his soft pubic hair and looked up at him.

"Damaged."

"Beautiful warrior. A gift from God," she said wanting him to believe it.

He swallowed hard, pulled her close and kissed her. Nothing could've prepared her for this feeling of drowning and being rescued at the same time. He took and gave. Her hands wrapped around his neck as she tried to climb him to get closer to his heat, needing more. His arm came under her hips as he lifted her with apparent ease.

They broke apart gasping.

"You're so damn beautiful," he said.

Her heart stuttered. She'd been called princess, sweetie, babes and a manner of other endearments, but no one ever told her she was beautiful with such earnest heat and care.

Her forehead touched his as she pulled her thoughts together.

"There's this light inside you, so bright, sweet and pure. The first time I saw you, I pretended to be looking at the house but you captivated me from the beginning. Didn't think I had a shot, not with all the shit going on with me. Then you smiled and I was gone. You light up my fucking life, I mean that, Mia. I mean that."

Tears leaked from her eyes and she scrubbed them away with the back of her hand. She never realized how much she needed to hear those words from someone. Never occurred to her that she needed to matter, to have someone believe she was special. After years of searching for the child of her womb, no matter how it was planted the babe was a part of her, she wanted her child to know he or she mattered. Know that she thought and prayed for them constantly. They mattered.

In less than five minutes Noah broke through the walls surrounding the failures of her past and watered her thirsty heart.

"What's wrong?" he rubbed her back as he lay her on the bed. With his thumb, he gently wiped away her tears. "Don't cry, I can't take it."

She scooted up and over so he could join her. "I'm not… sad," she said extending her hand to him. He took it and lay beside her.

"Lay with me tonight. Sleep here, hold me close," she said. "I need a moment to breathe."

His warm arms wrapped around her, pulling her close. "Whatever you need."

The hard length of his cock pressed against her and she smiled as she yawned again. Sleep pulled on her, there were a few things she wanted to say to him. But the darkness dragged her under.

CHAPTER 17

"You can't tell him."

Mia's eyes flew open as she sat up quickly, looking around. She lay in the middle of a rich, green field with rolling hills that smelled like spring. It was beautiful and unlike anything she had ever seen. She patted the grass, smiled at the smooth texture and wanted to roll around in it.

"You can't tell him." The words drifted toward her.

"Who said that?" She slid to her knees, gaze keen as she searched for the voice. "Who's here?"

A tall man with green eyes, long white hair wearing a black robe walked toward her. "Hello, Mia."

"Hello, Grandfather. You scared me. Is this your place?" She looked around again. "I've never seen this one before, it's beautiful."

"Yes, one of them. Come sit. Let's catch up." He folded gracefully onto the grass.

Inhaling deep, she sat back and looked at him. "You look good, at peace."

He nodded. "Things are changing but that's good I think. How about you? Still searching?"

Did she hear mocking in his tone? Possibly. Grandfather had been around as long as she remembered. He first came to her in a dream in her early teens when she first escaped the Liege. She'd been lost and afraid, he told her how to find Thomas and the others which literally saved her life.

"Yes, I am." She explained Thomas' mission and her working the case. When she discussed the murders her heart wept. Emotions intensified in dreams.

"There is much evil in the world. At times like these there must be a balance," he said. "You cannot tell the young man of your past. The time is not right. He's not ready."

Mia thought about what she had seen in the mist and agreed. "He's been through a lot, thinks he's older than me." She offered a bittersweet smile. "You're right, I cannot and will not betray the others by sharing our secret." She looked at Grandfather. "Will he stay? With me I mean?"

He smiled. "That's between the two of you."

She hadn't expected an answer but it never hurt to ask. "He changed. He's fully human but has similar powers to us. How's that possible?"

"Perhaps his injury required surgery that tapped into the same areas of his brain as yours. You're human with a little extra, so is he." He shrugged. "How would I know these things?"

"He's lonely," she said speaking of herself as well. She'd never realized just how lonely she had been.

"He's not alone. There are others like him, coming together because of the war. Choices and alliances will be made, could be good, could be bad. Who knows what's in the hearts of men?"

She took note of his words and didn't bother asking for explanations. Most times she thought he was an oracle with no idea of the things he said.

"What about us? Are we going to survive all of this change?" Granted she told Thomas she knew she'd die one day, but if that day was in the distance, she wouldn't be mad.

He gave her one of his rare smiles. Green eyes lit like shining shamrocks. "You will indeed survive dear child. One might think your journey is just beginning."

Warmth filled her.

"There you are," Noah said, taking her hand and pulling her to her feet from the rolling gray mist. "I didn't see you." He wrapped his arms around her waist, holding her close.

They stood in the middle of the campus, watching students come and go. She blinked several times to get her balance and waved at the fog. It rolled away so she could see clearly.

"I'll be glad when I'm able to do that," Noah murmured against the top of her head.

She leaned back and patted his cheek. "You will. Why are we here?"

Holding her hand they moved forward. "I don't know. Green's van hadn't been on campus."

"Could he have been here without his van?" she asked as they moved toward the student union.

"I suppose so." They stood just inside the large building for a few seconds. "There." He pointed. "Saul, the guy from the meeting."

Saul moved quickly through the building, turned and walked down a long corridor. He opened a door into a small office with Leviticus Club on the door.

Noah whistled as they followed. "Somebody made a serious donation for that."

Saul entered a small room in the back, closed the door and pulled out his phone.

Mia and Noah looked at each other and moved closer to look at the number. Noah wrote it down.

Moments later a male answered the call.

"Drum, we may have a problem," Saul said. "The FBI is investigating Green's death. My contact at the police department sent word to go to ground."

"FBI? Hmm. Okay, I'll pass it on. Your numbers are down for that area, what's the problem?"

"Working on it. But we may need to hit the other campus soon, give this area a break. Or should we work the streets and hostels? We have decent success with those."

"Not yet. Not until I speak with the Priest, see how he wants it to go. Sacrifice or worship? I'll let you know. Don't worry about the FBI either, that'll be handled and I'll let you know when the heat's blown over."

"Good to know." He disconnected and stared out the window.

"That was two days ago when you arrived in town," Noah said. "Someone called to let them know."

"Because they knew this guy and his group was involved in the murder." She looked at Noah. "But who? The Detective? Receptionist? Those are the only two I've ever seen."

"There are more," Noah said watching Saul pace. "He's nervous. Wonder why?"

"Murder makes a person nervous." She watched Saul bite his fingernail while staring at the wall.

"But that happened last week. I spoke to him last night, he seemed fine. Can you read his mind?"

"What? No, I can't do that, not fully," she said. They watched Saul a few moments longer.

"What next?"

"You're driving, I'm along for the ride," she said easing her hand into his much larger one.

"Wonder if we can find Peter Drum or Aaron Mosely," he said looking around.

Nothing happened.

Noah had no real idea how the dream-walking thing actually worked. In the past, he revisited places he had been before and was able to see what transpired in that location. But what if he could see places and people by choice, direct the dream to his specifications? That would be a big help.

"Look at me." He stared at her. "Think Peter Drum with me. We want to see Peter Drum." He squeezed her hand.

"We want to see Peter Drum," she murmured.

"We want to see Peter Drum with the Leviticus Club," he clarified staring at her.

She repeated what he said.

Seconds later the mist swooshed over them. They moved at a tremendous speed and stopped in an office. A man sat at his desk talking on his phone.

"Not yet. Not until I speak with the Priest, see how he wants it to go. Sacrifice or worship? I'll let you know. Don't worry about the FBI either, that'll be handled and I'll let you know when the heat's blown over."

Slender, blonde, well-dressed with every strand in place, he put down the phone and sighed as he made another call. "Henry, Saul needs a permanent vacation never to be seen again. The place is hot right now, make it happen in two days max." He hung up, stood and brushed his shirt. "I hate when people get sloppy and make excuses." He paused. "We may need to take out his contact at the police station as well."

"Last night may have been the last time Saul is seen," Noah said.

Mia nodded as Drum left the office. She looked around his desk to see if he left notes or anything lying around. Nothing.

"Can we follow him?"

"No, I'm wearing out," Noah said.

"Same here," she said as they disappeared into sleep.

The morning sky didn't burst onto the horizon with brilliant colors announcing its arrival. It rolled through the blinds in shades of gray, an omen of the day to come.

There was a bit of chill in the room when Mia woke. She stiffened at the arms wrapped around her waist and slowly remembered Noah's declaration of wanting her last night.

Her gaze flicked to the window noted the gray clouds and a darker lining on the horizon. They were running out of time. She desperately wanted to prove she could do this type of work, not just to Thomas but to herself.

Yesterday, she hummed as pieces to the puzzle locked into place. She knew, with uncanny certainty Leviticus Club was somehow involved the moment the skinny chick approached Noah at the buffet.

A clap of thunder rolled across the sky. She burrowed closer to Noah's warmth. They wouldn't be going anywhere soon.

He pulled her closer, brushed a kiss across her forehead. "It's a Texas morning."

She smiled.

"Thunder and lightning's the best way to greet the day." His warm breath rolled across her scalp. His masculine scent filled and touched her. Why hadn't she ever noticed that before? The men on the team had scents, everyone did. But she never thought of their scents as masculine. Interesting.

"Sleep well? No more dream-walking?"

"Slept great. Just woke." She turned so that her back was to him. He moved closer. They fit into a perfect spoon.

His questing hand ran down her outer thigh, returned and moved slowly to her stomach, breast, pinched her nipple and down to rest between her legs. The hard cock pressed against her back clearly said this was more than morning wood. The musky scent of his arousal filled her nostrils adding to the accumulating scents in the room.

This was different. He didn't roll on top, spread her legs and get relief. Frowning, she wondered if there was a problem. Turning, she met his gaze with a question on her lips. A question he kissed away.

His firm lips latched onto hers. The kiss obliterated every thought. All her concerns and questions evaporated like the early morning dew. He moved slightly, his big, strong arms tightened around her, drawing her closer still.

They broke apart, gasping. Pleasured shock raced through her. Her core throbbed in expectation. She stared into the heat filling his gaze, wrapped her arms around his neck and kissed him again. He deepened the kiss, probing with his tongue.

She moaned at the exquisite feeling of his tongue. "That was amazing," she said in a whisper when they broke apart. "Teach me how to do that."

He stared into her eyes for a few seconds. "Whatever you want."

"I want it all. Teach me how to do it all," she said excitedly.

His brow rose. "You've never had sex before?"

"Sex? Yes, of course. It's necessary to have a periodic release. But I want to learn about this." She ran her hand down his back. "What we're doing now."

"Kissing? Hugging? Hopefully foreplay?" he smiled.

"Yes. I want to experience it all," she said wholeheartedly. Her body burned. Her core throbbed in a way it never had before.

"Okay." He placed a quick kiss on her lips. "What if this time I show you how good it will be between us and start the lessons next time?"

Her heart slammed in her chest at the sultry promise in his gaze. Swallowing hard, she ran her tongue across her dry lips and nodded. "Okay."

His smile reminded her of a naughty boy who had just been granted his fondest wish instead of punishment. He ran his hand beneath her back and pulled off her shirt, removed her bra and pulled down her panties.

Exposed to his gaze, her breath hitched as his finger lightly grazed the tips of her breast.

"Like that?"

Her skin heated like an out of control forest fire. Tingles shot to her core. Moisture dampened her thigh.

"Oh yes. Feels so good," she moaned.

His tongue swiped across her nipples.

She jerked and looked down at the top of his head.

"Shh, let me work," he murmured against her breast, before drawing the nipple into his mouth. Each suckle from his mouth sent little jolts of electricity crashing straight between her legs.

No one had ever touched her this way. Shock turned into drowning pleasure as his hand eased down her quivering belly and rested on her mound. Those thick fingers played between her legs, teasing, rubbing and finally entering her hungry core.

"Ohmigod," Mia shouted. One hand held the back of his head to her breast the other pressed his hand between his legs as she rolled her hips. When he removed his hand, she groaned and then gasped in amazement when he licked his fingers. The expression on his face was one of joy. He smacked his lips and looked down at her.

"Tasty. I knew you'd be sweet but damn, woman. I've got to have more of you. This is better than breakfast."

Unsure what he meant she frowned. When he placed kisses down her body she moaned in delight. But when he kissed her between her legs her eyes flew open and she tried to push him away.

"What are you doing?" she asked.

He didn't move and didn't budge. "Beautiful," he murmured.

The oral assault included long, leisurely swipes of his tongue between her legs, kisses, sucking and moans from his mouth that shot through her. Never had she felt anything like this. When his finger penetrated her again and the kisses continued she pulled him closer rather than pushed him away.

"Noah... oh my, never...this is so... please..." her head tossed side to side on the pillow. Her heart slammed in her chest. She closed her eyes to savor the sensations traveling at warp speed through her body robbing her of breath. Something was building. She grabbed his arms and lifted slightly.

"Noah," she screamed as wave after wave of bliss crashed through her. Trembling, she sucked air into her starved lungs and stared at the ceiling. *What the hell just happened?* Seconds ticked in silence. Her heart didn't slow and the tremors took a few moments longer to stop. The bed moved.

"Ready?"

She couldn't speak if he paid her. Not that it mattered, her body had other ideas and clearly gave the answer he needed.

"This is just you and me. From now on, this is just us," he said and then slid into her. He didn't move, instead, he stared down at her, waiting. She met his gaze, saw the tension in his clenched jaw, the quivering of his muscular arms and realized it cost him to remain still.

"You're so damn tight I'm about to lose my fucking mind," he ground out.

Sensing his need was as great as hers, she relaxed.

He closed his eyes, dropped his head for a few seconds. "I need you."

"Take me."

His gaze locked onto hers. She shivered from the heat in the dark depths. He pulled out and rammed his whole length into her, stealing her breath. He had been so swift it took her by surprise. This was more than needing releases. The hard, fast thrusts were a primal taking. She shuddered in response, lifting slightly to meet each thrust, to give as much as she received. His grunts of pleasure lit a match to her need, spiraling her to another level.

He pumped hard and fast inside her, rubbing against her velvety walls. A cascade of fire spread throughout her body. Needing more, she dug into his hair, pulled his mouth to hers for a desperate kiss and received a short brush against her lips as she spiraled upwards, faster, and faster, she couldn't breathe from the intensity of it.

She opened her mouth, no sound emitted as her body shook wildly from the force of her shattering climax.

Bewitched, Noah thought as he pressed down onto her, moving his hips rapidly, matching her moan for moan. When her pussy clutched him through her orgasm, he didn't stop to let her recover. He continued thrusting into her as her screams filled the air and no doubt alerted the hotel guest in the next room of their activities.

He couldn't believe how tight she was, how sopping wet she'd been when he touched her. His balls literally dripped from her sweetness as they slapped against her. This was heaven. Teeth gritted, his nuts drew up, as he pushed into her. Just a few more.

His back arched as he called her name as he came so hard, toes curling, legs weakening and stomach tightening. He shuddered and fell like a weak cat. He gulped in air and tried to corral his splintered thoughts. He'd been sexually active since he turned 12 and he could say without question, she had the absolute best pussy he ever tasted or fucked.

He rolled to the side, pulling her with him. Outside, thunder rumbled and lightning flashed, a perfect complement to the shifting thoughts in his mind. Mia was his addiction. Just thinking about her tight pussy sent blood rushing to his dick. Regardless of how long it had been since he took a woman, he was hitting 40 and normally it took a few minutes to regroup.

Pulling her closer, he inhaled their mixed scents and knew he would never forget it or her. She snuggled closer and released what sounded like a contented coo.

He smiled. "Satisfied? If not, I can show you a little more." He pressed his semi-hard dick into her belly.

"Noah, I've never experienced anything like that." She leaned back, snared his gaze and he was struck by her sincerity as well as the tears in her eyes. "No one has ever given me so much pleasure or kissed me down there. I didn't know it was possible."

His chest expanded with pride.

"You do want me," she said as if it was some new or difficult concept for her to grab before looking at him again. Inhaling, she faced him with shoulders squared. "When I became of age, I was taken by force. Rape is what it's called now. Over and over until I conceived. When the child was born they took her or him. I have no idea if I gave birth to a son or daughter. I've searched for answers for years and have not had a real relationship with a man. I'm not sure I know how. You say you're damaged, broken, in that case, we are two of a pair."

"God, I'm sorry, Mia. I'm really sorry." Being stationed overseas in poor countries he knew things like that happened. People bought and sold infants all the time. It was a big business. He didn't know how to make this better for her.

She wiped the tears from her face and offered a small shrug. "I don't know who my family is. I don't know my real name." She sounded embarrassed.

"Orphan?" Not that it mattered to him. His parents were dead and he hadn't talked to his younger brother in at least 10 years. He considered Liam his kin but that was about it. Family could be a bonus or liability, it just depended.

"Yes, orphaned." She searched his gaze.

"I'm sorry for your loss, but it doesn't matter to me." He didn't know what else to say that wouldn't sound dismissive.

"That doesn't bother you? This lack of identity?" she asked leaning up on her elbow, staring down at him.

"No, should it?"

Her frown deepened.

Using his index finger, he stroked the small indentation between her brows. "I want you, the person you are today. The bold, strong, sexy woman I met a few days ago. I care about her, you. I'm not minimizing your losses, I can only imagine how much it hurts and how you suffered. Despite all of that, I think the woman you're today is pretty amazing."

Her eyes widened slightly. "You do?"

"Yes, I do." His gaze dropped to her full bottom lip and he pulled her close, urging her lips apart. His tongue slid in as if returning home as he rasped her tongue against his with increasing hunger.

She held onto him so tight, her fingers left marks. Badges of honor in his mind.

"You're incredible," she whispered. "I'm hot, trembly, and so turned on. What are you doing to me?"

Bewitched for damn sure by this woman. "Showing you my appreciation, how much I care for you, how much you mean to me. I want to give and receive pleasure from you."

She held his gaze for several heartbeats. "I don't know what to say. It's never... ever been like this." Then she smiled brightly and the sun outside joined her happiness as it peeked from behind a cloud. "I really like it. We can do it as much as you want."

His heart leaped in his chest. "I will always want," he said pulling her on top of him. "Are you sore?"

She frowned and then pursed her lips. "A little but I'm horny too, which makes no sense after what I've experienced already. It must be you. Because you make me feel things I've never felt before." She sounded as if she'd just solved a problem and now things were right in her mind.

Rather than join her one-sided discussion, he lifted her from around her waist. "Line it up and when I bring you close, it will slide in."

"Yes, I know this position," she said taking hold of him.

If her hands hadn't felt so incredible wrapping around him, he would've changed positions. Nothing they did should remind her of being with someone else.

As he eased into her, her heat welcomed him. He hissed his pleasure at the velvety warmth. She placed her hands on his chest, lifted slightly and worked her hips bringing him in and out of her.

He watched her face, eyes closed, mouth open with the tip of her tongue visible she fucked him. He knew when she found her rhythm, knew when she found the spot that would take her over. Her movements became jerky, her eyes flew open with a silent desperate plea.

He thrust his hips to meet her every move as her hips bobbed up and down on his cock.

"Noah," she screamed, moving faster, straining.

He grabbed her hips tight, pistoned in and out of her, faster and faster.

Her walls tightened. They were both close.

She screamed his name again and shuddered as she came once more. Her release triggered his, as she milked his cock with her pulsing warmth.

CHAPTER 18

Dressed in a white linen tunic, a blue robe and an ephod with 12 stones, the Priest faced the audience and lifted his hands. "Blessed are the meek, for they will inherit the earth. We are living in difficult times, there are those who despise God and His mighty works." He curled his hand into a fist as if grabbing Holy energy and shook it. "They mock the God of heaven while we worship and adore Him. He blesses the works of her hand and love in our hearts to please Him in everything we do."

People stood, clapping in agreement.

His heart soared, as it always did when he stood in front of them. When they responded to his words, peace filled his broken spirit. The Bishop had been wrong to excommunicate him, the penance had been unreasonable and wouldn't please God. No. God required sacrifice. His voice had been clear, the demands specific, the scriptures made him righteous.

The priest was specifically chosen to carry out the commands of God and would continue to do so until there was no breath in his body. The Bishop hadn't understood. Few did. God's ways were mysterious, but who could question them?

Not him.

He'd rather obey God's voice than the church and though it grieved him, he left the order beneath a cloud of misunderstanding. While the others continued singing he motioned for the 12 to follow him. They entered a small room lined with heavy plastic and a pile of red clay bricks in the corner. In the middle of the room, a blind man lay bound on the ground.

Sorrow filled the priest for what he must do to please God. Two decades of his life had been serving as a different kind of Priest until God called him away for this special service. As the others took up their places, he quoted a part of Leviticus 22.

"The Lord said to Moses, "Say to Aaron: 'For the generations to come no man who has any defect may come near: no man who is blind or lame, disfigured or deformed; no man with a crippled foot or hand, or who is a hunchback or a dwarf, or who has any eye defect, or who has festering or running sores or damaged testicles. Because of his defect, he must not go near the curtain or approach the altar, and so desecrate my sanctuary." He paused, looked at the blind man again.

The 12 Elders standing around him spoke together. "Yes, that is what Yahweh says."

Filled with righteous fervor the priest lifted his brick above his head. "What is the penalty for those who disobey the Lord?"

"They are taken outside the camp and stoned to death," the others said as they each picked up bricks, one in each hand.

"We will cleanse this earth of those who are not worthy to be in Yahweh's presence, for this is our mission. Do we accept it?" he asked.

"Yes, we accept it," they said together.

"In the name of Yahweh, we rebuke you, unclean one." The priest threw the first brick, hitting the man in the forehead. The others threw their bricks until the man's body was covered in red and blood ran on the tarp.

The priest lifted his eyes upward. "Thank you, Father, we obey you in all things. We vow to cleanse the earth of those who defile your temple and your presence."

Weary, yet elated he waved his hand. Those on the clean-up team moved forward to remove the body from their temple. He and the others returned to the sanctuary to finish the service.

It was the tenth sacrifice this week. Now that the incinerator was repaired they would be busier than usual. God had spoken to him last week, demanding more and more sacrifices.

CHAPTER 19

Feeling better than he had in years, Noah and Mia ate a late breakfast before she checked out of her hotel room to stay with Noah. It was either she stay with him or he'd stay with her.

Since the hotel room was much smaller, she finally agreed to move. On the way to his place, they stopped by the police station. Detective Gordon had left an envelope for her with the receptionist.

Inside were the forensics and toxicology reports. "Propofol," she muttered as she read.

"Huh?" he asked glancing away from the road to her.

"Fast acting drug that incapacitates you. Anesthesiologists use it. Not hard to find." She continued reading the reports.

"Never had oral sex before?"

"What kind of sex?" She looked at him, her brows furrowed.

"Oral. When I kissed you between your legs?" The question had been pushed to the back of his mind behind so many others. Her response from their sexual romp, the utter surprise, and appreciation in her gaze made him feel 20 feet tall. And made him wonder about her past, something they never discussed.

She grinned, leaned over and kissed him. "No, you're my first."

"And last," he said with an arched brow.

"You're a pre-cog? Can read the future?" she asked with a saucy grin.

"For that, yes." He held her hand and turned off the highway toward his home.

She laughed but didn't release his hand. When he pulled into his drive, he noted his cousin Liam's car and cursed. In the past if his cousin had a date, needed a place to bed a woman or just wanted to hang out, he came over. Today wasn't a good day.

Noah wanted to be alone with Mia to continue exploring her body and learning more about her. He didn't want Liam or anyone else around. Once he turned off the engine, he said. "Looks like my cousin Liam is here, he'll be leaving soon."

"Is that him?" Her gaze veered from him to his cousin standing on the porch, sans shirt and pants unzipped displaying his pubic hairs.

Noah leaned out the window. "Go put on some clothes."

Liam tilted his head, looked at Mia, nodded and returned inside. "Wait here for a minute."

He strode inside and released a frustrated breath at the sloppy condition of the living room. Clothes, empty beer cans, and half-eaten pizza were everywhere. Quickly, he picked up the clothes, tossed them into the hamper. By the time he returned to the living room, Liam helped clear the living room and kitchen.

"Shirley's in the shower, soon as she's done, we'll leave," Liam said. "Do I need to change the sheets in the spare room?"

"Yeah, toss them in the washer." No need to mention how sensitive his and Mia noses were. He'd toned everything down the moment he reached the porch.

Liam headed back.

Noah looked around and exhaled before returning to the truck. Ryan stood next to the door on the passenger side talking softly to Mia. So softly he couldn't hear what they said.

"Hey, how's it going?" Noah said offering his fist.

Ryan bumped it. "Good. Once you guys get situated, we've got some things to share with you." He nodded to the house. "Be back in a bit." He turned and walked off.

Noah opened the truck, assisted Mia down and wrapped his arm around her waist. "You're a pretty, little-bitty thing."

She pushed his shoulder. "No. Fully grown woman standing in your arms."

He grinned, loving her spirit. "Standing corrected, pretty, little-bitty, fully grown woman."

"You're bad." She smiled and accepted his kiss.

"Let me get your bags so we can get started."

Her smile eased away and he knew her thoughts were on the case. They were closer after last night hearing Drum. He grabbed her backpack from the back seat and computer bag, while she carried her purse.

"This is nice, Noah. Quiet, restful," she said looking around at the barn, large, old trees.

"It is. I like it." And hope you like it as well, he thought as they moved forward.

Liam and his date walked out as Noah reached the porch. He smiled at Mia, glanced at her bags and his smile widened as Noah introduced them.

"My name's Marie, not Shirley, asshole," the blond snapped at Liam and stomped off the concrete porch toward his car.

Liam's cheeks reddened as he shrugged, waved goodbye and headed toward his car.

"That was interesting," Mia said.

"Not surprising though. Liam gets around," he said. "I'll place your bag in the bedroom. You can set up the computer on the table, I'll get the internet code for you." Inhaling, he strode to his bedroom, placed the bag on the chair and quickly made the bed.

"Want something to drink?" he asked returning to the living room, handing her the paper with the code.

"Not right now." She typed in the information and sat at the table. Noah pulled his laptop onto the table next to her.

"What did Ryan discover?"

"Two years ago Aaron Mosely, the Priest running the Leviticus Club, was excommunicated for assisting a woman to abort his child" She looked at him. "The woman was in a wheelchair and much younger than his 57 years. It was hushed up because his brother is Senator Mosely from Alabama."

Noah whistled and sat back. "What the hell? That's like a flashing light saying pick me, pick me."

She nodded and stared at the monitor. A few moments later she shook her head and closed her eyes.

"What?"

"Thomas is dropping the case, turning over the information we uncovered by traditional methods, which is very little, to the FBI. With the connection to the Senator he doesn't want us involved, it'll become too high profile. He's letting the General know."

Noah frowned, trying to understand. "Turning over? Aren't you the FBI? And what General?" he asked, completely lost. She could've been speaking Arabic and he'd be just as confused.

"We can't share the stuff we learned in dreams, how would we explain that?" she asked.

"But—"

"Hold on." She typed and then stopped. "I have to get permission to share this with you." She bit her nail while watching the screen.

What did she mean, needed permission? He didn't know what to think. Was she leading him on? He didn't think so, but he could be wrong.

She tilted her head, typed more information and stared at the screen. Finally, she looked at him. "Ready to go on a trip? Thomas said for me to bring you in, let you see, and we'll explain it all to you."

Noah didn't want to go anywhere without answers. Fear of losing her, of losing what they were building locked him in place. Her eyes seemed sad, resigned, tugged at his heart. Even though he didn't understand what was going on, one thing was crystal clear. Life had become a thousand times better since meeting Mia.

"When do we leave?"

Her eyes widened and then went glassy.

"You thought I'd let you go? Leave me behind?" he asked incredulously. They were just getting started.

She nodded and turned away.

He placed his finger beneath her chin, turned her to face him. "Did you hear deceit when I said I wanted you? When I said I was the first and last to eat your fantastic pussy? How can I do that if we're apart?"

A tear rolled down her cheek. He caught it with the pad of his thumb. "Together, we are better as a team, Mia. Whatever I need to learn or do, I'll do it so we can stay together." At that moment he meant every word. He had walked through hell in the military on the battlefield for his country, he would do no less for the woman who was fast becoming extremely important to him.

She exhaled and typed. "We'll leave in a couple hours. The others are already there." She smiled at him and his world righted. "We're going to Wyoming."

Ryan and Ryder stepped on the porch. "Come in," Noah yelled. His thoughts on the upcoming trip.

The twins entered and looked at them. "Dad says Thomas canceled the op and you guys are headed home. To your home," Ryder pointed at Mia.

"Yeah. I just read the email. He sent it an hour ago and had been waiting to hear from me. We leave in two hours," Mia said.

"How long will we be there?" Noah asked, thinking about his home.

"I don't know. It won't take long to get the information," she said.

"In that case, we've got an hour to work with you Noah. You slept away the morning, let's get started, we'll grab some takeout from Lucky-G for you to take on the plane," Ryan said heading toward the door.

"You might as well come along, Mia," Ryder said. "Can't hurt to see what he's learning."

"As soon as I finish this report to Thomas I'll be outside. I need to tell him about Peter Drum." She looked at Noah.

He nodded and followed the twins outside.

CHAPTER 20

Mia stepped off the private jet onto the tarmac with Noah behind her. The twins promised to listen out for his house as he locked his truck in the detached garage and informed Liam he would be out of town. His cousin offered to stay at the house until he returned and Noah agreed.

They walked toward the small airport parking lot where Mia had left her car a few days earlier. Noah wasn't sure what was going on with her. She had been uncharacteristically quiet since he agreed to accompany her. During the flight, she held his hand and listened to music through a headset.

When they pulled out of the small parking area and hit Highway 80 he looked at the brown landscape. The drive was similar to the flight except light jazz played in the background. After an hour they turned off the highway onto a dirt road.

In the distance, he saw a gray stone, squat building wavering beneath the hot sun. The closer they came, the larger it grew.

She pulled up to a gate and ignored the box on the side. A few moments later, the gate disappeared and she drove down rather than toward the house.

Surprised, he watched as they pulled into a covered garage filled with several types of vehicles and parked. Neither spoke for a few seconds.

When she looked at him her eyes glistened. "I just want to say thank you for trusting me enough to come. This means a lot to me that you wanted to." She leaned over, captured his lips and kissed him hard. The kiss was over before he fully engaged and she was stepping out of the car.

Noah stepped out, grabbed both of their bags and followed her. She entered what he considered must be a decontamination area and was scanned. There were a few blasts of light, she stepped to the side and waved him through.

"First place your palm here. The system doesn't know you." He followed her instructions, felt the heat on his hand and waited until she told him to move it.

"Master Sargent Noah Sloan, welcome. Step into the unit," the machine said.

Surprised to hear his name, he stepped forward, the sensation of needles on his skin was over in a few seconds. The heat from the light hit several spots on his body. When it stopped the light turned green.

"Come with me," Mia said extending her hand to him. He accepted it and walked beside her to a heavy, steel door. She placed her palm on a pad. The door opened.

"Place your hand the same way I did," she said as she walked through. The door swooshed closed. He placed his hand on the scanner, it took a second longer than hers had but opened. He reached for her hand again as he walked through. The clip of her boot heels and his sneakers were the only sound on the polished concrete floor. They turned right, went through the palm security checks again and entered what could only be called an underground oasis.

A large waterfall with beautiful green plants stood in the middle, giving off delicate scents that teased his nostrils. There were sitting areas, large screens on the walls, light jazz played softly in the background. Delicious aromas floated through the air.

"Mali!" Mia yelled and took off running. Noah followed slowly while trying to see everything but there was no way. There were a lot of corners and halls he couldn't see into.

"In here, Noah," Mia yelled.

Hearing her excitement, he braced himself as he strode into the large commercial sized kitchen. A tall, slender, gorgeous woman with a heart-shaped face and light brown eyes stared down at Mia' smiling. "I returned last night. Max arrives later today. Tip is in his room." She looked at Noah and her smile dropped slightly as she inhaled.

"Damali this is Noah, my guy. Noah, Damali." Mia stepped back as the two looked at each other.

"Where did you meet?"

"Texas," Mia said looking at him.

"Thomas met him?"

"Yes, he told me to bring him with me. Noah has questions," Mia said moving back a few steps.

"And Thomas has answers," Mali said. "I see the energy around you like broad bands of bright color, good. It'll take a strong man to handle Mia. She's coming into her own and will probably be stronger than all of us."

She smiled and hugged Mia again. "Missed you, Princess."

"Don't you start with that," Mia said but it was obvious she and Mali were close. "We're going to put our things away in my room and come back for a bite to eat."

"This is almost done, see you in a bit," Damali said as she looked at Noah. "Call me, Mali."

"Nice meeting you, Mali." Noah accepted Mia's hand and walked with her down the hall. A minute or so later they stood in front of a wall. Mia placed her hand on it and it opened.

She glanced over her shoulder at him as she walked inside. He followed. Once inside the door closed behind him as he stood in what must have been the living room with a long curved sofa in front of a wide screened TV mounted high on the wall. He marveled at the ten-feet walls and spacious floor plan.

"Living or meeting area," she pointed to the room they entered and continued walking. "Kitchen, bathroom and bedroom." She pointed to a closed door, opened it and walked inside. A king sized bed was in the middle of the room and that was all. He looked around, noted a few doors and waited to be told where to put his clothes. She pressed the wall and it slid open revealing a large walk-in closet with a dresser, mirror, and hangers.

"Put your things in here." She placed her backpack on the floor and waited for him.

"Very nice, big space. You all have suites like this?"

"Yes, they're all basically the same," she said and moved to another wall, placed her palm on it. It led to an in-ground hot spring cut out of the rock. "Just a few of the rooms have these. A friend made it for me as a gift several years ago, I treasure it."

Steam rose from the water. He walked closer, the rock was smooth and lightly filtered from outside. Looking up he didn't see how that was possible, there was nothing but stone overhead. Patience he told himself. Don't start asking questions yet.

"This is great, I hope we can use it soon."

She smiled. "I'd like that. Let's eat, I'm hungry."

He moved slowly behind her, trying to take it all in. The comfortable temperature, solid construction, efficient floor plan. "Where's the bathroom?"

"Here," she said turning slightly and placing her hand on a wall. The door opened, and the lights came on immediately. The large room held a huge tub, large shower tiled in lavender and purple, double sinks and a large tower holding towels, soap and cleaning supplies. It was twice the size of his master bath.

Finished, he met her in the suite's kitchen. He had thought it was a kitchenette because of the size of the main kitchen, but it was larger than his kitchen at home with modern appliances. She stood at the counter eating a banana.

"Ready?"

He nodded and tossed the paper towel he used to dry his hands in the trash.

"Come on."

He pulled her close and stared down into her eyes. "You're simply beautiful."

She met his stare and smiled. "Thank you. I think you're sexy and ruggedly handsome."

"Rugged for sure." He kissed her, loving how she melted against him and wrapped her arms around his neck. Her tongue stroked deep inside his mouth, kidnapping his thoughts.

She moaned deep in her throat and it ran through him. He pressed her close to his hardness, wanting her to know how much he wanted her. Always seem to want her.

Breathing hard, she lay her forehead on his chest and took several deep breaths. "How… how hungry are you?"

"For you? Starved." Questions could wait, his need for her couldn't. "Here or in the room? Your choice." He slid his hand beneath her blouse, tweaked her nipple.

A red buzz went off.

Noah froze.

Mia groaned.

"What?"

"Call to meeting. Thomas and Max must be here." True regret filled her eyes as she looked at him and placed a soft kiss on his lips. "We've got to go." There was no hesitation, she could've been in the military the way she followed orders. He wasn't sure how he felt about that. Following her, he was completely lost until they arrived near the kitchen filled with several faces he didn't know. Mia launched into the outstretched arms of a pale guy who could've modeled for Adonis with his long blonde hair and beach bum look. He picked Mia up and spun her around.

"Good to see you, Princess. It's been too long," he said, smiling at her.

"I know, Max. I missed you, too. Now put me down. I want you to meet Noah, he's my guy."

Max's brow arched. "Your guy? Since when?"

"Since I said so. Now put me down and be nice." She pinched him.

"Ow." He looked at Noah. "Hope you realize how vicious she can be."

Noah met Mia's happy gaze and smiled. "She's good for me."

"Noah, this is Max. Max, Noah."

Max's nose quivered as he extended a hand to Noah. "Nice to meet you man, you've got a real Princess there."

Noah looked down at Mia. "I totally agree with you. She's very special." Max held his hand slightly longer and Noah looked at him. The two stared at each other and Noah sensed he was being warned not to hurt Mia in any way.

"Thomas and the others are in the dining area," Mia said claiming Noah's attention. He nodded at Max and walked behind Mia.

The dining area was huge with a long, wide, mahogany table currently loaded with food. Thomas, Mali, Tip and another female Noah hadn't met sat at the table talking softly.

"Lizzy, yes. Yes, yes," Mia yelled and ran to the woman with long dreds, sun-kissed complexion, and freckles. She was much taller than Mia and average size. They embraced and held each other for several moments. Lizzy held Mia's head to her and stroked it gently. "I'm home. We're here. There's a lot to talk about, a lot to do, sweetie," Lizzy murmured.

Mia nodded, stepped back and wiped her face. "I prayed every day for you. I'm so glad to see you." She looked at Noah and extended her hand. Moving forward he took it. "Noah this is Lizzy, Lizzy my guy Noah."

Lizzy smiled. "Hello Noah, it's great meeting you. Please have a seat so we can all catch up. It's been months since we've all been together, a lot has changed."

Mia and Noah sat next to each other. After grace was said, the food was passed around. No one talked until plates were pushed aside.

"Noah, thank you for your assistance in the stoning deaths case. Mia said we wouldn't have discovered the critical clues in the case if the two of you hadn't walked back in time."

"Walked back in time?" Max said looking at Thomas.

"Noah is a dream-walker, a very strong one," Thomas said to everyone at the table before looking at Noah. "Mia asked if she could explain the mission to you and I told her that it would be better for you to see first. Before I share our secrets, you've got to promise never to repeat them to anyone. Not your family or closest friend."

Noah thought about it. Honestly, who would he tell? He hadn't shared his dream-walking with Liam and that would've been the only person he would consider talking to. All of his closest friends died on the battlefield.

"You have my word I'll never share whatever you tell me, today or any day," Noah said, meeting Thomas' gaze.

Seconds later, Thomas nodded. "Accepted. Listen until the end and then ask questions."

<<<>>>

The next hour and a half, Noah listened to an unbelievable story of how all of them had either been sold into slavery or captured by force. Used as human guinea-pigs for weird experiments locked away in a lab someplace south of Russia. They underwent multiple operations which were the source of their mutations.

If they didn't die on the operating table they were given a week at most to recover and then experimented on again and again. It was a story of madness, misery, and hopelessness. Hundreds died and were discarded as trash. Baron Lords turned the other eye often selling children to the Liege for profit.

These guys barely escaped with their lives. Noah's stomach tightened with nausea. He couldn't look at Mia, instead, he took her trembling hand and continued staring at Thomas as he continued speaking. Noah heard the pain of loss of those came to this country and died over the years. No, for decades. They arrived after the civil war, watched the growth of this country and used their gifts to survive.

His initial reaction had been disbelief. But the methodical manner in which Thomas told the story, plus the complete lack of deceit made him slowly accept the impossible. "That's the bulk of it," Thomas said. "Anybody got more to add?"

No one said anything.

"The FBI thing?" Noah asked.

"A prop from our client, that happens from time to time. He's really pissed but understands the game has changed with the Senator being involved. I refunded his money minus our expenses," Thomas said.

"Is that what you do? Hire out for jobs like that?" Noah looked at Mia first and then Thomas.

"Sometimes, but we have to make some decisions regarding how we're going forward." Thomas looked at the others. "Mia sensed change in the air, she's been getting things lately and was right. We'll get to that in a few." He looked at Noah with an air of expectancy.

"How is it no one knows about you? How do they find you for jobs?" The idea that they remained hidden in this country for decades blew his mind. With satellites and new technology, it didn't seem possible.

Thomas pursed his lips for a few moments. "When we arrived in this country, we headed west where there weren't many people. We were too weird for the Indians they left us alone. Initially, we thought of moving into the Smokey Mountains but decided against it. One of our people had the ability to manipulate land, earth. Another could make anything grow from the ground, illusions, bend nature. Between us, we were able to create a place large enough to comfortably house us several feet below ground without being seen or disturbed. We burrowed in, fortified our new home and fought to survive."

Fascinated, Noah asked. "He tapped into water sources in the earth?"

"Yes, and fixed it in a way we always have water as well as a few hot springs. Jeri was truly gifted, an artist in his own way. The temperature here is always perfect, we're not bothered by atmospheric issues, uncontaminated water and he created a way to filter the sunlight into his below-ground greenhouse to grow fresh vegetables and some types of fruit. Back then meat was everywhere. Now we order from the butcher and hit one of the warehouses once or twice a month."

Thomas and a few others smiled in tribute to their deceased friend. "Jeri was a genius."

"Most definitely." Noah looked around at the architectural masterpiece.

"Through the years we purchased new furniture, spruced the place up, added security, that kind of thing. But structurally the place is the same as he built it."

Impressed, Noah looked around at the high sweeping ceilings, smooth walls, and colorful fabrics. Comfortable, he thought. "Are there more people like me who mutated recently? In this decade?"

"There may be. How did your mutation happen?" Thomas asked.

Noah thought about it for a few seconds. "Honestly I don't know. This last tour was a bitch. Surprise attack. Six of us returning to base. Never should've happened. We were outgunned. Firepower came from several directions. I remember getting hit, passing out. Woke up, saw body parts of my team everywhere. I lost it. Later I was told I died on the operating table and was resuscitated. They sent me stateside to recover. I'd only had my new rank for eight months and wanted to go back. But the dreams got worse. Couldn't tell the difference between what was real and fake. I would go places, see and talk to people who told me weird shit. I'd be rambling trying to make sense of everything. Didn't take long to be discharged, mental disability." He shook his head. "Fucking mist." He looked at the others around the table. "When I walk through dreams, this mist attacks me, like I'm dinner or something. Have you ever heard of something like that?"

"Let's first address when your abilities started. Before or after you died on the operating table?" Thomas asked.

Noah opened his mouth, recalled they all mutated after several operations and went still. "After."

Thomas nodded. "Fragment was lodged in your brain?"

Chilled by the similarities, Noah nodded. Mia rubbed the top of his hand.

"Do you know if you were resuscitated in the field or in the States?" Thomas asked.

Noah thought back. "In the field." He nodded. "Definitely before I was shipped back."

"Based on what I've recently learned I'd say your mutation occurred when you were resuscitated. It's very possible that the same chemicals that changed us, changed you. The mist is something you've got to master, it's yours to use. And to answer your last question regarding if there are more of you, yes."

Speechless, Noah stared at Thomas for a few moments and then looked at Mia. If he didn't know for certain he was awake, he'd think he was locked in a nightmare or dream-walking again. He pinched his thigh just in case. Yeah, he was wide awake and learning shit he saw on TV. "Ryder and Ryan? They've got something, but were vague," he said.

"I don't know them and can't answer that," Thomas said. "We have one hour before we meet with Hawke and his team for examinations," Thomas said. "Noah, will you come with us? You're an important piece of this ever-widening puzzle and we need as much information as possible to prepare."

Noah looked at Mia and then at Thomas. "What kind of examinations?" He hadn't agreed to have anyone poking on him.

"Physicals and some blood work. In order to have access to the library of information they have on the Liege, I agreed that we would share information. The physicals are a part of it."

Noah looked at Mia. "Did you know about this?"

"Not until just now," she said.

"You're okay with it?" he asked her.

She didn't say anything for a few moments and then looked at him. "We've never fully known or understood our bodies, what's good or harmful. People I loved died because we didn't know what to do or if there was anything that could be done." She nodded, met his gaze. "I'm okay with it."

"Alright, I'm okay too." Noah looked at the others and then Thomas as he pushed away from the table.

"We'll take two vans," Thomas said standing. "It'll take about 40 minutes to get there, any questions you have, feel free to ask Hawke or his team. They've been really helpful." He looked at Lizzy.

She nodded. "One of the things I want to know is what kind of shot he gave me. Definite miracle worker."

Thomas agreed. "I'm thinking we'll turn one of the rooms into an infirmary, bring in some of the same equipment they use in their clinic so we have it whenever we need it for repairs."

The others nodded and Noah wondered if he was the only one who thought the use of the word repair was odd.

CHAPTER 21

The Wyoming Clinic was a huge three-story, brick and glass building at the end of a strip mall owned by the Pack. There weren't many cars in the parking lot out front when they parked.

A tall, tanned female with dark green eyes and wide smile met them as they left the vans. "Hello, I am Trina, your guide. Please follow me." They were shuffled through an underground entrance and stepped into decontamination units much more sophisticated than the ones used at their complex.

"Remain still, this will only take a few minutes," she said while pressing keys on a panel.

Mia glanced at Noah and smiled. Back at the complex, his heart-beat had been off the charts, especially when Thomas told their history. She knew Noah didn't immediately accept it. Who would? But he hadn't run off screaming or left her behind.

The Liege was the stuff nightmares were made of. Monsters children feared in the dark. She knew the second he believed and accepted the truth of who he was. No one had to tell him he was different, he knew that. Just knowing he wasn't alone, that others experienced something similar and he could have a decent life, well, it was what they all wanted.

Coming to this country, they worked odd jobs until Marok took a mercenary job. The pay had been phenomenal and an excellent way for them to sharpen their skills, They invested their money, lived off the land and eventually placed large sums in offshore accounts. Each member received an equal portion of the interest to do whatever they wanted and while not billionaires, over the years they shared millions.

Noah's declarations regarding her and their budding relationship made her heart sing. To say she didn't have much experience with romantic relationships was quite the understatement. Fear of the Liege kept them in the shadows, amongst themselves. Survival trumped everything, even personal relationships. As the youngest who had been raped, it took a very long time before she allowed anyone to her bed. Even then it rarely happened.

When Max shook Noah's hand, he hadn't blinked or winced when asked questions. Not once had he acted inferior or impressed. Granted, he didn't know what any of them could do, but she doubted it would make much difference.

Noah was a keeper and she thanked God he was here with her. He said he wanted to be on her team, well, she wanted to be on his.

Once they all went through decontamination, they were given white robes and matching flat sandals to wear. Mia looked at Noah, looking yummy all dressed in white and winked.

He smiled as they followed their guide to a huge elevator. She wiggled back until she stood in front of him and leaned her head on his chest. He wrapped his arms loosely around her. All eight of them fit inside and remained silent as they rode upward.

Filled with hope, Mia had so many questions but understood the need to wait. Goosebumps raced across her skin as they exited the elevator and were sent into different rooms.

Separated, Mia sat on the chair, took several deep breaths to calm her rising fear and focused.

Raw emotions buffeted her. The last person in this room had been in a lot of pain. She frowned as she struggled to follow the thinning emotional vibrations and failed. The thick walls prevented her from picking up anything beyond the room which wasn't good. She didn't need this.

Accustomed to contact in some form with the others she stood, wrapped her arms around her waist and paced.

Another female entered with a smile. "Hello, I'm Rina. Please sit here so I can take your blood sample."

Mia took the seat, extended her arm and looked at the opposite wall. This wasn't her favorite part of physicals.

"Have you been in to see the others yet?" Mia asked.

"Each one of you has your own tech. Hawke believed it would be faster that way. As soon as I label these, I'll take them to the lab for processing. You'll have answers soon." She smiled again, easing Mia's concerns.

"Thank you," Mia said after the swab was removed from her mouth.

"You're welcome. Hawke will be in to see you soon." She left with the blood and saliva samples.

Mia stared at the floor, then the wall and then the ceiling. No matter how hard she tried to relax, she couldn't. How were the others doing?

Noah? She didn't want to lose anyone else. More to the point she had questions about the women in their group. No one had ever used birth control and there were zero pregnancies. Were they sterile? Had the Liege stolen the only chance she would have at being a mother? Her heart slammed into her chest at the thought. "Please God, don't let them steal that from me too."

Walking back and forth, she bit down on the edges of her nail and thought about how to frame her questions regarding the changes she noticed in her powers. The compulsion and empathetic abilities seemed stronger. Thomas was right, she picked up changes before he had, which was different. Listening to the bartender at such a great distance was a change too.

Deep into thought she hadn't realized the door opened until a cool breeze from the hall hit the back of her neck. Turning she looked up and froze. Goodness, he was huge. Bigger than Thomas which she didn't think was possible.

"Hello Mia, I'm Hawke." He remained utterly still just inside the door until she calmed down.

She cleared her throat. "Hello, Hawke. How are you?"

He smiled, and it changed the landscape of his face. According to Thomas, Hawke had undergone more surgeries than all of them combined. He was the Liege's poster child of mutations on steroids.

He stepped inside, Rina was behind him and closed the door before stepping to the side. "Please stand over there." Hawke pointed to a small white platform in the corner.

Trina assisted her and flipped a switch. The platformed hummed.

Warmth rose swiftly through the soles of Mia's feet to the top of her head, then down her arms and back to her feet as if it was a fast moving train on a specific course. It took less than a minute.

Hawke stared at the pad in his hand before looking at her. "Overall, you're in good health, Mia. Your energy levels are higher than all the others except Noah. What have you been doing that they haven't?"

Heat flew to her face. She opened her mouth and snapped it shut. "Noah and I are a couple."

He looked at her as if there should be more. "Sex? That's all you've done?"

Now she was confused. "That's all I can think of."

He nodded and tapped the tablet. "Do you have any personal questions regarding your health for me. I will be speaking to all of you as a group about the Liege serums and where you are with that." He stared down at her.

"Yes, there is one thing." She told him about being raped right after she started her menses, the pregnancy, and the delivery. "Will I be able to have children? Or is my womb dead? Did they destroy that too?"

He looked at the tablet, tapped it a few times. "I don't know the answer to that, but I will look into it for you."

She exhaled with a nod. A part of her believed her child was dead or wouldn't know her if they crossed the street together. Still, she couldn't put out that flicker of hope that they would meet each other one day so she could explain she hadn't abandoned the child and had wished things had been different.

Back then she had no choice in the matter. Things were different now and if she could have a child, she wanted one.

Trina brought Mia's clothes into the room and left her to dress. "When you're done, I'll take you to the meeting room."

Mia looked at the woman and smiled. "Thank you." She had no idea why she was so nervous her hands shook. She couldn't pull in calm thoughts or slow down her heart.

Before calling out to Trina, Mia sat in a lotus position on the floor, closed her eyes and found her center. She breathed in deep and released it slowly. It didn't take long but at the tap on the door, she unfolded and stood.

Just outside in the hall, Noah stood with Trina. His serious gaze asked if she was okay.

She nodded with a slight smile and took his hand as they followed the two techs down the hall into a mid-sized meeting room. A huge monitor took up most of one wall. Chairs were situated around a long table so that they faced the monitor and each other easily.

Hawke sat in a chair at the head of the table with his back to the monitor. He glanced at her and Noah when they arrived. The door closed behind them, leaving the members of their team alone with Hawke. He leaned back in the chair and looked at Thomas. "I'll start at the beginning since we have similar pasts."

Thomas nodded.

"I was given to the Liege when I was two or three summers, suffered through numerous operations." He held up his arm and pointed to the changed bones. "Titanium steel replaced my humerus, radius and ulna bones." He pointed to his legs. "Also both femurs."

Mia gasped and held onto Noah's hand tighter.

"Camera behind my eye, that's long gone. And a computer chip to control it all. It took a lot of surgeries before the metal fused correctly to the bone and I could see out of my eye. I refused to be dominated, controlled, which called for several more surgeries to ensure the computer chip worked in my brain, and eventually gave those bastards the control they wanted." He paused and ran his hand over his chin before looking at them again. "I told you that so you would know I understand what you went through. I've met others who've survived the horrors of the Liege compound and many of them will never be able to live normally." He paused. "I'm not saying you're lucky or that I am, just stating the facts."

Mia exhaled and looked at the others.

Max looked ill and Tip stared at the floor. Thomas and Mali stared at Hawke, while Lizzy met Mia's gaze with a small sigh. The Liege was the common denominator for everyone, except Noah, in this room. Time blunted the cruel memories, but nothing could destroy them.

"Once my mate rescued me from the Liege compound, my Alpha, La Patron, commissioned us to destroy the main lab and any of the others we discovered while on the Continent. He and a few other Alphas searched and destroyed the labs here in the States. Every time we destroyed a lab, we took their notes, databases, inventory, and equipment. We have a warehoused library on the Liege."

Max and Tip looked up at him again.

"They came to the States to continue their experiments and were destroyed," Hawke said.

"How can you be sure?" Tip asked.

Hawke held up his fingers and counted them off. "I was there when the council members died, we blew up the main lab, the building crumbled. I watched it fall. I saw Lancaster die by my mate's hand, as did Griffin. Lancaster killed Gordon. Alpha Barticus has three of their newest recruits locked away in prison. Roderick hides but is dying, could be dead already. We'll know if he resurfaces."

"Had no idea that bastard Lancaster was dead," Mali said on a surprised whisper, looking wide-eyed at Lizzy.

"Griff was a motherfucking animal," Lizzy hissed. "Good riddance. The air is much cleaner without his foulness in it.

"They've been dead a very long time," Thomas said with a kind of wonderment in his voice. "We didn't know."

"All those years of hiding," Tip whispered and shook his head.

Hawke looked at his tablet and then at them. "The serum you and the others received is deficient and needs to be upgraded."

No one spoke or moved at the change in topic. The Liege, those monsters were dead, time to move on. Hawke held their undivided attention.

"You were all given shots of an early formula before the serum was perfected which is the reason there are only six of you left. The others did not receive the same batch of serum as you. Even so, what you received wasn't the best and is failing."

Mia's heart leaped to her throat. She had no idea what that meant and hoped he had a solution to the problem.

"When Lizzy arrived, I gave her a small dose of a serum created for her from the Liege notes. It has been over 48 hours and her body has accepted the drug." He held up his finger. "Here is where we are, the decisions you will need to make today. "Do you want to continue living in this mutated manner? Or do you want to allow your expiration date to run its course? I cannot tell any of you how much time you have left, but I can say without taking this new serum you will continue to decline."

Noah squeezed her hand.

"That's the first part for you to consider. Here is another." He looked at Noah. "Master Sergeant Sloan received a similar shot as all of you. Which means the U.S. Military is using the serum on human soldiers to change them for some reason."

Noah's fingers tightened around Mia's. "Without our consent, you can damn well believe that," he ground out.

"That's normally the way it's done," Hawke said. "What concerns my Alpha is this. Is the military creating mutated humans as weapons of war? If so, how long before other countries do the same? Will this program spill over into the public sector? Cops? Robbers?" He sighed. "The serum was created specifically to enhance humans to be more than the norm. Not everyone can handle it and remain sane."

"Thought it was PTSD," Noah said sounding somewhat relieved. Both PTSD and being given a mutation drug were bad in Mia's opinion.

"Very similar symptoms, Mia helped you find your balance, which is a great thing. Now you control your mind instead of it controlling you," Hawke said looking at Noah and then his gaze broadened to take them all in.

She sensed distressing news and tensed.

"If you decide to take the new serum your abilities will strengthen. I need to tell you that. So if you controlled water, expect to be able to walk on it." He looked at Damali. "And if not walk on it, it'll be damned close."

"Why?" Thomas asked sounding as baffled as Mia felt. She didn't want to be stronger, she wanted to live.

"Because of the changes to your chromosomes and body over the years. Imagine a car with a good body but the engine must be replaced to run. Outwardly the car looks the same, but the juice beneath the hood is more powerful. If you put the same engine in that car, created the same year the car was developed, you simply carry over the same problems."

Thomas looked at the others. His gray eyes appeared worried. "Lot to think about."

"Not for me," Lizzy said. "My engine was dying, I don't want to go through that again. I want a new one."

Mia smiled and knew she wanted the same thing.

"Is the shot a onetime deal?" Tip asked. "Or will we need to keep getting them?"

"I don't know the answer to that," Hawke said. "You're the first. That's why my Alpha insisted I give you all the information I have, to allow you to make your own decisions. There's one more thing."

He waited until they all looked at him. "I'm a full-blood wolf. Dual-natured human, that's my extra. Our pack is large and everywhere in this country. You can never share knowledge of our existence. La Patron went through a lot to help you, which meant getting permission from the Goddess to tell you anything. If you betray him by telling anyone what you've learned here today or about our pack, you will be killed. I need to make that crystal clear. Thomas knew and agreed before we started down this road."

They all nodded.

"Understand, we, our pack is not allowed to interfere with humans at all. But the Goddess has decided your situation is different and placed you in another category. Chimeras."

"What?" Max said, sitting straight. "We're weird but that's taking it too far. We're not fire-breathing monsters with a lion's head, a goat's body, and a serpent's tail."

Confused, Mia stared at Hawke.

"That's a mythological creature or definition. From a biological point of view, the Goddess' view, Chimera is a person containing a mixture of genetically different tissues, formed by processes such as fusion, grafting, or mutation." He paused, must have read their confusion and said. "How about this, a person with a DNA molecule derived from two or more different organisms, formed by laboratory manipulation."

Max leaned back in the chair. "Happened in the lab."

"She's saying because of the serum, what happened in the lab or in the operating room, we mutated into who we are?" Mia asked. "That's the definition of a chimera?"

"Yes and yes. It's how She classifies you. How La Patron will classify you and the pack as well. This allows us to assist you, otherwise, as humans, we could not," Hawke said.

"It's accurate," Lizzy said.

"Yeah," Tip said. "We're chimeras."

"Hawke, forgive me for asking but I'm from a different era than everyone else and was raised believing few people did things from the goodness of their hearts, expecting nothing in return," Noah said. "Personally, I'm grateful for everything you and your Alpha have done for Mia and the others. But what is your Pack getting out of this? What's expected in exchange for your help?"

Hawke smiled, it was nice, friendly even. "La Patron seeks human allies. As I said, we cannot interfere with humans, but you can."

<<<>>>

"Explain interfering with humans," Thomas said in a low voice.

Hawke's expression never changed. "Pretty much the same as what you're doing now. We looked over your jobs for the past three decades and noticed you never interfered with the Pack and took jobs that fought against humans. We don't want that to change. Once the military learns of you, they'll attempt to recruit you."

Thomas frowned. "To fight against you? The Pack?"

Hawke nodded.

"That would be suicide," Mali said looking at Max.

"But if they're injecting dying soldiers with that serum like they did me, they would train them to use their gifts and could direct them to attack the Pack." Noah looked at Hawke. "What would you do then if you cannot be involved with humans?"

"We have always been permitted to protect ourselves. If they attacked, we would defend in an instant. Part of this bargain is you cannot fight against us in any capacity, whether for the military or any other group, " Hawke said in a hard, cold voice.

"Can't blame you for requiring we don't work for the military, because hiring others to attack you is something they would do," Noah said looking at Thomas.

The two men stared at each other for a few seconds before Thomas nodded.

"Understood, thanks for explaining that Hawke. Are there any other requirements in exchange for your assistance?" Thomas asked.

"Not so much a requirement as a strong suggestion, at this point anyway. As I said the serum will enhance your gifts. A concern is that one or more of you may turn rogue. I understand that your system of democracy has worked brilliantly in the past, but you've never experienced this level of power. Remember, the Goddess has given you a separate designation, Chimera, not human."

"Which means you can interfere, even kill us if we go, rogue," Mali said slowly. "Even if we're not doing anything against the Pack, if we harm humans you'll take us out." They all stared at Hawke.

"Yes, you're right. What La Patron would prefer is for you to police yourselves, answer to your own leader. He or she would be enhanced to handle that."

No one moved or spoke. It was one of those moments when you realized life was fucked regardless of the direction you traveled. A strong suggestion to pick a leader or being killed by wolves when they think you've stepped out of line.

Hawke stood. "I've told you everything, if there aren't any questions, I'll step out, so you can discuss what you want to do among yourselves."

"Thank you," Thomas murmured as he turned to face them with his eyes closed.

When the door shut, Mia exhaled and looked up at Noah. He ran his finger down her cheek and leaned forward. "Get the shot and live with me, baby. Please live."

She exhaled and nodded before leaning against his shoulder.

When no one spoke, Lizzy sighed. "The way I see it is each person has to decide whether to take the shot to prolong their life. With the understanding that you'll be changed, internally anyway. We don't really know what that means, do we?" She looked across the table at Mali.

"No. Just that we'll be enhanced. I'm not sure what we'll do with all of that. For several decades we focused on hiding from the Liege but they're dead now."

"Chimeras," Max snorted. "No longer human."

"Haven't been simply human since we left the Liege," Tip said. "Not with the things we've done."

"True, but we had that nice illusion, some ESP, or a sixth sense, all this time I've always considered myself human," Mia said.

No one said anything.

"If you don't take the shot, you'll die. Fading is an extremely painful process that I will never choose. I'd rather be shot, or incinerated, get it all done at once," Lizzy said with feeling. "To become a prisoner in your mind and body, like that... no. Just no. I'm taking the shot and will do whatever is necessary to survive. Now that I know what's what, and have access to answers, I can start living. Maybe live near a beach or on an island." She smiled.

"You plan to leave the team? Leave the complex?" Mia asked, concerned.

Lizzy pursed her lips. "Depends on what everyone decides. This is a personal choice; each person has to make their own decision. I've made mine and feel good about it."

"I'm taking the shot, too," Mia said and glanced at Noah.

Lizzy smiled at them.

"Same here. Hawke says I need the upgrade because the one I received isn't the best," Noah said. "Going backward isn't an option, can only go forward, deal with each day as it comes."

"What would we do?" Mali said. "Take the same kind of jobs? Mercenaries? School teachers? What do enhanced people do?" She looked around the table.

"We had a case where a fanatical group's killing disabled people for no good reason. Stoning them to death. If I were enhanced I'd definitely stop them. Not kill them but make sure they paid for that," Mia said in a low voice.

"Humans hurting humans, lots of work in that field," Tip said in a dry tone. "I think there'll be tons of work if that's what we decide to do. I'm taking the shot, regardless."

"Crimefighters? Seriously guys? Is that all we can do?" Mali asked.

"What do you want to do?" Max challenged her.

"Start a business, fashion maybe, I don't know. But I want to do normal. We've never done normal like buy a house, live in a neighborhood. Walk to the corner store for stuff or hang out with friends at a club dancing." Excitement brimmed in her gaze as she looked at them.

"But that's living a lie, Mali. We aren't normal. We're chimeras and people will begin to notice you're not aging or changing in any way. Some will see your aura and ask questions. You're too pretty not to be hit on or even attacked and you'll defend yourself, someone will capture it on their camera, put it online and before you know it the whole world will know who you are," Max said. "We're not human or normal, Mali. Haven't been since the Liege fucked us over on the operating tables."

Mali's jaw clenched for a few seconds and she huffed while releasing a sigh. "Sounded good, though."

Max nodded. "Yeah, it did." He looked at Mia and Noah. "There's one thing no one mentioned."

Mia watched him.

"Wolves mate for life, right?"

Thomas nodded. "Yes."

"What if there's such a thing as mated pairs for chimera, for us?" He continued staring at Noah and Mia. "We could buy land, create our own gated community, live in homes with our significant other, have some semblance of normal. Is that close enough for you, Mali?"

She looked at Mia and Noah. "That would be close enough. We could have backyard barbecues, hang out at the pool, play tennis or basketball, throw parties. If we buy enough land no one could build near us, we could do it." Her eyes lit again.

"What do you think, Noah?" Max asked.

Noah shrugged. "I have no idea about mated pairs, but I like the idea of living with Mia. The whole community thing sounds good too. Ask Hawke about the pairing thing when he comes back."

Max nodded and looked at Damali. "What do you say? In or out?"

She bit her lip for a few seconds. "Not all the military guys or women are joining that other group. There have to be other enhanced guys walking around," she said. "In the past we were afraid, but now…" she looked at Mia. "I'm in. I don't want to live enhanced alone and I don't plan to hook up with any of you guys. That would be incest in my mind."

"True," Thomas muttered.

Lizzy and Tip nodded.

"For real," Max said. "We're family. I don't want us to split up if we don't have to."

"Neither do I," Thomas said. "I'm going to take the shot. As far as working, I agree with Mia. There are some ugly things happening and we can help save lives. Hawke hinted that they'd pass information along to us regarding the types of work we'd like to do. We decide when to step in and make a difference." He looked at Noah. "Are you going to join us?"

Noah met Mia's calm gaze. "Yeah, like I said, can't go backward. I'm a chimera and this is home for me now. I've got a house in Texas I'll deed to my cousin and grab my things. He's the only family I have. I hate to give him up but we're the same age and he would notice if I wasn't aging." He brushed a kiss against Mia's forehead and light brown curls. "For me, it's a simple choice."

Thomas nodded. "Max, what's your decision?"

"I'm taking the shot."

"We're all taking the shot which means we are accepting La Patron's terms. The two go together," Thomas said.

"Anyone going against guys like Hawke is crazy," Noah said.

"They don't all look like him," Thomas reminded him. "Ryder, Ryan, their dad, Tyrone look more like the majority of dual-natureds. Their scents will give them away, just as our scents give us away. That's why we'll never be able to say we didn't know if a person is human or other. We'll always know."

"That's true," Tip said. "Let's vote on that part. This way everyone is responsible for what we learned today."

"Good idea," Lizzy said. "All in favor of entering into and following La Patron's terms, speak."

One by one, each of them agreed.

"Hello fellow chimeras," Mali said before breaking into a wide grin.

Mia waved, leaned forward and bumped Mali's fist. "What's up, Ms. Chimera?"

"You, girl. It's all you," Mali said with a large smile.

The others smiled.

"The last thing," Lizzy said looking at Thomas. "I know you stepped into the leadership role after Marok died and it wasn't what you wanted. But you're a natural. Over the years you've proven you'll put what's best for us first. When I set up my home in our gated community and one day bring in a significant other, I trust you to keep us safe with wise words and a steadfast heart."

Mia leaned forward. "Thomas I'd rather you tell me to straighten up and fly right than have La Patron do it. Consider taking the leadership role, please."

"I just assumed Hawke meant Thomas," Max said looking at the others. "Didn't he?"

"Whether he did or not, we should ask Thomas if he wants to do it and not assume he will," Tip said. "If he refuses, we'll knock him out and tell Hawke he agreed."

They laughed.

"That's a great idea," Mali said, lifting her fist above Thomas' head.

He laughed and shook his head. "As long as this is what we all want…" He looked at Noah who hadn't said anything.

"I'm good with whatever decision the group makes," Noah said.

"You have to give a vote," Mia said.

"Oh. I vote for Mia and promise to be good and—"

Laughing she pushed his shoulder. "No. Tell the group how you feel about Thomas leading."

"Oh, that. I didn't think I had a vote since I don't know anyone. For the past 21 years, I've been a soldier, got no problem following orders." He frowned and looked at Mia. "I've never had a woman to care for, whose life means everything to me. So I shouldn't make a blanket statement that I'll follow orders. What I'll say is I follow orders, as long as Mia's life isn't in danger. I'll always choose her first. You should know that. Otherwise, I'm fine with Thomas."

Thomas nodded and for several moments no one said anything. "I'll have Hawke return." Thomas looked at them. "Last chance before we get the shots."

No one changed their minds.

"Chimeras," Thomas said standing and shaking his head. "I'm a chimera, who knew?" He opened the door and walked out.

Mia squeezed Noah's hand. "You're going to give away your house?"

He nodded. "I didn't know about the slower aging and other stuff. Eventually, it would've been a problem."

"Military would've come looking for you," Tip said. "Probably still will. Either you die from that damn shot or you live changed, enhanced. It's that simple. You didn't die and are still on their radar. Someone's watching to see if you change or show any signs of being different."

"Good point, probably right. My therapist may have already turned me in," Noah said. "Liam doesn't know I'm in Wyoming, just that Mia and I went away for a bit."

"Military searching for you is an issue that'll need to be handled. They can be like pit-bulls," Lizzy said.

"Noted," Noah said as the door re-opened and Hawke walked in with Trina wheeling in a tray.

Trina left the room and closed the door.

"Before we start with the shots, I'll reiterate what we discussed and agreed to. Let me be clear, you owe no allegiance to La Patron, he is not, will never be your Alpha or leader. Thomas is your leader and anyone who joins your group will need to be approved by him and then bond with and through him so that everyone in the group is connected."

He waited until they all nodded. He discussed the fact that each person will be changed, supercharged but could not say what that change would be. He made no guarantees to how long they would live, how often they may need to take shots in the future if ever, he assured them that Thomas would have access to the serum and would work closely with him to make improvements.

They all agreed.

"Thomas asked about mated pairs and I confess I don't know the answer. I will say this. Mia impacted Noah's abilities, strengthened them and he impacted hers as well, she is keener, sharper since they came together. Maybe you'll know your significant other by how well your abilities mesh together. That's the way it worked for them. Don't expect your significant other to always have the same gifts or powers as you. The key is to complement, to make you better," Hawke said. "Oh and it won't matter what you think of the person initially if they're the one, you will walk through fire to get to them."

"And it won't take long to get to that point, either," Noah said squeezing Mia tight.

"True. In fact, it will happen quickly so toss all the human stuff away and pay attention, not to how you feel but how well you work together," Hawke said.

"Which means we have to get out and meet people," Mali said looking around the table at them.

The others laughed.

"After you receive your shot, the tech will take you back to the exam room for you to rest. You'll be here for a couple days, after that you can return home to work out the kinks to control your gifts." He looked at Noah and Mia. "We changed your rooms so you'll recover together."

Pleased, Mia smiled.

"Thanks," Noah said holding her hand.

Hawke picked up a pair of latex gloves. "I can't catch or give you anything. This is more for your peace of mind. Do I need to put it on?"

They all said no. There were eight needles on the cart. One for each of them and an extra one for Thomas.

Hawke gave each of them a shot in their thigh and sent them out the room. Thomas was the last person to receive both shots.

"You'll have the extra power to stop the others in their tracks, to literally break their minds, to forcibly call them all together, to find them anywhere in the world and to open frequencies for them to speak telepathically. This is the serum the Liege attempted to create but failed. It's a gift to you from La Patron. He believes others will come to join your team and you'll need to check their hearts before deciding to give them the serum to correct that crap the military is using. You need this to be their Alpha Leader." He gave Thomas the shot.

Liquid fire shot through Thomas. He fell to the floor.

Hawke lifted him and carried him to his room.

CHAPTER 22

Mia woke slowly, blinked a few times until the room came into focus. Her heart pounded in her chest as she took several breaths to slow it down. She and Noah were in her bedroom at the complex. No wonder the bed felt so good and comfortable beneath her. Sounds from the bubbling hot spring lingered in the air. An interesting mixture of citrus and pine teased her nose.

She turned slightly.

The aroma changed to include Noah's unique masculine scent. He lay next to her with his arm around her waist, snoring lightly. Scooting closer, she stared at his face, taking in every line on his pale skin, the high cheekbones, firm lips, and narrow nose.

He was so handsome. Her heart clenched when he snorted and snored louder. She loved that sound and hoped to hear it for years to come. Heat from his body caressed her skin. Pushing back, she snuggled closer.

His arm tightened around her waist.

Seconds later, his cock hardened against her back. Her mouth watered. Nipples hardened into tight pebbles. Her eyes drifted closed as his hand inched up to her breast, cupped and squeezed it gently before tugging the nipple.

Tingling sensations raced to her core.

She shuddered as he continued teasing her breasts. Goosebumps exploded on her skin followed by sensitive tingling and moisture pooling between her legs. She fought the moan rising from her throat and lost the battle when his fingers eased between her legs, toying with her pubic hair for a few moments. Perched on the edge of expectation, she panted like a bitch in heat waiting to feel what he would do next. Those talented fingers worked her swollen clitoris and then slid inside, stroking the length of sex using her juices for natural lubrication. Drenched, hungry and gasping for more she pushed back against his hand. She groaned and twitched against him, her walls flexing against his fingers as he added another finger, preparing her for his thick length.

Every stroke took her higher as if magnified in some way. She ached to reach her peak. To fly in the wind with him and dance with the stars. He gave this to her. Freed her from her cares and fears.

She humped on his fingers, increasing the pace. The scent of their joint arousal washed over her and intoxicated her as a sweet drug. Her head spun with lust and desire, the best cocktail. She was so wet, so hot against his fingers, his moaned in her ear letting her know he wanted more.

Close but not quite there, she pulled on her nipples, pinching and stroking them. Tingles of pleasure shot between her legs, inciting her core. Her pussy tightened. The contrasting sensations blew her mind, she lost her rhythm.

She tugged her nipple harder sending little jolts of electricity to her throbbing core. Demanding her body give her what she needed. What she wanted.

Noah's thumb pressed her clit.

"Noah," she yelled as sharp bursts of pleasure rippled through her body. Shuddering, she stiffened against his fingers until she stopped moving. He eased his fingers from her between her legs and licked them clean. "Like that?"

"Umhmm."

He cupped her bottom and ground his thickness against her slowly. She moaned as the head of his cock teased her opening.

"What about this? You like this?" He eased the wide, thick head inside.

She gasped, closed her eyes and placed her leg over his for easier access. He accepted her unspoken invitation and slid deeper into her from behind. She placed one hand behind his head as he leaned up and surged into her over, and over again.

Faster, deeper and harder than before. His grunts and moans were rough and urgent. He held her close as if she were a precious gem. Together they danced. Their sweat-slicked bodies moved in an intricate, erotic tango with the sole purpose of giving each other pleasure.

"Mia," he said on a long moan, with his mouth against her head. He chanted her name as his balls tightened. Lost in the exquisite sensation of being one with her, he jerked hard into her, as his world exploded into total bliss.

"Baby, that was," he said as sleep dragged him under.

"I know. I know," she murmured and drifted off.

<<<>>>

Noah stood in the middle of a wide, long field and looked at the snow-covered mountains in the distance. Inhaling the cold air into his lungs he turned slowly, wondering not only where he was but why was he standing on green grass in frigid weather, wearing nothing but a short-sleeved shirt and jeans.

No shoes. No hat. No protective gear. Why didn't the cold bother him? Weird.

There had to be a reason he stood here like this. Peering into the distance he noticed what appeared to be a small cloud drifting slowly toward him.

His chest clutched, and he didn't know why. The closer the cloud came, tension rolled through his body, all but paralyzing him. He wanted to look away, but for some reason, his gaze locked onto that cloud as if it was the returning Messiah.

Maybe it was.

His heart raced a million beats per second as the cloud drew near and he recognized the rolling gray mist. He couldn't catch his breath. His hands trembled madly as the mist inched closer to his naked feet, covering them like a pair of well-worn boots.

Pinpricks of pain registered everywhere the mist touched. Why couldn't he control the damn thing?

His head throbbed as he battled to remain in the present. Sounds of gunfire, the acrid smell of blood, gunpowder and the sight of body parts littering the ground wrenched a cry from his chest. He covered his ears.

A sharp pain tore through his heart as yelled with unmitigated grief. His entire squad, dead. Gone. With his hands covering his face, he fell to his knees, shaking, crying and begging anyone listening to save Rex, Gordie, Jake, Parker, Pablo, TJ, and Rhodes.

There was no answering voice.

The mist tightened around him, stealing his breath.

It hurt to breathe. He curled into a ball on the ground, reliving that last battle. Being hit, flying through the air, overlooked by the enemy and eventually found by others.

"Why?" he moaned thinking of his friends. They were good men, most had wives, kids, parents who loved them. It didn't seem fair.

The more he wailed against the injustice of his friend's death, the tighter the mist became until it choked him. Struggling to breathe and break free, he realized he couldn't. Trapped and entwined he stopped struggling and looked at the mist.

"This is crazy."

The mist pulsed against him as if it were alive. "Why do you always come to me? You don't follow Mia." He wiggled a finger free and poked the dark mist.

"Ow." It stung. "Being trapped by mist makes no sense," he muttered. What had Mia said when he asked her how she controlled it?

"Back off," he said taking Mia's suggestion to talk to it. Nothing happened, but it wasn't as tight as before. He could move a bit.

"Get out of here," he said and sighed. He thought of Mia, the team, Hawke and everything he'd learned so far. Somehow he would learn how to control this stuff.

If Mia could, he could. Thinking of her lightened his heart. He thought he was too old for her when it was the other way around. Although she looked much younger than him, she had him by several decades.

He stretched and was surprised that he could. The mist hovered but didn't twist around him or hold him captive. Frowning he sat up, reached out and touched it again. No pain. It curled around his finger, up his wrist, and around his arm sending tendrils of warmth through him.

"What the hell? One moment you're choking me, the next you're doing this?" Curious, he watched the mist curl around his midriff as if dancing with light touches. "No one would believe this," he muttered and tried to cup it in his hand, it was much lighter, almost translucent now. "What are you? Why are you here? Why do you torment me?"

There was no answer, not that he expected any.

"Back off," he said.

It darkened a bit as it rolled away but remained closed as if waiting for additional instructions. He eyed the rolling mist that looked as if it bubbled up from a cauldron.

"Is Mia the key to controlling you?" he murmured thoughtfully. "I was thinking of her and you backed off." He lay on the ground and searched the sky for answers. "If she is, that's cool." His thoughts drifted to the military giving him the shot that changed him into a chimera when he died.

He frowned. The others believed the military would search for him, wouldn't leave him alone." Anger rose in his chest. After all his years of service, they changed him without his knowledge or permission.

The mist darkened and rolled closer, tightening around him.

"Get back." It continued wrapping around him, growing darker. For several seconds he stared at it while thinking of the possible reasons.

Are you channeling my emotions? When I'm sad or angry, it's dark and painful. But when I thought of Mia... the mist lightened like now.

"Go away," he said firmly. It rose high in the sky like a child sent to its room peeking through the stair rails.

He stood. "Come to me."

The mist returned.

He looked around, didn't see anyone and opened his hand. "Come onto my hand." Sounded stupid but then none of this made a lot of sense.

The mist wrapped around his hand.

"What the fuck?" he whispered seeing the mist on his palm. This was cool, he couldn't wait to show Mia. He walked a few feet to a boulder and looked at it. "Wrap around that stone."

The mist moved, hovered over the stone and then covered it.

Stunned, he wondered if this was the enhancement Hawke mentioned but wasn't sure since the mist had always been around.

"Tighter. Wrap around it tighter."

The mist thickened. It looked as if it formed bands within itself.

What kind of super-power was that, he thought. "Crush the rock."

The mist darkened. The bands disappeared. Noah stepped back as the rock shuddered and burst apart.

He dropped back onto his ass with his hand covering his mouth as he stared at the dust and pieces of rock. "What the hell?"

Gradually the mist lightened but remained over the rock. Freaked, he stared at it for several minutes, trying to process what happened. Obviously, the mist wasn't normal. Not doing stuff like that. It obeyed him, but it obeyed Mia too. Would it obey anyone? He frowned. That wouldn't be good.

He stood, wiped his hands on his pants, and stared at it a little longer. "If the mist responds to my emotions, then I should be able to control it. But how? When it was dark, it didn't obey him at all.

Clueless what to do next he released a sigh and spoke. "It'd be nice to control you, have you in my pocket when I wake up," he muttered.

The mist disappeared.

Noah stood and turned in a circle, searching for it. He wanted to work with it a bit more.

"Damn."

CHAPTER 23

Dr. Higgins stared at the report on the screen. She was obligated to report this change in Master Sergeant Sloan but suspected it would cause him problems down the road. His nightmares were getting worse. Peculiar.

She shuddered in remembrance of his chilling recounting of what happened to her the previous weekend. She hadn't told a soul and she knew the Lieutenant hadn't. It would cost him everything and after his hundredth apology, she agreed to keep his secret, as long as he stayed far away from her.

She hadn't seen or heard from him since that night and had verified he'd been transferred to a base in Virginia. The report glared at her. Trifled with her professional responsibilities and sense of right and wrong. The only thing Sloan wanted was to be left alone, hadn't he suffered enough. If she sent in this report, they would come for him. Chances are he'd be taken somewhere like the others, even though he was now a civilian.

Indecision pulsed against her forehead. She hadn't said much about Sloan in the past two months, this month she had to answer the unasked question. Was Sloan enhanced?

If it wasn't for that damned dream, if he hadn't named the Jeep, she could've blown it off, said there was nothing special. Just PTSD. But he had said the Jeep. He'd seen it. And for that, she had to send this report.

She pressed send, grabbed her purse and left the office early. She needed a drink.

CHAPTER 24

Noah gasped as he woke with a start.

"Easy," Mia said, her hand on his chest as she stared down into his eyes. Her gaze held worry, concern and something more. It eased whatever bothered him before. He rubbed his hand down her arm and took a deep breath.

"You're here," he said.

She smiled. "Yes, I am." Leaning forward, she brushed her lips against his. "We have a meeting."

He frowned. "What?"

"As we wake, we're supposed to meet with the others. Hawke has to re-examine us, make sure we're okay." Her gaze locked on his. "You're okay? Anything strange happened?"

Looking around, he realized they were still at the clinic. "We made love, right?"

She nodded. "You forgot?"

"I'll never forget when you give yourself to me like that, it's just I thought we were in your bedroom, at the complex."

"Me too." They stared at each other for a few seconds before he exhaled.

"That dream was too real," he said and then remembered the mist and exploding rock. "The mist changed."

"How?"

He explained what happened.

She whistled. "Definitely ask questions about that."

He nodded, rolled off the bed, stretched his legs and arms. Everything felt the same.

"I did the same thing when I woke," she said finger-combing her hair. "I feel the same."

He looked down at her and froze. "You're taller."

"Huh?" she looked down and then up at him. "Taller?"

He nodded. "Yeah." He stepped closer and placed his hand on top of her head. "See." It was a few noticeable inches and her body seemed lusher. He rubbed his palm down and across her hips. "Bigger here too, firmer."

She jerked and tried to look behind her. "Wow, really? I didn't notice with these leggings. Like it?" She looked up at him.

He pulled her close. "Hell yeah. More cushion for the pushing."

She blinked and then laughed. "You're corny."

He grinned.

"Take off your shirt so I can see if you've changed," she said watching him closely.

He pulled his shirt over his head and immediately noticed it was tighter.

"Your chest is wider." With a wicked grin, she ran her hands over his chest and flicked his nipple.

Tingles shot straight to his cock, hardening it immediately. Intrigued by her boldness, he remained still as she continued touching him.

"Sixpack right here." She tapped his belly. "More muscular," she said slapping his chest with approval and stepping away.

If they had more time, he'd toss her on the bed and sink deep inside her tight warmth. "I feel good," he said replacing the shirt.

She grinned at him, understanding the double meaning of his statement.

Leaving the room holding hands, the hall seemed a bit brighter than before. The sound of his shirt ripping startled him. He stopped, looked at Mia and laughed. "Told you," she said.

Rina greeted them before they reached the corner.

"This way."

They followed her in companionable silence. As they turned the corner, he heard the others talking and eating. His stomach growled as spicy aromas filled his nose.

"Food," he growled. They entered the same meeting room as before. A long row of covered trays filled a wall. The rest of the team sat at the table eating.

"I hope there's something left," Mia said picking up a plate and serving spoon. When no one responded, she looked over her shoulder at them.

They stared at her.

"What?"

"You changed," Thomas said, his voice deeper and eyes lighter.

"So have you," Mia said turning back to fill her plate.

"I think we all changed physically," Lizzy said. "What about internally? It's been two days since the shot."

Noah's head whipped up. "Two days?" How had he missed two days?

Thomas nodded. Still big, but not as compact. "Yeah, takes that long to repair and stuff. This is my first meal since the change."

"Mine too," Damali said tearing into a drumstick. "Starving."

Noah took his plate to the table and pulled out a chair for Mia. Lizzy inhaled and looked at them. "How long you guys been awake?"

"In and out," Mia said.

"Been busy," Damali muttered.

"Absolutely," Mia said unashamedly.

The meal continued in silence, with Noah and Mia refilling their plates twice more. When they finished they placed the dishes on the cart and returned to their chairs.

"How does everybody feel?" Thomas asked looking around the table.

The responses were positive, not much different.

"Hawke will be in soon to start post-op exams. Anything you notice that's different now is the time to get it checked. My stuff is evolving and eventually, I'll be able to help but talk to him for answers."

They agreed.

"Also, within the next 24 to 48 hours I'll start reaching out to each of you to open channels for mind-speaking. Once that connection's in place, we can talk to each other privately."

Mia looked at Noah. "Sounds like what happened that time we dream-walked."

He nodded.

"What happened?" Thomas asked. Everyone looked at her.

"We were investigating the case." She looked at Noah. "In the library and I wanted you to fast-forward."

"Yeah, she called my name, I heard her in my mind."

"You didn't mention that," Thomas said in a considering voice. "Can you speak to each other like that now? Outside of your dreams?"

"I don't know," Mia said. "Never tried it."

"Definitely something to look into," Thomas murmured.

"Mind speaking is a new skill," Max said, bringing the subject back front and center. "Do we all have it? Or is it your skill that you're sharing with us?"

"The way it was explained is it's my gift to share as leader. Also, I share in all of your gifts and can boost or cancel them," Thomas said.

"You can strengthen my gift or take it from me? Is that what you're saying?" Tip asked leaning forward.

Thomas nodded slowly. "Yes, that's what he said."

"Wow, that is new, didn't expect that," Tip said.

"What other powers do you have that affect us?" Max asked.

"I mentioned telepathy, the ability to find you, force your attendance, break your minds, and stop you from breaking the law." He looked at them.

They stared at him for several seconds without speaking.

"That's not what I had in mind when I asked you to be our leader," Lizzy said.

"Same here, sounds like a judge and executioner," Mia said.

"Definitely an executioner," Mali said rubbing her neck.

"Did you know all of that before you accepted the position? Or took the shot?" Max asked.

"Hawke told me right before he gave me the shot," Thomas said. He spread his palms wide. "I don't know what to say. I hear the doubt and concern in your voices. Damali looks horrified."

"I don't like the idea of you or anyone being able to kill me if you don't like something I've done," Damali said meeting Thomas' gaze.

"I agree. I don't want to be the person to make that call, either," Thomas said.

When he didn't say more, Lizzy spoke. "But someone would be that person. In the past, we didn't need it. Things have changed. I'll admit I'm stronger, not with the extras, I don't really know what they are yet. But my mind is sharper, keener than it's ever been before."

The others nodded.

"So maybe there is a need for discipline," Lizzy said.

"Not without rules," Noah said. They looked at him. "No rules, no discipline. Otherwise, how do we know we're in the wrong? There are the 10 commandments and if that's the only thing that governs this team, cool. We all know and accept that. But if that's not it, if the rules are different or there are more rules, that has to be decided up front. Which would also include some way or person any of us can talk to if we don't agree with your decision, Thomas."

"I totally agree," Thomas said. "When we return to the complex, we'll draw up rules to live by and the consequences of breaking those rules, me included. Good point, Noah."

The tension eased in the room.

"Any body's gifts kick in yet?" Max asked looking around and stopping at Noah.

He didn't say anything.

"Hawke mentioned the gifts will evolve over time. Not months but days and that we'll need to remain in the complex to work on them. If we need help, we can ask," Thomas said looking at them. "How's your head, Mia? I hope you don't lose your gift, we need our empath."

She shrugged. "Everything feels the same. Just have to wait and see."

Thomas nodded and exhaled. "Look. I know it's scary. I can't say I won't change, Hawke told me I would because your fates, and he did use that word, rests on my shoulders. If for some unfathomable reason somebody fucks up, I've got to handle it or give an answer why not."

"Who do you answer too?" Mali asked.

"Hawke or La Patron," Thomas said. "La Patron is allowing him to help because he understands what we went through. Hawke made it plain no one wants to interfere with us but if we endanger their secrets, if our behavior starts humans to seek out dual-natureds, they will protect their way of life."

"By eliminating us," Tip said.

"Yes. As long as we don't share who or what we are with others either directly or indirectly by our actions, or allow them access to the serum for unauthorized changes, they'll leave us alone."

"Unauthorized changes?" Max said. "Who authorizes changes?"

"I do," Thomas said. "I'm the only person, other than Hawke with access to the serum. It's my life if I fuck up with that."

"Should we be writing these rules down?" Damali asked.

"Not yet. Hawke's on his way," Thomas said.

"You can feel him?" Tip asked.

"No, he told me. We're already linked." Thomas leaned back in the chair. Moments later the door opened and Hawke entered with his tablet.

"Hello, Chimeras."

<<<>>>

Mia searched the faces of her friends and noticed changes. Some were subtle like a streak of red in Lizzy's dreds and larger eyes. Other changes were more dramatic. When she first saw Thomas she had been stunned. It was as if someone stretched his limbs and neck while enlarging his chest. He was the same size as Hawke. It was startling. Noah, Tip, and Max were all an inch or two taller, closer to 6'5", plus they just looked bigger, like some of the wolves she saw earlier. Of all of them, Damali seemed the same but she could be wrong.

Hawke accepted their greetings. He had to sense their discomfort regarding Thomas' new role in their lives but didn't address it.

"Anybody have any problems waking up?" Hawke asked.

"No," they said.

"Pain, constipation, any physical problems at all?" he asked. They all said no. "Good. I'll take you one by one for a brief examination and then you can return home."

"Thomas." Hawke waved Thomas out of the room.

Thinking about the changes and turns their lives had taken, Mia sat back in the chair with her hands clasped across her stomach.

No one spoke for several minutes.

"Am I the only one freaked out by all of this? There's a lot happening in a short amount of time," Damali said.

"We voted and agreed to it," Tip said.

"Yeah, but we didn't... I didn't know we'd live with our executioner," she said.

"Only if you break the rules we set in place. Makes sense to me," Max said surprising Mia. Normally, he was the wild one in the group.

"Did you hear me say, executioner?" Damali snapped. "He can kill us."

Max nodded. "If it comes to that, if I'm that out-of-control, I'd prefer he be the one to put me down. I don't have a problem with that. There will be others joining this team. We all want that." He glanced at Noah and Mia. "That's risky but necessary. Living a long life is hell if you have to do it without that special person. So I'll live by whatever rules we agree to and make damn sure anyone who comes into my life does as well so that I, we, don't mess anything up for the rest of you. We're fam."

Mia thought about what he said and agreed. Seeing Thomas in his new role would take time, but she agreed there had to be a gate-keeper if they were going to let others in.

Damali balled up her napkin and threw it across the table at Max. "Why you got to make so much sense? Is that your new gift or something?"

He ducked the napkin and grinned at her. "You're the one wanting normal, it comes with a price and we'll pay it."

Lizzy nodded. "Nothing's free."

<<<>>>

Hawke took the hand-held wand and moved it slowly in front and then behind Noah. When he finished, he looked at his tablet.

"Looks good. Numbers are better than before, tissue mass is good, blood pressure, heart... all looks good." Hawke looked at Noah. "Dream-walked lately?"

Noah nodded. "Yeah." He told him about the mist. "What do you think that's about?"

Hawke's eyes widened at the news of the stone breaking. "Off the top of my head, I'd say your emotions drive the mist which could be a problem. It comes to you, which means on some level there's a link. But the ability to use it like that is amazing."

Noah agreed the rock deal was cool.

"With the shot, your gift is still evolving. Be prepared for it to strengthen as time goes on."

"Trailing mist is my gift? Seriously, that's an enhancement? What am I supposed to do with it?" He didn't see it. Most of the time the mist attacked him, where was the benefit in that?

"Once you're able to control it, to call it at will, you can shape it to whatever you need it to be, it's a formidable tool." Noah must not have looked convinced because Hawke continued. "Imagine the various shades in a mist, from clear, allowing you to see through it or dark enough to blind you. In a fight or escape, that ability alone can mean the difference between winning and losing. Weaponized, it is better than rope, handcuffs or plastic ties. Plus it will torment your enemies with their own dark memories. Don't forget what it did to the rock, it'll do that to anyone or thing you tell it to." Hawke inhaled. "It's one of the most awesome enhancements I've ever seen." He looked at Noah. "It appeared before the shot?"

Shocked by Hawke's depiction of the mist, it took Noah a moment to respond. "Yeah, it did."

"I suggest you work with it every day until you're comfortable using it as an extension of you. Just as you'd practice arming and disarming a weapon, do the same with this. Every day you'll grow stronger, master it in the dream and during sunlight."

That surprised Noah. "I can use it awake?"

"Of course. I'd bet the only reason it's so strong when you're asleep and dreaming is that your conscious mind blocks it during the day." Hawke raised his hand. "That's normal. But when you're asleep, your subconscious allows the mist to rise because it's an intrinsic part of you. Begin calling on it while you're awake, see what it can do and how you can use it. Once you accept it as a part of you on a conscious level it'll always be available."

Noah sat heavily on the chair. "All this time I thought it was the PTSD."

"That may be part of it or the trigger. It's possible that the anger and grief you experienced created the mist as a coping or defensive mechanism after you were resuscitated. Coupled with your brain injury, the induced coma, and long recuperating period it's highly feasible that you walked through dreams with the mist as an extension of you. That's probably a better way to explain it."

Noah had no words. He couldn't begin to think along those lines and stared at Hawke for a few moments. "Will Mia control it too?"

"Time will tell," Hawke said. "Soon you'll know more, but it is a powerful gift. Be prepared for some sort of backlash or limitations."

"Backlash? Limitation?" Noah asked.

"Something that powerful has to be limited or you could place large areas of the world in darkness," Hawke said with a soft smile.

Noah hadn't thought of that.

"The greater the gift, the higher the cost to use it. It may drain your energy leaving you weak if you use it for prolonged periods, or if someone suffers from it, you might feel some of their pain. Or you could black out. It varies. You'll learn what they are once you use them."

"Anyway to learn them before I need to use them? It'd suck to be in a sticky situation and fall asleep," Noah said.

"Time will tell, everyone's different," Hawke said as he clapped Noah on the shoulder. "Let me know how it turns out, I've never heard or seen that particular power before."

Still processing their conversation, Noah nodded, took a deep breath and stood with his hand extended.

Hawke shook it.

"Thank you. I appreciate you making sense of this." He ticked them off with his fingers. "The hit to the head, dying, the injection, induced coma, nightmares, dreams, it all started there. That's where chimera started." He shook his head. "Makes a lot of sense now."

"Good," Hawke said. "Things will be easier to accept now that you see how the enhancement evolved."

Noah nodded and walked with Hawke to the door. "We're good to leave now?" Noah was the last one examined.

"Yes. Thomas will visit the compound after he gets a handle on his enhancements. By then the scanning and other equipment I'm revamping for your team should be ready."

Noah hadn't known about any of that but nodded anyway. "Thank you again." He and Hawke walked in companionable silence down the hall toward the conference room. Thoughts tumbled and jockeyed in his mind for dominance.

Control the mist. It's a part of me. Triggered by the trauma to my brain. Control it. Backlash. Limitations. By the time they reached the conference room, he wanted a quiet place to sit and think.

The look on Mia's face alerted him something had happened. She stood and handed him his cell phone which she kept during his exam.

His cousin Liam had sent a text:

Two guys in military uniforms came by looking for you. Wanted to know where you went and when you'll be back. I don't know the answer to either and didn't tell them. They said it was important for you to contact them. Got their information for you to contact them.

"They're looking for you already?" Mia said looking worried

Noah thought of Dr. Higgins and his stupid comments. He never should've shared that information about her personal life. He'd been so pissed, so angry… now they were looking for him.

"Seems like it." Unsure of what to say or do, he read the text message again. If they saw him now, they'd suspect he was enhanced.

"Is Liam safe?" she asked surprising him.

"Why wouldn't he be? He's been a civilian for eight years." Noah wasn't sure why she asked that question. The military didn't want Liam for anything.

"Will you call them?" she asked.

"No. There's no reason to do that," he said.

"In that case, they will continue looking for you and Liam is their only link." She met his gaze with an earnest one of her on. "Even if you don't join them, they will want to know how the experiment turned out. That's how the Liege operates, the reason we hid for decades. It's more than what happens on the operating table, the really important information is how the shot or surgery impacts you. It's data to improve or scrap a project. They will always want to know how the shot affected you, Noah."

Her words rang true but he didn't know what else to do. "I don't have to return their calls or go to see the therapist or report for a physical. The most they can do is stop sending my retirement checks –"

"The moment you do those things, your value rises exponentially because they'll know that you know you're enhanced. The question then becomes what to do about it. The others are probably in a training program, someplace far away from society. Can't let the media or anyone know the government's giving dying soldiers' injections that change them into enhanced humans, right?" She looked up at him with a cocked brow. Every word she said made perfect sense

"Worst it may get to a point that they decide to put you down rather than leave you alone. Kind of, it's with us or no one else," she said.

"Motherfuckers can try, but I'll be kicking asses till Sunday if they step to me with that shit," Noah said, growing pissed.

"Just putting all of this out there so we can decide what to do. I don't want to put the team in their crosshairs any more than you do," she said.

He hadn't thought of that. "I'll leave," he said quickly.

"We'll leave," she corrected and took his hand. He pulled her close and held her tight.

"No one has to leave the team," Thomas said. "If they come for you, we'll deal with it together. If you deviate from normal behavior, you shine on their radar instead of being a blip. We'll deal with it when we get back to the complex."

Noah looked down at Mia. These were her friends and family, whatever she wanted to do was fine with him. She nodded and leaned against his chest.

"Okay," Noah said hoping his cousin would be okay.

CHAPTER 25

"We need a meeting," Damali said when they entered the main area of their complex. She spun and looked at Thomas. "We need to correct this right now. I want a meeting."

Frowning Thomas looked at her. "What's wrong?"

"Dropping out, quitting should be against the rules."

No one spoke.

"Things are going to get hard, I get that. But don't... just don't break our circle because of that." She spun and looked at Mia. "We can't do that, I can't do that. Anything you need, we've got you but to quit, to think of leaving because of potential enemies or problems... no. No." She inhaled and the room whirled. "No," she yelled and everyone stumbled forward.

"Calm down, Mali," Mia said when she could breathe.

Damali looked at her with tears in her eyes. "You would walk away, leave after all these years? Just like that?"

"No. Not just like that," Mia said moving closer to her friend, seeing the pain in her eyes, she tread carefully. "But I'll be with Noah wherever he is or goes. The military isn't going to just let him walk away. We all know that, whether we admit it or not. Eventually, they'll find him. When they do they'll discover there are chimeras who aren't a part of their group." Mia looked at the others. "That might be a problem." She shook her head. "That will become a problem, especially if other military people have taken the shot and aren't on their team. Will they risk exposure? What if one of those enhanced soldiers had blood work done? Or talked to the press? Do you see the fallout? They are going to try and squash this, him to protect themselves."

"They're coming after one of ours," Damali said crossing her arms, glaring at Mia who now stood eye to eye with her.

"Fighting the military? That's a battle that no one will ever win," Mia said in a morose voice. "We're trying for normal, how will that ever happen with them constantly coming after us?" She searched Damali's hostile gaze, hoping she would understand the risks involved.

"I want a meeting, let's vote," Damali said undeterred.

"Mia, if the regular military was coming after Noah I'd concede your point," Tip said taking a seat on the sofa. "But this is a covert group probably not sanctioned by the Pentagon. They're operating in the dark, and need to be hush-hush about what they do. As far as living normal lives, we can still do that. We knew there'd be constant upgrades to security to make it happen." He paused rubbing his chin. "Losing our first mated pair, our princess." He shook his head slowly. "I'm with Mali. I don't see it. Makes my stomach twist just thinking about it. You're our hope deferred, can't take off now that we've just had our tanks refilled."

"If they bring the fight, we'll deal with it as a team," Max said. "I agree with Tip. Stateside, we'll be fighting military trained chimeras. It'll be good information to know what they can do, how their training stacks up against ours, that kind of thing."

Damali moved forward and took Mia's hand. "I know your heart. You don't want to draw us into you and your man's fight. I get that and totally respect the hell out of you for thinking of us. But you're my sister, used to be my little sister, but now you're all grown up and setting up house. I'm happy for you but hell if I'm letting those assholes come after you and sitting on the sidelines. Don't you know if they attack you, they attack me? They attack us all, don't matter if you're here or in a damn cave somewhere. We're family and I'm not losing anyone else." She kissed the back of Mia's hand and wiped the tears from her cheeks. "I want a meeting to make this a rule, turn this team into the mafia or something like that."

"Only way out is death? Is that what you're saying?" Lizzy asked with a slight smile.

"Yeah, exactly," Damali said.

Mia inhaled and looked at Thomas who had been silent. As their leader, it was his call.

"All in favor of that rule say yeah," Thomas said surprising her.

Everyone, except Mia and Noah, said yeah.

"Against, say hell no," Thomas said.

No one spoke.

"It's a new rule, no dropping out." Thomas winked at Mia. "We've got your backs on this. There are a few ways to handle this. You'll need to eventually respond to your cousin or he'll think something bad happened to you. I'll set it up on the computer so you can't be traced to here."

"Liam's going to respond, I would," Mia said. "I'd ask questions, want to know if Noah was okay if he needed anything. I'm sensing we don't have a lot of time before this blows up."

They all looked at her.

"Imminent?" Thomas asked concerned.

She shook her head slowly. "No, but not long either."

"In that case, we need to secure the complex and prepare for company," Thomas said walking out the room.

Mia grabbed Damali and hugged her tight. "Love you, girl."

"Love you and these blond curls too," Damali said stepping back. She extended her hand to Noah. "Family."

"Family," he said taking her hand and wrapping the other one around Mia. "What can I do to help?"

The day had been long and punctuated with Noah learning security protocols, accessing the vast training areas equipped with gym equipment and several large private rooms. Mia explained those were the spaces they practiced their gifts.

Mia and Tip prepared dinner while Thomas and Lizzy took Noah through several tunnels and entered his information into their database. After dinner, they sat down to create the first draft of the rules and regulations governing thing.

It was an interesting affair considering they had very few opinions. Basically, Thomas repeated the rules handed down from Hawke, added a few housekeeping rules, and the mafia condition and they were done. Their shared background of surviving the horrors of the Liege coated their regulations and Noah didn't think they would ever shake it.

Holding hands, Mia and Noah returned to their suite. Neither spoke, their eyes were heavy with fatigue, another side-effect from their recent injection.

Stifling a yawn, she peeled out of her clothes and glanced at his glorious body. "I planned to play with you in the hot springs but..." She yawned again. "I'm about to fall down, I'm so tired." Her clothes hit the floor and she made a straight line to the bed.

"Same here. All day I kept thinking of all the wicked things I wanted to do to your sweet, luscious body. It's what fueled me until we sat for the meeting. I'm exhausted." He crawled across the bed, pulled her close and tucked her head beneath his. "If I see you in my dreams, I promise to take good care of you."

She chuckled and placed her lips on his naked chest.

Noah woke crouched in the corner of a small, dim room. Confused he looked up at the burning candle in the wall sconces. For some reason, the flickering light captured his gaze and deepened his confusion.

A low keening wail caused him to turn and peer in the direction of the pitiful sound that tugged on his soul. He could not ignore the wretched pain from the voice, it called to him. He stood slowly and looked at the floor of uneven concrete and block. Frowning he watched his step and followed the weeping filled with sorrow.

With each step, he realized differences in construction. High sweeping archways. Cracked and peeling masonry plaster, it all seemed dated, even smelled musty, old. He stopped in front of a heavy wood door and listened.

The wailing and sobbing tore at his heart. What happened? Why was she crying like this? He tapped on the door. "Miss, are you alright?"

She didn't acknowledge him.

He knocked and spoke harder. "Miss, can I help you?"

It seemed as if her crying and tears increased.

Stumped, he looked around, hoping someone would tell him what was wrong with her. A woman dressed in a long black dress with a crisp white apron and a little cap on her head walked toward him holding a tray. He waited for her to acknowledge him, when she didn't he realized this was a different kind of dream.

She unlocked and opened the door, Noah stepped inside behind her as she closed the door and placed the tray on a small table. The woman sat on the side of the bed next to a small female curled in a tight ball. Her hair was long, thick and wavy. Her arms were wrapped around her waist and she shook like a leaf beneath the covers.

The nurse? The woman stroked the young girl's hair and made an interesting cooing sound before speaking. "Now, now, you have to eat and regain your strength. Master's assigned you to work with me and the others doing cleaning and whatnot. No more working near the labs or... anything. But you must eat."

Noah noticed another plate on the floor near the bed and moved closer. That's when he noticed the metal cuff chained to the bed and the other around the young girl's ankle. "She's a prisoner," he whispered shocked and looked around the dingy room.

"You'll have more wee ones in time. Be patient. Now come, eat a little of the meat and broth I've brought you. You've got to get stronger."

"My...my... baby," the young woman cried as she turned into the older woman's warm embrace and buried her face into her chest.

Noah froze. Mia. His Mia. He looked around the room, took note of the smallest details so he could tell her about it when he woke up. He moved to the side to get a better look at her.

"Don't think on it anymore. Time will heal your sorrows." The woman picked up a hard roll and placed it against Mia's lips. Eventually, she bit off a tiny corner and chewed.

Noah moved to the end of the bed and watched. She was smaller, younger with long hair but she was Mia and in pain. The baby. The Liege had taken her child at birth. He would find out what happened to the child for her.

Armed with determination, he placed his hand on the door, realized he could walk through it and left the room. "Take me to Mia's child," he said.

Nothing happened.

"I want to see where the infants are kept in this place," he said hoping that would work. Immediately he stood in a room almost as dim as the room he had just left. The sound of crying babes marked the difference. Small metal cribs line the wall. Women with white nurse's hats, long white dresses, and aprons in the same color, interacted with the infants, either feeding, changing diapers or simply holding them.

How would he ever find Mia's child? Did they keep records? Of course, they did, the Liege would insist on it. He looked at a chart of the infant nearest him and frowned. There were no names, only numbers, and initials. He had no idea how he would keep his promise to find out what happened to the child.

Mia might know. Where was she? Why hadn't they met in the dream like they had before? "Mia?" he called. "Mia, I need your help. If you hear me, I need your help."

"Where are you?"

Should he tell her? Of course. He explained his location and problem.

"How do I find you?"

"Think about me, reach for me mentally and I'll connect with you," he told her. A few seconds more she stood next to him in the nursery. He took her hand.

She shuddered. "I swore I'd never step a foot back here again."

He wrapped his arm around her waist. "I know. We can leave if it's too much." He rubbed her shoulder to help stop her trembling.

"I hate this irrational fear of being caught and locked up again. This is a dream, they can't see us, and I'm still scared. Shaking like a leaf," she said in a harsh, brittle whisper.

"Let's go. This is too much for you," he said.

"No. Give me a minute." She took a deep breath and coughed a few minutes. "This place smells like shit."

He waited until her breathing slowed and she could stand without leaning completely on him. The trembling hadn't stopped, but she moved toward the crib and read the notes. "Look for the number 0217JG, that was me." Her voice sounded off, sad by recounting the sole identifier for finding her child lay in six digits.

"Have a seat while I look," he said concerned by how drawn her face had become. The vibrancy he equated with her had fled and a left a pasty flush on her complexion.

Thankfully, she sat in a hard-wooden rocker, eyes closed and rocked gently. He moved quickly, searching all the charts for the alpha-numbers she had given him. By the time he searched most of the floor, he grew worried. He hadn't found the baby and prayed for the best. Occasionally, he glanced at her and his concern grew. She hadn't rocked the chair or opened her eyes in a while.

At the last crib, his heart dropped. Not one infant bore the number or alphabets she gave him. When he looked over at her, she met his gaze.

"He's not here," she said.

It wasn't a question, more like a statement of fact.

"None of these babies have those numbers you gave me," he said rather than agree with her correct assessment. He didn't want her to give up hope.

"This is where they bring all the infants. Doesn't matter if they're sick or healthy, this is the only place," she said staring at him.

Noah realized she was dangerously close to the edge as she wiped the tears from her face with the back of her hand. "We have to check the log to see if he or she died." She pushed up from the chair and he hated ever bringing her back here.

"I'll do it," he offered, softly. "Sit back down or –"

"No. I need to know what happened." She looked up at him. "Can we go back a little further? To when I had the baby?"

He could but didn't think it was a good idea. "I won't handle hearing you in pain well."

"They gave me a shot right after, knocked me out. Take me to the time right after that so I can see the child, see what happened to him." She pulled and clutched his arm. "Please. I need to know, Noah. It's been driving me crazy for years. No matter what, I need to know."

Unable to deny her, he asked a few more questions to get the timing close and moved back in time a little more. They stood in the back of an extremely, crude and bloody operating room as a doctor wearing thick glasses worked feverishly on an infant. Mia's inert body was on the table nearby. The child's piteous cries pierced his heart.

Mia stood next to him, tears running down her cheeks shaking so hard he was afraid she would fall. Her hand covered her mouth as if fighting to hold back a scream or shout.

Her legs gave out and she hit the floor, but her eyes never left the doctor as he worked on the child. In a heart-wrenching situation like this, there was nothing to say. He had never experienced anything remotely close but he could wait by her side to give her closure. Good, bad or ugly, she wanted to know if she gave birth to a son or daughter and if that child survived.

He moved closer to the table, looked at the child in the doctor's hands and stepped back. Noah didn't have Mia's abilities to read emotions, but the doctor didn't look optimistic.

"Suction," the doctor snapped at the nurse. She moved to the other side to obey his request.

"Come on, come on," the doctor murmured.

Noah's heart ached as he looked at Mia. Her expressionless gaze remained on the doctor as if willing him to perform a miracle.

"Bah," the doctor muttered, took a deep breath and backed away pulling off his bloodied gloves. "What a waste," he said with another glance at the infant lying on a small metal table, eyes closed and chest still.

Mia stood, walked closer and stared down at her daughter for several moments. The doctor left the room, leaving the nurses to clean up and dispose of the child. Mia turned and looked at Noah, with puffy, sad eyes and tear-streaked face. "Get me out of here."

CHAPTER 26

The Priest sat on his brother's patio drinking a sweet tea, half-listening to his niece, Pamela, drone on and on about her upcoming nuptials.

"Uncle Aaron thank you for agreeing to officiate," Pamela said.

Hearing his name he turned toward her with a smile. "I'm honored you want your old uncle around."

She hugged him and kissed his cheek. "I can't imagine anyone else taking me through my vows. Love you." She left him and her father alone with a quick wave.

"How are things going, Aaron," his brother asked taking a sip from his glass.

"Good. Good. The organization is growing. We've our annual conference next week in Denver. You and Jill should come." Stuffy Senator Mosely wouldn't be seen dead or alive at a Leviticus Club function. He'd call the group a cult and made his disdainful thoughts quite clear.

"No thanks. You will show up for Pamela's wedding, she's been quite insistent that you handle it for her and Jonathan."

Aaron waved his hand and frowned at his brother. "I've already agreed to do the blasted thing, why are you questioning me about it?"

"Because you've been jet-setting all over the country and missed the last three family get-togethers you promised to attend. I don't want her big day ruined because you get a sudden itch to see Niagara Falls or some bullshit like that. Am I making myself clear?"

Aaron glared at his brother. "Crystal. Now I'll make myself clear. Back the hell up and stay off my case. I'm not a child, certainly not your child, who runs at your beck and call. If I have other pressing matters to attend, that's what I'll do, just as you've canceled on us when your job demanded it,

I'll do the same. To me, what I do is just as important as what you do."

"Bullshit," his brother snapped and scooted closer. "You created this cult to assuage your guilt over killing your own child. It'll never bring back the babe or change what you did or get you back in the Priesthood."

Aaron held up his finger with an arched brow. "That's where you're wrong, I'm God's priest, not the Church. Even you have to agree serving God is a higher calling."

"I still say this whole thing is BS. Just don't get in trouble again. I won't help you a second time."

Fury raced through Aaron at the reminder of his brother stepping in, paying off Amelia to remain quiet about the abortion, making a large donation to the church to release him of his duties gradually rather than a big media stink. "I didn't ask for your help then and wouldn't ask if I ever needed it. Plus, we both know you didn't help me for me, you did it because it was an election year and you'd be hammered—"

"That's right, and you didn't give a damn about that," his brother yelled.

"So my personal, intimate life should be put on a schedule around your career? Is that what you're saying? Do you hear how ridiculous you sound? I fell in love with someone. That went against my vows. I assure you I wasn't thinking of you or anyone else when I accompanied her to that doctor. She wanted an abortion, I refused to allow her to go alone. Get the fuck over yourself, it was never about you," Aaron said in a hard voice.

Silence fell in the room.

Neither spoke for several minutes. Aaron pushed up from his seat and brushed imaginary lint from his pressed trousers. Still irritated and ready to be amongst people who understood his mission and passion he headed toward the door.

"I'm sorry, Aaron. I know you didn't do it to get back at me. You'd called and tried to talk to me several times but I'd been too busy with the campaign. I've always wondered if I could've helped if we'd talked when you needed me before things went too far. Guilt rides me hard that I wasn't there for you when you needed me."

Surprised and yes, pleased. Aaron looked over his shoulder into his brother's gaze and turned fully to face him. "I wanted you to tell me to step away from her. Needed you to remind me of my calling because things were so twisted in my head. The first time we had sex, I felt dirty, guilty and exhilarated. When I called you that night, I had questions, sexual questions. By then I knew I wouldn't give her up, wouldn't stop."

His brother frowned as he stared back at him. "She was crippled?"

Aaron nodded. How to explain the euphoric joy that filled him when he had sex with someone completely dependent on him? There were no words. Quite simply he preferred sex with imperfects. Their deformity made him feel like a giant or a god. Amelia wasn't necessarily beautiful, but she was good, untainted, pure. He had been her first and her virginal offering had been exquisite.

"Yes, a car accident when she was in elementary school." He smiled in remembrance of their long conversations where she shared her life and history.

"The sex wasn't... difficult?" his closed-minded brother asked.

"Not at all." He waved off the comment and heaved a sigh. "She's gone, back to her family I think. Haven't heard from her since she took your check." When Aaron saw the check in Amelia's purse he snapped. After all, he'd given up to be with her, she sold herself to the devil. She had been the first person he stoned to death.

"Are you seeing someone now? Will you bring her to the wedding with you?"

"Her?" Aaron said teasing and fighting back a grin at his brother's scowl.

"If it's a he, leave him at home. He's not invited to the wedding."

"I'm heading to Denver for our annual conference. I'll be there a week." Several stonings would be done before the event and he would oversee the cleansings as Yahweh demanded. All 12 disciples were in Denver waiting.

"Enjoy," his brother said.

"Believe me, I will." Aaron smiled as he left his brother's home.

CHAPTER 27

It took Mia two days to leave her suite and face the team after seeing the death of her daughter. They'd been kind and understood her heart had taken a beating. Seeing the child lying so still, brought back memories of her pregnancy. The nights rubbing her belly and singing to her baby. Bittersweet memories of the baby moving, stretching and wanting ridiculous foods at crazy times of the day. Today she packed away that important time in her life, pleased that it no longer controlled her thoughts or actions.

Walking through a dream to see the past was one thing but there was no going back to relive the past, no do-overs in life. She received closure on the fate of her child and would move forward. There were things that needed to be done. Preparations to be made.

When she strode into the main room, Lizzy and Max sat on the sofa talking softly. Mia looked around for Thomas as she approached them.

"How're you feeling?" Lizzy asked stretching a hand toward Mia, who took it.

"Better. Much better. I wanted closure and got it." She looked at Max and back at Lizzy. "We've got to get moving, where's Thomas?"

Lizzy's gaze sharpened. "With Noah and Damali in the training area. What's going on?"

Mia stood. "Come on, I prefer to tell everyone at once." She strode down the hall toward the rear of their complex. *Noah, I need you,* she thought.

"I heard that," he said.

Mia stopped looked around at Max and Lizzy, who stared at her curiously. She continued. *"We mind-spoke?"*

"This is great, I hear you plainly. How're you feeling?" he asked.

The past couple days he brought all her meals to her, wiped her tears, rocked her gently and was constantly by her side.

"Better. I've been picking up something this morning. We're on our way to the training are to talk to the rest of you. Is Tip there?"

"Yeah, he just walked in."

"See you in a bit."

Mia and the others entered the large training area. Thomas stood watching the others in separate training rooms. Not wanting to interrupt, Mia stood behind him and watched Noah work with the mist. He had mentioned it to her, but she'd never seen him handle it before.

"Are you spinning that like a lasso?" she asked him moving closer.

"Yeah, watch this." The spinning stopped and it settled like a cube in his hand. *"Now this."* The room darkened to the point she couldn't see anything. Then it went gray and finally clear.

Impressed, she moved closer to the room where he worked. *"What else can you do with it?"*

"It's a weapon." He glanced at her over his shoulder, opening his hands wide. The mist stretched between it. *"This can harden to any density I need. Come inside."*

She opened the door and stepped in.

"Touch it," he instructed.

She placed her fingertip on it and jerked back. *"That hurt."*

He nodded and flicked the mist outward.

"Ouch." She rubbed her butt where the mist landed. *"That was hard. You sure that's mist?"*

He shrugged. *"I don't know what it is anymore, just that it's a part of me and I'm still learning how to control it."* He wrapped it around her and stepped back. *"Try to get out of it."*

She moved. The mist tightened. The more she struggled to get out, the tighter it became. Mia looked at him, smiling. *"This is great. I can't get out."*

"Imagine putting that around someone's neck and tightening it with a thought," he said releasing her. *"It will torture as well, play on your darkest fears, amplify them."* He looked at the mist wrapped around his wrist and then at her. *"Hawke really liked this enhancement, and I'm beginning to see why."*

She walked toward him and placed a kiss on his lips. *"Hearing you in my head feels funny."* She giggled.

"I like it." He pulled her closer.

"Not now, we've got unfinished business."

His brow arched. *"You've got something?"*

"Yeah. I'll tell everyone at the same time." She took his hand and they left the room. The others stood around Thomas talking and watched her approach.

"Leviticus Club?" Thomas said.

For Mia and the others who lived through unimaginable cruelty as lab specimens and slaves, Aaron Mosely, the Priest, reminded her of the Liege. Men who did nothing but take as if it was their right simply because they believed it was a good idea. If they didn't stop him, hundreds would die, because he was killing more than before. Her vision had been drenched in blood, something she hadn't seen since her days in the Liege compound.

Mia nodded. "We've got to finish it. Plus the military is ramping up their search for Noah. He's got to respond to Liam otherwise his cousin will get hurt."

"We're in sync on this Mia," Thomas said. "I picked up on both of those this morning. Once Noah goes home, which I agree he needs to do to close out everything, he's up on their radar. It's possible they'll track him back here. Then we'll be on their radar." He looked at each of them.

"Here's another option. Noah goes home, tells them no thanks, set things in place with his attorney to give his cousin the house and then leave with Alpha Theron's help. All they'd know was Noah went on pack land and didn't leave," Thomas said watching Noah.

"I'm going with him," Mia said quietly.

They all looked at her as if waiting for an explanation. She had none. It was the way things were going to happen.

Noah's gaze flitted from her to Thomas and back to her. She knew he wanted to object, would try to protect her. He needed to understand she wasn't ever going to remain behind while he went out to face danger and fight. They'd go together or not at all.

"Mia, I can go, get it done and be back in a day," Noah said.

"Yes we can," she faced him with a stubborn tilt.

"If something goes wrong —"

"We deal with it together," she said resolute.

He ran his fingers through his hair while staring at her. *"If anything happens to you—"*

"You'll go batshit crazy like I would if something happens to you. We're still learning how all of this works. So this is how we do it, together or not at all. I'm serious, Noah. We do this and everything together. That's what being a pair means to me."

He stared at her a few moments and nodded.

"What the hell was that?" Max asked his gaze going between them. "Were you talking to each other? You're linked to mind-speak?"

Mia's gaze slid to Thomas. She assumed they all could. "Yeah."

"When did it kick in?" Max asked.

"Today when I got up, first time I used it," she explained.

"How did you activate it?" Max asked but they all watched in anticipation.

"I thought about him and said words in my mind, he answered." It had been as simple as that.

"Do you hear me?" Thomas asked her.

Her gaze widened as she looked up at him. *"Yes. Yes, I do. It's a different channel or link or path, whatever you call it than what Noah and I share."*

"How?"

"There's a more intimate feeling in Noah's link," she said not knowing the exact words to use to explain it better.

"I see," Thomas said, his gaze flicked to the others. *"I've linked with everyone. I don't know when you guys will link with each other."* He paused. *"Can't talk you out of going with Noah?"*

"No. I'm going," she said leaving no room for doubt.

"Okay. I'll contact Tyrone, see if he's still in Texas and explain the situation. Contact Noah's attorney so the papers will be ready for signing."

"He doesn't have an attorney, we've got to find one," she said.

"In that case, I'll take care of it. Makes things easier. He can sign them here or anywhere."

"We still need to deal with Liam," Mia said.

"Can't you just talk to him on the phone since you don't need to meet with an attorney? Tell him you and your lady are going to be traveling for months at a time and will contact him when you can. In the meantime, the house and truck are his to use. It's a clean break, you take nothing, and he thinks you're following your heart," Lizzy suggested.

Mia looked at Noah who was following the conversation. "That might work," she said.

"Liam's just worried that's all. They've contacted him again, plus he can't reach me when he calls. He thinks I'm in trouble and covering things up," Noah said.

Mia sensed his deep discomfort over discussing his cousin like this.

"Can he meet you guys someplace? Take a trip to New Orleans or the Blue Ridge mountains, something like that, so we have room to maneuver?" Thomas asked.

"We can do that," Noah said' slowly. "Take them away from my backyard. If he really wants to see me, I'll suggest he meets us someplace."

"The moment you call it'll be traced. If it can't be traced, that's a red flag that you're hiding something. If it can be traced and turns out to be fake, it's another flag that'll buy some time," Thomas said.

"Even if you drive into your garage at midnight, they're going to trace and try to track him," Tip said. "Just like they're tracking you financially through your credit card and bank account. If you contact your cousin for any reason, the tracking starts. That's a given. We've got to decide how to minimize it so they can't find you after the contact."

"Is there a way to do that without my cousin getting hurt or involved?" Noah asked.

No one said anything for a few moments. "The only way your cousin isn't used as a trigger or pawn is for them to think he's not important to you," Thomas said. "You've got to understand that. They will use him to get to you."

Noah's face tightened and he looked down. Mia knew to face that particular reality hurt.

"I don't like them fucking with his life like this, none of this is his fault."

"I know," she said.

"Do I tell him? Warn him the shit might hit the fan?" He looked at her.

"Ask the group, ask Thomas. It's not just your secret, all of us could be at risk if you warn him."

Noah asked Thomas.

"What could you say to him that would not require a full explanation of what happened to you and your new reality?" Thomas asked.

Noah opened his mouth and snapped it shut. Mia tried to think of something but came up with nothing.

"I can't think of anything right now," Noah finally said. "But the idea of his death because of me, for something he's got nothing to do with is messing with me."

Thomas nodded and clasped him on the shoulder. "We understand and will try to help as much as possible."

Mia took his hand and held tight. *"We'll think of something, maybe ask Ryan and Ryder to keep an eye out for him. Call us if they see something."*

After a few seconds, he nodded.

"There have been two more reported deaths since we dropped the Leviticus Club case," Thomas said. "The FBI has covered considerable ground but because we couldn't turn over all of our information they haven't connected the dots to the Leviticus Club yet. In fact, they've made no progress in that direction."

Mia's gaze narrowed. "What? All they have to do is go arrest the Priest,—"

"Senator Mosely's brother? That Priest?" Thomas asked with a cocked brow.

"We have to finish it, there are a lot more deaths than two," she said quietly.

"I know. And we will," Thomas said watching her. *"The need to finish that case is intense, isn't it?"* he asked her.

Realizing he understood, she nodded. *"Yes. Very intense and it won't go away. It's getting stronger, I hope that doesn't mean he's preparing another sacrifice."*

Thomas looked at the others, most had been silently following the conversation. "We have to stop the Priest from killing more disabled humans and put Liam's mind at ease."

"Where is the Priest?" Max asked.

"I'll get that information," Thomas said. "This is a live FBI case. We have no authority to work on it and can be arrested. We have to be really careful."

"What are we doing? Gathering evidence or stopping the threat?" Tip asked.

"I vote for stopping the threat," Mia told Noah.

"I agree," he said.

CHAPTER 28

General Strait buried his cousin Nate two days ago. It had been a difficult day, made worse by what appeared to be a stalled case. His contact at the FBI was no further along than the team he hired to look into matters. How could multiple stonings take place in this country without leaving any clues? Impossible.

Obviously not. The stonings had been going on for months and the FBI didn't have one solid lead. It made no sense. Sitting in his home office, he used a burner phone to place a call to Gil Schmidt, the trainer he bought on for the Olympus Project.

"Do you have anyone who can hunt down a serial killer?"

"Yes. What do you need?"

The General explained what he knew, advised him on the FBI's involvement but didn't mention the other team he hired. That was a private card he would hold close.

"Sounds like more than one person, maybe a group," Schmidt said.

"I'd been thinking along those lines, myself. No way one person could commit the same type of crime in several states by themselves, the deaths have been too clean. So far the FBI has found no mistakes."

"They're good. But my guys are better. Send me what you have and I'll send two of my best hunters to handle it."

"Try to stop whoever this is. I want them to hang publicly for what they've done."

"Any vets been killed?"

"Not yet," the General said.

"Not ever. We'll nail the bastard," Schmidt said.

Feeling better that he would fulfill his promise to his cousin, the General relaxed. "Sounds like things are going well with the program. You've resettled on the Compte?" He had approved the group's request to access a training facility in the US Virgin Island.

"Yes. Three days. Training has been good. They're learning to use their enhancements better and soon it should become second nature to them."

"Do not allow them to fraternize with the natives."

"Understood. When we're ready and in control, we'll return stateside to the base."

The General would need to introduce the concept of enhanced human soldiers to the Joint Chiefs as a replacement for La Patron's Knights.

Most of the Joint Chief would accept the new team. Admiral Blue and General Williams might give him a hard time. But once they saw what these men could do, it would change their minds. At least he hoped it would.

The General cleared his throat. "Before you return, prepare a presentation for high ranking members of the military. Make sure it's damn good, no mess-ups. We need them to approve additional funding to build that corps. To get beyond the fact of injecting soldiers who flat-lined with a serum that enhances them to become more than human, I've got to show the benefits outweigh the methodology."

"Yes, Sir. We'll be ready."

"Two weeks."

"Done. Just the ones we're training now, not anyone who comes in after today," he said.

That was fair. "Got a lot coming in?" the General asked.

"One or two a month survive the shot and remain sane."

"What happens to the ones who aren't sane?" the General asked.

"They're put down."

"Which is the end result of what would've happened if they hadn't been given the serum," the General said thinking that's the line he'd give the others.

"Exactly."

"Tidy. No loose ends," the General said.

"None, Sir. My team's got this under control. We'll be ready in two weeks."

"Counting on it. Let me know when you get more information on the serial killer," the General said.

"Yes, Sir." Schmidt disconnected,

CHAPTER 29

Noah and Mia returned from a quick flight down to Las Vegas where he called his cousin to let him know he was alright. Understandably, Liam had a lot of questions which Noah artfully avoided. Finally, he told his cousin he was traveling with Mia and would see him whenever he returned to Texas which would be whenever. They talked for 10 minutes about the house, truck and Noah's future plans to be with Mia for a while.

Noah said he probably wouldn't contact the military guys who were looking for him because he was finally enjoying retirement. When they finished talking, Noah immediately powered it down and turned it off before sticking it into his pocket. He and Mia returned to the small private airport where Thomas and Lizzy waited for them onboard a chartered jet to Denver to attend the Leviticus Club's annual conference.

The two men monitoring Liam's phone listened in on the call and immediately traced Noah's location. They called it in.

Schmidt answered the call on the first ring. "Yes?"

"Sir, Sloan called his cousin. He's currently in Las Vegas walking along the strip with someone."

"Do we have anyone in Vegas who can put eyes on him?"

"Who do you want involved?"

"Never mind, I know someone. Continue watching Liam, I'll get back to you in a few."

"Yes, Sir."

Schmidt called an old friend he'd served with several years ago. Glass retired to Vegas, worked in a casino. There was no answer. Schmidt tapped his finger on the table unsure if Sloan posed a threat. Probably not. Regardless, he was a loose end that had to be snipped.

He made another call, this time the phone was answered. "I need you to follow someone until my people arrive. They'll take it from there."

"Usual rates?"

Schmidt nodded. "Yes, usual rates. He's on the strip walking with a date." He gave him the longitude and latitudes of the moving target. "He may not be there long."

"I was headed home, am turning around now. Send his pic and I'll let you know when I see him."

Satisfaction soared through Schmidt. Torr wasn't military or anything close. He was a thug who'd make your problems disappear for a price. Schmidt rarely used him.

Schmidt sent the picture and then a message to Zeus and Hermes, sending them to Vegas.

"They're heading to the private jetport. Pulled in and boarded a plane. Just took off."

Schmidt frowned at Torr's message. "Private plane?" He sent Torr a message to find out where the plane went. Next, he told his men to wait. No need to send them to Vegas.

Torr responded with a call. "The flight plan has them heading to Denver. The name on the manifest was your guy. No mention of the female. But she was with him."

"Did you see them enter the plane?" Schmidt asked to be certain.

"Yeah, it's a small jetport. I parked on the side and watched."

"Which airport are they landing in Denver?"

"Centennial."

"On it." He sent Zeus the message to take the jet to Denver which was much closer than Vegas. They might arrive at the same time as Sloan.

"Sending the bill," Torr said.

"Thanks."

"Has the mission changed?" Zeus asked via text.

"No. This is clean up. Something that was missed. I'll send you information for his termination. Once he's eliminated continue the search for the perpetrators in the stoning case."

"Yes, Sir."

Schmidt looked out the onto the training area at the men and few women exercising or working to control their abilities. For some, the additional abilities were too much and they snapped, had to be terminated.

Others, like Zeus, Apollo, Hermes, Hypnos, Janus, Athena, and Hera, thrived. They believed the hype that they were gifts to men, better than the rest and used their gifts with eager abandon. They concerned Schmidt the most. Right now, they listened, followed instructions but how long would anyone who believed they were gods listen to men?

Onboard, Thomas sat back reading his tablet. Noah checked to make sure he had his handicapped placard Liam had overnighted. He was going in as bait. As a cripple, he'd get close to the Priest and take him out.

"We've got a handicapped van reserved at the airport in addition to a car. Tonight is the kick-off for Leviticus club's Annual Conference. Noah, you're going in using a wheelchair. We'll have you there early. They've got special sections for the disabled," Thomas said. "I'll give you a shot that will numb your legs in case they test you. It'll last for 30 minutes." He looked at Mia. "I'll give you another dose for him, just in case."

Mia nodded.

"I've got your change of clothes, Mia," Lizzy said. "That wig will work but it'd be better to wear something with hidden pockets." Mia had worn a long, dark brown wig while in Vegas with large sunglasses. Noah wore a baseball cap and sunglasses as well.

Lizzy passed her a bag. "Change before we land. If anyone checks cameras at the airport, they need to see your alias."

"Okay," Mia said.

"We'll all be linked," Thomas said. "Once the Priest appears, Mia compel him to choose Noah as his next victim. Draw his attention to Noah, we're trying to avoid another murder. Lizzy will cast a glamour on Noah that will make him look helpless."

Mia nodded and placed her hand on Noah's thigh. He covered her hand with his.

"Whatever excuse they give for separating you and Noah, go with it's an honor and appear excited for him." Thomas looked at Noah. "If they remain true to how they've operated in the past, they're going to shoot you with a fast-acting drug that'll knock you out." Thomas held up a small plastic bottle. "Before we leave for the conference you'll take these to negate any effects. Hawke doesn't think the drug will work on us because of our physiological changes but I'm not taking a chance."

"Agreed." Noah took the small bottle and slid it into his pocket.

"Once behind the curtain, use the mist to take him out," Thomas said. "Make it quick and clean.

"Any idea how many of them there'll be waiting for him back there?" Mia asked.

"No. but we know the Priests have others that surround him for the stoning. He doesn't do them alone," Thomas said. "He would have 12 at a minimum, crazy bastard."

"That sounds about right," Lizzy said.

"Is the Priest the only target?" Noah asked.

"Yes. Unless you've got to defend against any others," Thomas said. "Then do whatever is necessary. But terminate Mosely."

Noah opened his hand and the mist sparkled as it danced in a short spiral in his palm. It became dark, then disappeared. He'd come a long way controlling the mist and wasn't sure it was still mist. "Gladly."

"Mia what did you tell the dispatcher at the jetport?" Thomas asked.

"Instructed him what to say if anyone asked questions about us and to contact the toll number if it happened. He called?"

"Yes. Sent a video of the conversation too." They watched the mousy looking man at the counter asking about them.

"They know we're headed to Denver," Thomas said.

"They know Noah's headed to Denver, he's the only one on any paperwork and we used his credit card for everything. If they follow us to Denver, we know exactly who they want and why," Mia said.

"That guy's not enhanced," Noah said pointing to the video.

"No. Chances are he's local. You weren't on the phone long. Once you turned off your phone, you were off the grid. They would've sent someone local to the area where you were on the phone to follow you. If they're coming for you, it'll be in Denver," Thomas said.

"Will that interfere with the op?" Noah asked, concerned.

"We won't let it," Thomas said. "There's a chance they're coming to reclaim you as their property."

Noah snorted. "Doubtful. Termination of loose ends. Can't have crazies with unknown super-powers running around."

They looked at him.

"Be interesting to see what they've got," Noah said looking at the others. "They aren't expecting any of you."

"No they aren't," Lizzy said sitting back, crossing her legs. "You're right, it will be interesting to see what their version of the Liege drug can do versus Hawke's."

"Any bets?" Mia said before breaking out into a wide grin.

"Hawke for sure," Noah said tossing the sparkling mist into the air watching it fill the cabin and dim before returning to his palm.

One moment they sat on leather seats in the middle of the jet, the next they sat on the beach hearing the roar of the ocean with drinks in their hands.

"Liz, girl this is awesome," Noah said.

"No fair, it doesn't work on me," Mia said. "I want to see."

Lizzy laughed and removed the illusion. "Stop pouting, illusions never work on empaths. Believe me, that's a good thing when dealing with strong illusionists."

"Like you," Mia said.

"Yeah, like me," Lizzy agreed.

CHAPTER 30

When the plane touched ground near the Mile-high city, the team was ready. Mia had changed. Noah was carried down the steps and placed into a motorized wheelchair. He and Mia entered the handicapped van. She drove away. The jet moved to the other side of the airport and parked.

"The black SUV is still behind us, think that's them?" Mia asked Noah.

"Probably," he had sensed them nearby the moment he was carried off the plane. "Damn controls," he muttered pushing the knob.

"Don't hit the door, you might fall out." Mia laughed. "Thomas hasn't been able to read the guys in the SUV. He still wants us to go to the hotel."

"Mm-hmm." Noah pressed the knob, the chair bumped into the side of the van. "I need to get this before we reach the hotel."

Mia glanced in the rear-view mirror and smiled at his concentration. He could wield mist with whipcord accuracy but had problems navigating an electric wheelchair. Following the GPS' instructions, she turned off the highway and onto the feeder road leading into Denver. It was a beautiful place, she wanted to return when they could spend some time.

"Go ahead and pull into the front of the hotel, let Noah out. Lizzy has the glamour locked on. If either of these guys is an empath let me know," Thomas said. *"We're pulling into the garage and will be there in a few seconds."*

Mia saw the name of the hotel and pulled beneath the canopy. The SUV pulled close but not behind them. She was certain they could see their every move as she released door, it slid open and the gate extended.

Noah steered the chair onto the gate and it lowered to the ground. Mia grabbed their bags and watched Thomas and Lizzy in the distance as she locked the van.

She walked slowly next to Noah as they headed to the lobby and sensed

189

probing fingers into her mind. *"Mindlock,"* she told Noah.

"Been locked all day," Noah said as they entered the doors. *"Did you sense them?"*

"Yes. Definitely enhanced. One is quite strong. Neither are empaths, so the illusions should hold." She approached the counter, gave Noah's information and credit card. Once they received their room key, Noah moved out of the way as Lizzy entered and checked in. Thomas was still outside as Mia moved the van to a handicapped parking spot. She jogged back inside, placed her hand on Noah's shoulder and they went to the elevators.

"Those two are discussing Noah. He's not what they expected and isn't sure they're supposed to terminate a disabled vet," Thomas said. *"They're contacting someone named Schmidt for further instructions. Mia, are you guys in your room?"*

"Yes," Mia said pulling off the wig and tossing it on the dresser. *"I've scanned and sealed the room already."*

"Good because this Schmidt person just told these guys Noah is supposed to be enhanced and that he's no cripple. Claims it's all an act to fool these guys. Guess what their names are?" Thomas said.

Mia heard the laughter in his voice.

"What?" Lizzy asked.

"Zeus and Hermes. They gave them names after Greek gods."

"Wow, don't tell Mali," Mia said and the others laughed. *"I guess this means we can't take a nap?"*

"Rest if you can. Delay that, they're leaving their truck. One tall blond, big, other reddish-brown, triangle-shaped face, goatee. They have on sunglasses and just passed me. They're bypassing the counter and going to the stairs which mean they know where you are."

"What should we do with them?" Noah asked laying on the bed with his feet crossed at the ankles.

Thomas didn't immediately respond. *"Protect yourselves if they break down the door."*

"I can fix it that the door won't break," Noah said.

"Try that first," Thomas said.

Noah opened his palm. The mist spread from top to bottom along the entire wall, covering the door and changed colors to solid black.

Mia knew the moment the two men stood in front of the door. *"They're here,"* Noah said.

She nodded, stood and faced the door. If the seal didn't hold, she would go after their minds, while Noah attacked their bodies.

There was a knock on the door.

She looked at Noah and they moved to the bathroom just as something slammed so hard into the door the wall shuddered and dust sprinkled to the floor.

Mia looked at the window and pointed.

Noah immediately covered it with the same black hardened mist. The door was hit again and again.

Mia wondered why security hadn't come, surely they felt the vibrations.

"We're in a bubble, you sealed our room. They probably sealed the hall too," Noah said.

She nodded and jumped as glass from the window broke. *"They just broke the outside window,"* she told Thomas.

"They blocked your floor, we've been trying to get to you but the doors won't open to that floor, we're stuck in the stairwell," Thomas said.

"Go to the room above or beneath us," Mia said watching the window and trying to be calm like Noah. He stood watching the window and listening.

"They're going to try to come from above or below or through another wall," he said as he spun, sending mist to cover every corner of the room. The wall behind the bathroom shuddered. Water turned on, as the walls bowed inward but didn't break.

Noah glared at the wall.

Trickles of mist flowed from his palm and into the pipes. The wall on the opposite side of the room shuddered as something hard slammed into it. The door shuddered as it was hit immediately after the wall. Next, all three walls were hit at the same time. The bathroom wall bowed but didn't break.

"Do they mind-speak? I haven't heard anything from them," Noah said.

"Good point. Maybe it's the room seal. Do we need it with the mist?" she asked him.

"No. I've solidified the mist to unbreakable steel. Hawke helped me master it."

She removed the shield. Now they heard the murmurs and footsteps. *"I thought there was just two?"* she looked at him and sought the men.

"Hermes can duplicate himself but it weakens him after he does it for any length of time." She flicked through his thoughts and sent the information to Thomas regarding the organization led by Schmidt. Hermes realized someone had tapped into his mind and tried to lock her out but it was too late, she had a foothold and drilled down to find the box of locked-away memories everyone hid.

His horrified scream filled the floor. Footsteps thundered down the hall. "What happened?"

Hermes couldn't answer. He wouldn't talk to anyone for a long, long time. Mia amped his nightmares a hundred percent. His nightmares would have nightmares.

"We're on your floor, are you alright?" Thomas asked. *"Good lord, they destroyed the wall and the door. Is that the mist?"*

"Yeah," Noah said. *"Titanium grade created a rectangular box inside the room."*

"Awesome," Thomas said, admiration coming through their link.

"Taking a nap," Mia said scooting back on the bed and replacing the

shield to drown out Zeus' cursing.

"What did you do to that guy?" Lizzy asked sounding impressed. *"He's bleeding out of his nose and curled in a ball. Every time his partner tries to help or move him, he cries out in terror. Security finally arrived, with the cops. Zeus is walking away, leaving his partner on the floor. I guess he prefers to let the human's deal with it."*

Noah joined Mia on the bed and pulled her close. "That was a solid, wicked move," he said near her ear.

Mia turned into him. "I was only able to get into his mind because you drained his energy trying to get in here." She placed a soft kiss on his lips and rolled over on top of him. Looking down she stared into his face grinning. "We make a good team."

He slapped her butt. "Told you that days ago." He kissed her hard, robbing her breath. "But you know it's not over, right? There's another one, Zeus, the god of thunder. Any idea what he does?"

"My guess would be hitting the walls, trying to break in." She snapped her finger. "I pulled information from Hermes memories." She focused inward. "There's nine of them, they've lost quite a few lately. Zeus is a team leader, uses his voice and massive strength to fight. Has some kind of sonic boom. He has to gear up for it and can only do small hits fast or on the run. We have to keep him moving, not allow him to build it up or he can do major damage."

Noah nodded.

"Hera releases poisonous odors that will paralyze you. There's Apollo, wears gloves to keep his fingers covered, or he hurts himself with a similar toxin found in Dart Frogs but much more concentrated. If it enters your bloodstream it can paralyze and kill you."

"Those are vicious, I don't see how they can be used to help anyone," Noah said.

"Aren't you glad you're a dream-walker?" she teased.

"Hell yeah." He kissed her again.

"That's all I've got, either he doesn't know the others or I didn't go far enough into his memories to get them," she said.

"Those are bad enough," Noah said. "We'll need to learn to defend against them."

She nodded as Thomas knocked on the door.

"The cops and ambulance have left. Lizzy let them see the damage but not the hard mist. They're sending a maintenance crew up in a few. I told them you'd stepped out of the room and would be back soon."

Noah and Mia rolled out of bed. He removed the mist. The door fell forward into the room. They all stared down at it and the cracks in the wall. Thomas and Lizzy stepped inside and looked all around the room. Zeus and Hermes had hit the walls from every side, top, and bottom.

"Get in your wheelchair and let's get out of here," Thomas said. *"Good thing the*

police is charging Hermes for the damage. Zeus left before they could get his name or information but some of the guests saw him hitting the door before they blocked the floor."

Noah sat in the chair and headed toward the elevator. It opened just as Zeus stepped out of the stairwell and stared at them. He took in the wheelchair, inhaled and released a sound that rolled through the hall knocking them backward. Noah fell out the chair and hit the ground.

Zeus ran forward, grabbed Noah and kept running toward the stairs on the other side of the floor.

"I've got this," Noah said as he released the mist to cover Zeus' mouth and eyes. Within seconds the hall darkened.

Zeus kept running.

Anger ripped through Noah, he charged the mist with electrical currents. It snapped, crackled and popped against Zeus' face, arms, and wrapped around his legs, tripping him. He hit the ground hard.

Noah fell from his grip and rolled along the floor.

Zeus tried to stand but the mist tightened around his legs. Suddenly he stilled and took several deep breaths through his nose. Eyes closed, he kept inhaling, chest expanded and then he released it through the mist.

The halls shook, lights flashed, but not much more.

Mia ran to Noah and dropped to her knees holding him close. *"You okay? We can fuck him up if you want."*

Noah tied Zeus' hands together with the mist as well before Thomas helped him back into the chair. "Here, let me help you, Sir."

Zeus stared daggers at Noah and then Thomas, Lizzy, and Mia. Noah darkened the mist in front of Zeus' eyes so he wouldn't see them leave down the hall.

"He pissed you off, didn't he?" Mia said walking alongside him.

"Yeah. Asshole wouldn't let go," Noah said. When they reached the elevators, the hotel manager and maintenance guy stood in front of their room.

The manager stepped to the side and handed Thomas an envelope with his new room keys. "Again I apologize for the inconvenience."

"Thanks," Thomas said as they entered the elevator and rode up three floors. *"Try and get some rest. We'll be leaving in a few hours and then heading out."*

Noah nodded as he stood, pushed the wheelchair to the side and sat on the edge of the bed. Thomas and Lizzy left. Mia sealed the room and joined him on the bed.

"How long will you leave him tied like that?"

"Until I wake from my nap," Noah scooted up the bed and slid beneath the covers. Mia joined him.

"I used a lot of energy, and need to rest." He pulled her close and she sealed them inside the room.

CHAPTER 31

Mia looked around the large, packed out, auditorium in awe. Who would've thought this many people followed a cult that stoned imperfect people.

Yes, after listening to several individuals in the audience, Leviticus Club was all about being physically perfect, supposedly in the eyes of God. It boggled the mind how they came up with such a crazy notion, worst, that thousands of people bought into it. There was always a market for people who needed to feel they were better than others, she guessed and looked over at Noah. He sat in the second row with other handicapped persons. Lizzy assured her that anyone, other than her or other empaths, looking at Noah would see a drawn, defeated looking older man and not the strong, viable soldier he was.

Several individuals in priestly robes strode onto the stage as the band warmed up. They took seats on a slightly raised dais while singers stepped to the microphones.

"Where is the priest?" Noah asked.

"I'm not getting anything," she said straining for information backstage. She hoped Mosely and his crew weren't somewhere stoning another innocent victim.

The intolerably long program included songs that roused the crowd to screams of agreement with whatever the person on the mic said. Mia tuned out and searched for clues that the Priest was on the premises and not actively hurting someone. After an hour, she wondered if he would appear.

"How much longer?" she asked Thomas as if he would know these things.

"Soon," he answered.

She didn't bother asking any more questions. The volume of the crowd

194

doubled as a man of average height and stature, dressed in a white linen tunic, a blue robe and an ephod with 12 stones walked onstage waving as if he were the Catholic Pope.

Standing to get a better view of him, she moved to the side but couldn't see because so many were jumping up and down in front of her.

"Move into the aisle," Thomas said.

Hands raised in the air, she yelled in excitement along with the crowd as she moved toward the aisle, avoiding the eyes of the usher a few feet away. She would need to be quick before they hustled her back to her seat. Turning, she looked at Aaron Mosely standing in the middle of the stage smiling and waving at the crowd.

"Aaron Mosely," she called him with her mind, searching for him. He didn't respond, didn't change his behavior. Undeterred, she added more compulsion and whispered his name, sending it on the airwaves.

His smile slipped as he looked in her direction but would never see or know who called him.

"The man in the wheelchair with the gray and yellow shirt is pathetic and needs to be eliminated. Take him away. Stone him. Take him away. Send for him. Take him. Send for him, now. You must take him and purge the earth of this pathetic creature. Yahweh demands this sacrifice." Mia tried to think of something else to say, nothing else came to mind, so she repeated her earlier commands.

The Priest walked back and forth now, searching the audience. She knew the moment he saw Noah. "Gray and yellow shirt. Pathetic creature. Sacrifice to Yahweh. Take him now. Send for him now."

"It's working," Noah said. *"He just looked at me."*

"Good." She told him what she said to the Priest.

Noah chuckled. *"Ouch. Do I look that bad?"*

"Not to me," she said as she nodded to the large usher who told her to return to her seat.

The Priest waved for the audience to be seated and spoke when they obeyed. "Yahweh be praised."

The audience repeated his words, some jumped up but most remained seated. He spoke in moderate tones about love, peace, and happiness through God. The best speaker she'd ever heard he was not, but there was passion in his words as if he truly believed the BS he spouted.

Staring at the Priest, she watched as he stepped back and someone else approached the microphone. He spoke to someone dressed in a black suit who nodded and disappeared.

"This may be it, everybody knows what they're supposed to do?" Thomas asked.

"On it," Lizzy said from her vantage point on the far side of the stage. Mia didn't see either Thomas or Lizzy as she waited for whoever was coming to get Noah to approach him.

She didn't need to wait long, the same usher who demanded she return to her seat walked down to Noah, knelt beside him and spoke to him.

"The usher says the Priest wants to pray for me in the back," Noah told Mia. *"Of course it's a great honor to be chosen, blah, blah, blah. We're heading their now. You see her?"*

"Yep, got her and will follow you guys in a bit. I'll make sure she won't remember anything after she delivers you to the man waiting for you in a black suit," she told him.

"Everybody hold positions," Thomas said. *"There's an old woman stopping them."*

"She's praying for me," Noah said. *"She put some oil on my forehead in the sign of the cross. This guy in the black suit is pissed at the delay."*

"Some of these people really are true believers," Lizzy said.

"We're moving again," Noah said. *"Is this guy in the suit a part of the stonings? He hasn't said a word since he started walking behind my chair."*

"I don't think so, possibly just security," Mia said watching the stage. The musicians returned to the stage. *"The Priest is leaving, so are the others on the dais."*

"Got it," Thomas said. *"Noah are you ready?"*

"If you're asking if I took those pills to block the drug, yes, Been ready to drop kick this pompous asshole since the first," Noah said.

"Okay. I'm heading to the side where we rendezvous," Thomas said.

"I'm heading back," Mia said slipping out of the row. The usher glanced at her but said nothing. Mia spoke a few words, and added a healthy dose of compulsion to them to make sure the usher didn't remember her or Noah. She walked out and down the bustling corridor where people stood talking, eating and standing in line for the restroom.

Inhaling, she opened her senses, alert for danger and also information. Always interested in information, she moved in the same direction Noah traveled earlier.

"This was awesome, I told you so," someone said.

"It was, I'm so glad I came. I feel so much better," someone responded.

Mia walked around them and ignored other similar conversations. When she reached the end of the corridor she sensed three security guards nearby. *"Did you go through a door with three guards?"* she asked Noah.

"Yep, real friendly fellas, watch your back. If you need me…"

"I've got it, just checking to be sure." She didn't look at them, instead, she reached out to each of them and compelled them to let her through the door without question.

When she approached them, the one closest to the door opened it for her. She stepped inside and inhaled. *"Have you gotten your shot, yet?"* she asked Noah.

"Yeah, stung a bit. The guy handed me off to someone and is standing guard someplace. I'm in a room alone, not real big. There's a cross, black tarp on the floor, a

pile of bricks, and the smell of blood. Fresh blood." He sounded disgusted.

This was the tricky part. *"Someone's going to come to bind you to the floor. I don't know if it's before the Priest enters or if he's involved. Can you play the role?"*

"I don't want to be bound. We discussed that," he said.

They had. But nothing had been agreed on. *"I'll try to grab the person before they get to you."* She crept up the hall and stopped to scan the area. *"You're close."*

She spun and ducked, barely missing the punch from a guy dressed in a black suit. He turned and pulled out his gun. She jumped and kicked it out of his hand and then spun to kick him across his face.

He slapped her foot as he jerked back while staring at her. She grabbed his mind. "Stop."

He grinned at her and shook his head slowly. "No."

She slammed into his mind, pushed the compulsion. His head jerked back as surprise widened his eyes.

"No," he whispered as he fell to his knees. Blood trickled down his nose. Staring at her, he shuddered and fell forward. Mia dragged him from the middle of the floor into a janitor's closet. She picked up his gun and dropped it in a nearby trashcan.

"You okay?" she asked Noah while making her way to the room. Her energy levels dipped. Leaning against the wall she took several breaths before moving forward.

"Still waiting for them to show up." He sounded bored.

She stepped inside the room and closed the door behind her. Noah sat slumped in his wheelchair in the middle of the room. Tarp was spread on the floor near the cross. There was nothing in the floor to attach the rope, this was a convention hall and not the place Nathaniel Green died. She looked around for a place to hide and eventually slid into a shadowy corner.

"You good?" Noah asked.

"Yeah, couldn't find a place to hide. The whole tie down thing might be a moot point, nothing in the floor," she said.

"Good." Again he sounded bored as they settled in to wait.

The minutes passed and no one came.

"What's going on?" Thomas asked.

"He's in the back waiting," she said and then explained the set-up in the room.

"Did you check for cameras?"

She hadn't and did a quick check. *"No, I didn't. Had a small run in I had to take care of."* She told him about the guy in black.

"I checked on the way in. Didn't pick up anything," Noah said surprising her. He rarely spoke to anyone through links unless it was her or if directly asked a question.

"Let me know when someone comes in," Thomas said.

"What are you thinking about?" she asked Noah a few minutes later.

"Hmm?"

She repeated the question. *"You look distracted."* Not like you're expecting a murdering psychopath to enter the room and stone you to death any second.

"Liam. Being the only link to me he's in the middle of a shit storm. When we finish this I've got to get him out of there. Whatever we need to do, I'm not having him destroyed over my decision to stay with the team," he said.

She gave it some thought and realized he was right. The only reason the military was after him was because he wasn't on their team. If he chose to work with them, Liam would be safe. *"Have you talked to Thomas?"* She heard footsteps.

"Not yet. Someone's coming," he said.

The door opened.

Mia watched the tall man dressed in white pull Noah from the wheelchair and position him on the black tarp on the floor. He spread out his arms and pulled his legs together in the shape of the cross.

She updated both Lizzy and Thomas what was happening.

Once the man had Noah how he wanted him, he headed toward the door.

Mia grabbed his mind and gave him last minute instructions. He halted for a few seconds and then left the room.

Minutes later, Mosely and the others walked into the room. He read a scripture from a huge Bible as he entered, performing what she assumed was a ritual before the stoning.

"Mosely and the others are in the room," Mia told Noah and the others.

"Take him out," Thomas said.

Mia didn't see the mist leave Noah, she didn't have to. Mosely stopped reading, dropped the Bible as his hand flew to his neck. Gradually his face turned red, his eyes widened in watery shock as he struggled to breathe. The tightening mist held him securely as he fell to the floor, trying to inhale.

Initially, those around him didn't move, not until his face turned colors. Then they huddled around him, searching for the cause of his problem. One guy tried CPR before Mosely but stopped when they yelled the Priest was still alive.

"Call 4-1-1," a female yelled.

The others looked at her, then at Noah stretched out on the floor. "Move him so we can help the Priest," she yelled as Mosely stopped moving.

It was as if they couldn't believe he was dead that fast. One person ran out of the room.

A brave soul pressed against his fingertips against Mosely's throat and looked at the others. He shook his head.

For several moments, no one spoke. "What do we do now?" someone whispered.

"Jennings was second in command and he just ran out of here like a bitch on fire." This unflattering remark from someone else.

"What about the guy on the floor?"

Mia prepared to take out anyone who attacked Noah. The man who laid him on the floor spoke. "Leave him. He'll wake and go home believing he's been blessed."

She waited to see if the others accepted the instructions she'd given him just before he left the room earlier.

"I'll put him back in the chair, take him out."

The others nodded. "What about the Priest, do we call the paramedics? We have to call them otherwise it looks like we're hiding something."

Two guys picked Noah up and returned him to his wheelchair. "Once we get him out of here, we'll call them." Someone else rolled up the tarp.

"What about the bricks?"

"Leave 'em. I don't know how they got in here, do you?" the guy said.

"No. No, I don't."

"We don't touch anything other than remove the guy and the tarp. The rest of you go on, I'll call it in," he said on a low sigh. "I'll call it in."

The others filed out of the room after giving the Priest one long look. The guy pushed Noah out of the room toward the security checkpoint.

"*They're heading back to the front,*" Mia told Thomas and Lizzy after reporting mission accomplished.

"*I'm waiting to receive him,*" Lizzy said. "*Are you leaving now?*"

"*Yes. In just another moment.*" She left her hiding spot and stared at the face of the man who killed hundreds of innocent people. Granted he wasn't alone, but he was the head. She'd given each of the others something to think about if they ever decided to restart the stonings. She sidled out of the room, avoiding going in the same direction Noah had been walked and went an alternate route that wasn't handicapped accessible.

She reached Thomas in the van before the others. Nervous, she didn't say anything until she saw Lizzy and Noah approach the van and released a pent-up breath. When everyone was in the van, Thomas pulled out of the near-empty parking area and hit the highway on the way to the jet-port.

"How're you feeling?" she asked Noah who left the wheelchair as soon as they were on the highway to sit next to her on the back seat.

"Good. It went well. Be interesting to hear the spin on his death," Noah said pulling her closer.

She rested her head against his shoulder and inhaled his unique scent while listening to the steady beat of his heart. "He'll be glorified in some way, not that it matters. For right now, no one else will be stoned to death. I planted seeds in the minds of the people in that room to stop them from ever doing anything like that again."

Noah looked down at her with a slight smile. "Did you now?"

"Might never be right with what they did, now that they know Yahweh was angry over the innocent deaths and destroyed their leader because of it," she said.

Noah, Thomas, and Lizzy laughed.

"That's perfect," Lizzy said. "You're scary with those new skills."

Noah brushed a kiss against her forehead. "Well done, babe."

"Hadn't thought to take it that far, but that's brilliant Mia," Thomas said winking at her in the rear view mirror.

CHAPTER 32

Zeus looked around slowly as the bonds holding him disappeared. He was on the floor in the stairwell. How long had he been here? He sensed the sun had set and muttered a curse. He stood stretching the kinks from his body and patted his pocket for the keys.

Relieved Hermes had given him the keys earlier, he walked down the stairs, his thoughts in disarray. As soon as he reached the car he would contact Schmidt to find out about Hermes and to report what happened.

He frowned, uncertain as to what exactly happened. The door to the room with Sloan wouldn't open, he couldn't break it down or any of the walls. There was a force preventing him from getting to Sloan. He didn't know if it was the cripple or the woman. Schmidt said Sloan wasn't a cripple, the wheelchair was fake.

It made no sense. There was little activity in the lobby. The agents behind the desk stared up at him as he strode out the door. As soon as the cool night air hit him he pulled out his phone to contact Schmidt.

The phone was dead. It took a few moments to realize the dark screen wasn't returning to life before he shoved it into his pocket, pulled out the keys and hit the open button.

Nothing happened. No beeps. No sounds. He hit the panic button. Still nothing. Moving quickly, he noticed the disabled van was missing and so was the SUV they arrived in.

"Damn it," he said looking around. Anger bubbled beneath his skin as he stormed back inside to ask about his truck and was told it had been towed. The clerk gave him a card with the towing company information.

Zeus stared at the card for several seconds wanting to rip it into tiny pieces before stuffing it into his pocket. "Call me a cab," he growled.

The clerk placed the call and stepped away from the counter. Zeus took several deep breaths to calm his anger and walked outside to wait. Waiting allowed him to review the disastrous day.

For the first time since joining the Olympus Project, he failed an assignment. He still wasn't sure how it happened. Hermes lost it, was now in a hospital somewhere and Sloan was still breathing. He looked up to the sky, clasped his hands behind his back and rocked on his feet. From the moment Sloan arrived in Denver, his actions had been off. He didn't act like one of them, there was no proof he had received the same injection. Despite the wheelchair, Sloan hadn't been helpless or afraid.

Zeus stopped to buy a charging cable before checking into a hotel and ordering food service. Once the phone was connected to the charger he saw several missed calls and text messages.

He called Schmidt and was told to return to base. No explanations. No discussion.

Curiosity got the best of Zeus. Instead of returning to home base, he directed the jet to Littleton, Texas. He needed more information on Noah Sloan.

<<<>>>

It was close to midnight when Zeus arrived at Sloan's home. The lights were on and he heard music and singing. Not professional singing, more like someone was drowning their sorrows off-key. The bio on Sloan stated his cousin lived in the house now that he left to be with the woman. He parked on the road and walked up the long drive until he reached the wide porch.

Lights blazed from several windows. The singing stopped and the front door opened. Zeus waited a heartbeat and coughed.

The cousin's head jerked up and he peered into the darkness. "Who's there?"

Zeus strode forward with his hands up. "You don't know me but I have a few questions about Noah."

"You are?"

"Zeus."

"Seriously?" he said as Zeus walked forward and he looked up. "Guess so," he muttered. "Lots of people have been asking about Noah. You military too?"

Zeus hadn't realized others had been here before him. "Yes." He rattled off his name, rank and serial number out of habit, before realizing none of it applied anymore. He and the others were a part of a new, elite task force Schmidt and the brass was setting up. But they didn't know there were others with similar powers who weren't on their team. If they knew, they never shared that information with him or any of the others. Hermes paid for that ignorance. Zeus refused to follow in Hermes footsteps and no longer trusted Schmidt, to be honest with him.

"Want a beer? I've had a few already," Liam said.

"No. Noah left with his new girlfriend?" Zeus asked.

The cousin snorted and extended his hand. "Liam."

Zeus looked at it for a second before accepting it. When was the last time he did something so... human? He couldn't recall.

"New girlfriend? That's accurate I guess. They hit it off, he fell hard. About time, since he hasn't really dated since he became a civilian," Liam said.

"Since being discharged?" Zeus said standing on the opposite side of the porch.

"Yeah, it's been rough. But all of those who served had it rough, at least he survived. A lot of good men and women didn't," Liam said.

Neither spoke for a few seconds.

"What happened to put him in a wheelchair?"

Liam frowned. "Wheelchair? What're you talking about?"

"The reason I'm here is that I saw him in a wheelchair in Denver and when I tried to get to him, I couldn't. What happened to him?" Zeus glared at Liam as if the failure to destroy Sloan was his fault.

"Noah's not in a wheelchair. Only time I ever saw him in one was when he left the hospital after his surgeries. He's been driving for months, I don't know who you thought you saw, but it wasn't Noah," Liam said.

"Why was he in a wheelchair? What kind of game is he playing? Has he been changed from the shot?" Zeus asked moving closer to Liam.

Liam frowned and stared up at Zeus. "He's not playing any games, asshole. He's not in a wheelchair, you've got the wrong guy. What shot are you talking about?"

"Where did he meet the girl?" Zeus asked.

"In town someplace. She worked for the Feds. Was here on a case,"

"Has he been acting differently lately?"

Liam stilled. "Differently? What do you mean?"

"Different, better than before. Stronger, faster, that kind of thing," Zeus said.

"Faster? Stronger?" Liam frowned, thinking back. "He didn't run or go for walks, so I can't say if he's faster or not. Stronger?" He rubbed his neck. "I have no idea. Last time I spent any time with him, he had found the body of the dead guy and I knew it spooked him."

"PTSD?"

Liam nodded. "Bad dreams about the war, then seeing it home, I knew it'd bother him and stayed the night. We had a few beers, talked shit and watched TV. If he was stronger than before I didn't see it."

"These bad dreams, did he have them before taking the hit to the brain?" Zeus asked recalling Sloan's file.

Liam's brow furrowed. "If he did, they were nothing like this. Nothing like this. They make him sick the next day if, they're really bad a couple days. Ever happened to you?"

"No."

"Did you serve time with him?" Liam asked.

"No."

"How do you know him?" Liam asked, confused.

"I was sent to kill him and he escaped."

"What the fuck?"

Zeus' arm shot out, grabbed Liam by the throat and lifted him. "Where is Sloan? If you don't tell me what I need to know, you won't see the sunrise.

Liam struggled to break the hold but the man's arm was like granite. "I won't see it anyway," Liam said taking small gasps of air as his feet dangled in the air. What the hell had Noah gotten into to have this mammoth come after him, Liam wondered desperately.

"Problems, Liam?"

Standing near the porch were Ryder and Ryan, Noah's friends. Liam wanted to weep in relief but couldn't take in enough air to do that.

Zeus stared at the two men, inhaled deeply and opened his hands. Liam hit the porch and winced. Between his bruised throat and knees he wasn't sure which hurt most.

"What are you?" Zeus demanded turning to look at the two.

"Neighbors. Friends of Noah. And you are?" Ryder asked.

"Zeus."

The twins looked at each other. Ryder smiled. "Of course you are."

Ryan walked up the steps and went to Liam. "You alright?"

Liam nodded but kept Zeus in his sight. That big motherfucker was crazy as a bedbug but strong as fuck. He walked down the step with Ryan and stood behind the two brothers. It looked as if Zeus had grown taller or something. Liam didn't trust him not to come after all three of them, he prepared to fight like his life depended on it. Because it did.

"I will not ask again, what are you?" Zeus demanded as he changed position to stand with his arms loose at his side and feet apart.

"Neighbors," Ryder said but this time there was no teasing in his voice. In fact, it was as deadly as the big guy's on the porch.

Liam wasn't sure what was going on but knew the twins were friends of his cousin. They'd stopped by yesterday to check on things. "He's looking for Noah to kill him."

"Is he?" Ryder said, his voice dropped an octave and sounded cold as ice.

"Do you know where the coward is hiding?" Zeus asked.

"Why would we tell you anything?" Liam asked, anger rising.

"To save your lives. You're simply prolonging his death by hiding his whereabouts," Zeus said and moved so fast across the porch railing, Liam hadn't seen it. He fell backward and rolled several feet away until a large tree stopped him. Unbearable pain shot through his back and side. He almost blacked out.

Liam shook his head and tried to get his bearings. He must be dizzy delusional because the twins were moving as fast as Zeus and kicking his big, blond ass. The world spun. Liam closed his eyes until he could see straight again. He heard a thump and groan.

One of the twins lay a few feet from him. That was not good. He watched as Zeus picked up the other one and tossed him into the side of the barn. The sound of flesh splintering wood made Liam flinch. He needed to help and tried to move. His leg refused to oblige as blood rolled from his forehead into his eye. Leaning forward he dragged himself toward the nearby twin to check on him. This wasn't their fight. As much as he needed and appreciated their help, he didn't want them to die or get seriously hurt because of him.

The next moment something slammed so hard into Zeus he flew backward, hit the porch railing and pole causing that entire side to collapse on him."

"What the fuck?" Liam said trying desperately to see but his vision wavered in and out. "I'm dreaming this shit. Got to be dreaming it."

Shaking his head, Zeus stared up into the eyes of a giant who grabbed him by the throat, shook him like a rag doll and punched him in the face several times.

<<<>>>

The moment Tyrone sensed the twins were in trouble, he left Rose and the girls at a run with instructions to lock down the house. He sensed their location and ran the 10 plus miles through several fields and copse of trees.

Something snapped when he saw Ryan thrown into the barn and felt Ryder's pain. He morphed into his two-legged form without turning into a wolf and moving like a speeding bullet slammed into the tall, blond guy who never saw him coming. The posts on the porch snapped in half like twigs, and that entire side of the roof crashed down on the guy. If it hadn't been for the concrete porch breaking the asshole's fall, he may have skidded through the exterior wall into the house.

Rolling to the side, Zeus tried to stand. Tyrone grabbed his shirt, pulled him up and punched him in the face again.

Zeus tried to push Tyrone off him.

A low, warning growl rumbled from Tyrone's throat just before Zeus punched him in the belly hard enough for him to stumble backward a couple steps. Tyrone ducked the next blow, and came up with a punch to his adversary's stomach, knocking the wind from him. Followed by an uppercut beneath his chin, which lifted him off the ground and sent him flying backward into a large oak tree which shuddered on impact.

Zeus didn't move.

Tyrone rolled his jaw and checked on his sons. Ryder groaned and was coming around. Tyrone was concerned about Ryan who hadn't moved. "Check on your brother," he instructed as he morphed to his regular size.

"What's going on?" La Patron asked.

"Stranger on Sloan's property. I think he's one of the military experiments," Tyrone said. *"Strong, big dude goes by the name Zeus. At least that's what he told the twins before he attacked them."*

"What?" Silas roared. *"He attacked? When? Why?"*

"A few minutes ago. They stopped him from attacking Noah's cousin, he didn't like that. He kept asking what they were," Tyrone said standing over Zeus. He wasn't surprised when his father merged with him to see the guy.

"Are the twins alright?" La Patron asked.

"He knocked them both on their asses. Ryder's helping Ryan now. I plan to send them to shift, finish healing. Liam, the cousin is passed out, needs to get to a human hospital," Tyrone said glancing over his shoulder at his sons. They stood looking at the guy at his feet wanting to kill him. Their anger vibrated through the air.

"Shift, finish healing," he said in a tone that left no room for discussion or debate. With a final glare at Zeus the two ran off, no doubt headed to the ranch. Tyrone alerted Rose they were on their way and went to find Liam.

"Alpha Theron is sending someone to drop Liam off at the hospital emergency room," Silas said. No sooner than the words came across, two men ran up the driveway, looked at Zeus and then Tyrone.

"Not this one, the one beneath the tree," Tyrone instructed.

They nodded, left and carried Liam away.

Tyrone watched Zeus closely. *"He's healing fast like we do. I'm watching the bruising disappear. It's amazing. Does all chimera heal that fast? Or is it just the military injections?"*

"I'll consult Hawke on that. Can you get a sample of his blood?"

Sometimes doctors required patients to take all kinds of samples from excrement to urine to mouth swabs. Maybe Sloan had supplies for that kind of thing. Tyrone went inside to the bathroom.

Beneath the sink, Sloan had several medical supplies, most were in unopened boxes. Tyrone finally found a blood testing kit in the back and took it outside.

"Found a kit," he told Silas.

"Good, I'll let Hawke know."

Zeus would wake soon if not once he felt the prick in his finger. Tyrone shifted to the same form as before, grabbed Zeus' hand and applied extreme pressure leaving no doubt that he would break his bone if Zeus fought.

As expected Zeus eyes flew open just as Tyrone pricked his finger. He tried to break free but couldn't. Tyrone finished taking the blood and slipped it into his pocket. He met Zeus' confused gaze.

"What the fuck are you?" Tyrone asked to mess with him.

He frowned. "I am … I am Zeus."

Tyrone squeezed the hand tighter and blocked the fist that came at him like a hammer. Zeus wasn't human and had no protection from the wolf community. That knowledge unfurled and tempted his beast to destroy this chimera.

"No. Do not kill him. Teach him manners, but don't kill him," La Patron said.

Tyrone head-butted Zeus, three times, breaking skin which sent rivulets of blood down Zeus' face before releasing him. Tyrone stepped back as Zeus hit the concrete porch step hard and released a loud groan but didn't move.

Theron approached and stared down at Zeus who was trying to stand. *"Pity La Patron won't allow us to kill him. Feels it's unfair, says the other chimera will deal with him and his kind,"* Alpha Theron said sounding like a kid denied his favorite toy.

Tyrone gave Theron the blood testing kit. *"This needs to get to Hawke asap. I'm still here a few more days, can you take care of it for me?"*

Alpha Theron nodded. *"Will do. So this one just walks free?"*

"If he had attacked one of ours with no humans involved, we could destroy him. But the twins were protecting the human, so he gets to see the morning sun." Tyrone shrugged. As much as he wanted to rip this asshole a new one, he understood his father was setting the game rules in place. Thomas would be notified of this trespass and Hawke would communicate anything he discovered from the blood sample.

As far as La Patron was concerned, this fight was between the mutated humans unless they came after Pack.

Tyrone left and was halfway home when the ground and trees shuddered and shook. The crash and boom of buildings followed, wreaking havoc on the otherwise quiet night. The ground rumbled again.

The twins met Tyrone in the copse of trees. *"What was that?"* Ryan asked.

"I don't know, I'm contacting Theron, now," Tyrone said heading back toward Sloan's home.

"This guy does something with his voice," Theron said. *"Un-fucking-believable. He flattened the house and barn. Nothing but rubble, trees fell, looks like a tornado hit it.*

Fucking asshole. When he got to the road, the dick yelled, "I am Zeus." Got into a truck and drove off. La Patron sure the other guys can beat this guy? What he did to the house and barn… it's fucked up."

"That's a question for Hawke," Tyrone said as he and the twins approached what used to be Sloan's home.

CHAPTER 33

Mia, Noah and the others arrived home from Denver later that night. Hungry they sat around the dining table eating whatever was in the main kitchen, discussing the Leviticus Club operation.

"Do you think the FBI will ever connect the dots to the club and the stonings?" Lizzy asked the others in a dry tone.

Thomas shook his head slowly. "Hard to say, but doubtful unless someone confesses." He looked at Mia. "Which is a strong possibility."

Mia shrugged thinking of Nathaniel Green. "Glad that's over. No one deserves to be stoned to death." She shivered and took another sip of her soft-drink.

Noah covered her hand with his before looking across the table. "Have you discussed Hermes and Zeus with Hawke or shared what Mia discovered about their team?" he asked Thomas.

"I told him bits of it and sent the information during our downtime at the hotel. We'll probably talk tomorrow when he's had time to go over it," Thomas said. "He knew we were in the middle of the op and didn't respond on it today."

Noah nodded. On the flight home, they had discussed possible strategies to protect Liam but hadn't finalized anything. It didn't sit right with him that he had placed his cousin in danger, the sooner they came up with a solution the better.

In the middle of Lizzy's next comment, Thomas straightened, stared ahead and then closed his eyes. Everyone at the table watched and waited for Thomas to tell them whatever he just learned.

He looked at Noah. "Zeus attacked your home. Liam was taken to the hospital. He used some sort of sonic waves on your place, destroyed,

209

leveled the house, barn, and surrounding trees," Thomas said meeting Noah's shocked gaze.

"That motherfucker," Noah yelled, slapping the table and standing so fast his chair hit the ground. Sparks flew all around him as the mist leaked from his control. The air dimmed and trailed behind him as he strode away from the dining area to their room where he kept a spare phone.

He placed the call to find out Liam's condition. Fortunately, they were each other's points of contacts and while the person didn't tell him a lot, she assured him Liam was in the hospital receiving care.

Sloan sat in the chair, shoulders slumped with his arms hanging between his legs. Despair swamped him. He didn't know what to do. Mia had become his world, his dream deferred, he couldn't leave her or let her go. She was an innate part of him. Which meant accepting a role and place in the team. Besides they were safer with Thomas and the others than on their own.

The sane side of his brain told him all of that. The other side, the dark mist rumbled, sparked and rolled urging him to go after Zeus and anyone else who posed a threat to him, Mia and Liam.

"Noah," Mia called just as the door to their suite opened and she walked inside. *"What do you want to do?"*

He inhaled deeply. Her scent filled him. Calmed him. He extended his hand to her. She took it and sat on his lap as he wrapped his arms tight around her.

"I want him safe. But I won't betray the team, or us by going off half-cocked to get him. Plus, where could I take or send him that they couldn't find him?" He shook his head. "Nowhere. If I go to him now, they'll always use him as a lever to get a reaction from me." He exhaled. "Seriously, I don't know how to help him and it's killing me inside."

She stroked his back and held his head to her chest in silence. "We'll think of something."

"Sloan, Mia, we've got pictures of your place if you want to see," Thomas said.

Eager to see the damage to his home, Noah said. *"Where?"* He and Mia left for the main area where Thomas stood in front of a monitor. "I'm sending this to the wall."

Noah looked up, opened his mouth and snapped it shut. His home was nothing but rubble. The truck had been stored in the garage and was buried beneath the timber and bales of hay.

Mia gasped, her hand flew to her mouth.

"Zeus uses sound to create sonic waves, booms and this is the result," Thomas said.

"Is that what came against our hotel room?" Mia asked, reaching for Noah.

"Maybe a variation of it," Thomas said. "For this much destruction, it takes time to inhale enough air for release. If he'd been fighting, running or doing anything that required energy he couldn't do this kind of damage."

"This happened after the fight with Liam?" Lizzy asked.

"That's what I've been told. He must've left Denver, flew to Texas for information about Noah. No doubt he has access to your file. He was asking Liam about you when Ryder and Ryan got there. From what they're saying, Zeus kicked ass," Thomas said. "Tyrone knocked him out before things got out of hand."

"Did he kill him?" Noah asked, hoping he didn't. He wanted that pleasure.

"No. They won't either. If the military chimeras attack the Pack, then they'll defend themselves. In this case, the twins were attacked because they helped Liam, a human," Thomas explained.

"I'll call and thank them," Noah said.

Thomas nodded before continuing. "Tyrone took a blood sample from Zeus. Hawke will check to see the differences in their serum and ours. We need to know who we're dealing with."

The others nodded in agreement.

"Where is Zeus now?" Noah asked in a low voice, vibrating with anger. He wanted another shot at that dude in the worst way.

"Took a private jet and left the area headed to DC. We don't have a way to get him, yet. But we will address this shit, believe me," Thomas said, his eyes taking on an unnatural glow. "That motherfucker crossed a line."

Mia took his hand and squeezed it. "We'll get him, just not tonight, okay?"

Noah looked at the remains of his home, inhaled and nodded. He would perfect his skills and return the favor to that asshole when they met again. And he was certain that was just a matter of time. Guys who called themselves gods needed to strut their stuff. "Okay," he said calming down.

Mia leaned into him and brushed her lips against his.

"Tomorrow we start preparing our defense against the Greeks," Thomas announced. "Next time, we'll be ready for them."

Noah tugged Mia close and walked toward their room. This was truly home now. Her, the others were family. "Next time," he said.

Hello,

Thanks for checking out Book one in the Olympus Project. This story is set in the same world as La Patron with Hawke as the bridge between the two groups. I specifically like that the Goddess named Thomas and the others and from this point on, that's how I will refer to them. I love the hope this group have for their lives to change now that they've taken the new serum. I get the feeling they hadn't really lived before, now they're ready to come into the sunshine.

You're invited to journey with me through all the books in this series. If you like fast paced action, suspense and great love connections like me, you won't be disappointed. Feel free to drop me a line, SydneyAddae@msn.com or join my Facebook group, La Patron's Den, where discussions regarding Silas and the Wolf nation abound. Also, you can find me at my website, SydneyAddae.com.
Knight Chronicles is a newsletter for my Readers Group from the characters of the series to keep you informed of what's going on in the Wolf Nation. Each issue has a personal message from Silas Knight, La Patron, or his mate, Jasmine. Character profiles with in-depth interviews and thoughts you won't find anywhere else. Also works in progress, new releases and special giveaways in every issue. If you would like to receive **Knight Chronicles** click this sign up link! Thank you. (http://eepurl.com/bb3csz)
La Patron, the Alpha's Alpha is my first paranormal series and I'd like to ask a favor. When you finish reading, **please leave a review**, whatever your opinion, I assure you I appreciate it.

Thanks again

Sydney

BirthRight
BirthControl
BirthMark

BirthStone
BirthDate
BirthSign
Sword of Inquest
Sword of Mercy
Sword of Justice
La Patron's Christmas
La Patron's Christmas 2
La Patron's New Year – w/Catherine Marsh, & Leigh West
KnightForce 1
KnightForce Deuces
KnightForce Tres'
KnightForce Damian
KnightForce Ethan
Angus
La Patron's Den – Jackie's Journey
La Patron's Den – Alpha Awakening – Adam
La Patron's Den – Renee's Renegade
La Patron's Den – David's Dilemma
Knight Rescue
Knight Defense

Booksets
La Patron Series Books 1-6
La Patron Series Books 4-6
The Sword Series – Books 1-3
KnightForce Collection 1
KnightForce Collection 2

Vampires:
Last in Line

Bear:
Bear with Me
Jewel's Bear

Olympus Project
The Leviticus Club

Hi,

Thanks for joining me on this new and exciting

www.ingramcontent.com/pod-product-compliance
Lightning Source LLC
Chambersburg PA
CBHW070456260626
47161CB00004B/1323